Turk's kisses, gentle at first, became more forceful, waking every sensual spot in her body, until she became limp with desire. Myrhia had never responded to passion before in this way. It was becoming all-consuming, almost frightening, and she was reveling in its primitive fierceness.

"Myrhia, Myrhia." Turk said her name over and over, pressed against her as if he would never let her go. "You were never out of my thoughts these past weeks. Is it possible you missed me too?" His lips came down on hers, making any reply impossible for the moment.

When Myrhia caught her breath she whispered softly, "I did miss you. I tried not to think of you, to hate you, but I couldn't help—" She was not allowed to finish as his lips closed over hers once more. Turk's tongue was sweetly exploring, seeking her own, arousing an ardor too strong to resist. "Myrhia, my lovely one. You are my torment!"

Dear Reader,

It is our pleasure to bring you romance novels that go beyond category writing. The settings of **Harlequin American Romance** give a sense of place and culture that is uniquely American, and the characters are warm and believable. The stories are of "today" and have been chosen to give variety within the vast scope of romance fiction.

Lois Carnell chose for her first romance characters who are incompatible by profession—an architect and a real estate developer. You will enjoy watching the hero and heroine emerge before your eyes and their problems dissolve into a passionate partnership.

From the early days of Harlequin, our primary concern has been to bring you novels of the highest quality. **Harlequin American Romance** is no exception. Enjoy!

Vivian Stephens

Vivian Stephens
Editorial Director
Harlequin American Romance
919 Third Avenue,
New York, N.Y. 10022

Beyond the Flight of Birds

LOIS CARNELL

Harlequin Books

TORONTO • NEW YORK • LONDON
AMSTERDAM • PARIS • SYDNEY • HAMBURG
STOCKHOLM • ATHENS • TOKYO • MILAN

Build tall a dream—beyond the flight of birds,
Hold close the ecstasy of love—there is no need for words.

—L.C.

For Steve, my architect, with love and appreciation

Published October 1983

First printing August 1983

ISBN 0-373-16028-3

Chapter One

Myrhia Lassiter was wearing a smile as big as Dallas itself when she stepped from the lush offices of Muldrow Associates. Preoccupied by her exciting news, she tripped over two large feet planted firmly outside the office doorway and fell into a pair of muscular arms that closed tightly around her shapely figure.

"Oh!" she gasped, looking up into cold steel made more startling gray by contrast with olive skin. "I'm so sorry. I didn't see—"

"I noticed!" came a terse reply as the blue-gray gaze raked intimately over her body and back to her face before releasing her without further comment as all six feet three of him walked into the doorway she had just left.

"Conceited prig!" she snapped, shaken by the encounter. But her anger was short-lived. She wouldn't allow anything to dim the excitement of the news she had just heard from the Muldrow Associates that the committee had voted unanimously to accept her design proposal for the Tarrington Building. Carl Muldrow had told her it would be erected in the very near future somewhere near the Turtle Creek area in Dallas.

Carl himself had forewarned her that the competition would be fierce with at least fifty other submissions. She smiled to herself, thinking how hard her good friend had pushed her into making a bid for it. A glow seemed to emanate from her face as she caught sight of her reflection in the glass paneling of the outer door of the Muldrow Building. She sighed, feeling a wave of relief. The struggle had been worth it and now she had taken her first step in becoming recognized as an architect worthy of notice.

At twenty-seven Myrhia was beginning a new phase in her career. It seemed to her now as she looked back over the five years she had spent at the University of Texas at Austin that the time had moved swiftly. She recalled her nervousness the day she took the Texas State Architectural Review exam and waited to see if she would become a registered architect and remembered her disappointment when she was not immediately asked to design anything spectacular until now. It seemed to her she had plowed a painful rut while designing private dwellings, two-story nondescript buildings, and an occasional shopping center.

Some minutes later her enthusiasm soared again as she stepped into her own modest office to find an expectant look on the face of her secretary, Trish Martin. "I'm dying to know, Myrhia. Did you get it?" The girl asked expectantly.

"I can tell by your expression that you already know the answer, Trish. You can't keep a straight face. The Muldrow office called again, didn't they?" Whirling in a slight dance step, Myrhia continued.

"Yes, I did it! I can't believe it yet and I won't until I see my building rising twenty stories into the Dallas skyline." She felt like shouting as the excitement welled up inside her.

The slim, brown-eyed secretary rose from her desk

and came to Myrhia, putting an arm around her shoulders in a brief hug before turning away, as if embarrassed to show emotion to her employer.

"Thanks, Trish!" Myrhia touched her friend's arm briefly. "I'm happy you're here to celebrate with me." Trish turned with a smile, looking relieved.

Stepping toward the window in her office Myrhia looked out at the already heavy traffic gathering in Lemon Park. The call to the Muldrow office had delayed her plans to leave early in order to avoid the weekend flotsam of bumper-to-bumper traffic, but it had been more than worth it.

She turned back to Trish. "I'm glad I was still here when the call came from the Muldrow Agency."

"Me too." Trish's plain face took on a glow of admiration. "I told my boyfriend last night that it's a privilege to work for a woman architect with real talent." She gestured to the colorful renderings and sketches that adorned the office walls. "Honest, Myrhia—your delineations look like museum pieces. They're so complete—with trees and people on the sidewalks, fountains, and the complete scene. Did you ever consider commercial art?"

Myrhia laughed. "No, not really! But my mother opted for that career for her daughter. She preferred that I not follow in my father's footsteps. She's so feminine. She wanted a career in art, interior design, or modeling for her daughter. Since I'm not tall enough or willowy enough for the latter, she decided on one of the first two pursuits."

Trish sighed, looking almost calf-eyed with what Myrhia suspected might be called employer worship. "Nevertheless, Myrhia, I'm happy to be working for you. It's something new and glamorous every day and I suspect now we'll see more glamor after the Tarrington goes up."

Myrhia smiled at her secretary. She was fond of Trish, who was only four years her junior at twenty-three, but sometimes, as at this moment, she seemed teen-aged. "Well, I've got to come back to earth and get out of here. Tell you the truth, I believe I could fly home at this moment, but the reality of facing that five-o'clock traffic on the Central Expressway might clip my wings."

Trish interrupted. "I almost forgot. While you were out, you had another call from Carl Muldrow. He said to tell you he would have to meet you at Elan's; he's been detained in Denton. He's running late, said something about the high Dalai Lama detaining him. Whatever that means." A slight frown nudged her eyebrow. "Anyway, he said to congratulate you all over and he was sorry not to have been the one in his office to give you the good news."

"I suppose you told him you knew already." Myrhia grinned at her secretary.

"Yes, I couldn't keep it in. You see, I eavesdropped on your conversation with the vice-president of Muldrow before you went over there."

"See you, Trish." Myrhia started to the door but turned back. "The Dalai Lama must be Dirckson Vaughan, the man with all the money to construct the Tarrington Building." She stopped as a stunned expression washed over Trish's face. "Are you all right?"

"You can't mean *the* Turk Vaughan who was the Dallas Cowboys' leading rusher a few years back?"

"I believe he's the same. Dirckson Vaughan—or Turk—to you is the elusive, chauvinistic, wealthy financier and probably one of Texas's biggest developers. Carl said he got out of football a few years back—leg injury of some kind. But I understand he is one shrewd operator."

"And you haven't met him yet?" Trish said, appearing to be in a state of bliss. "I used to go to the Cowboy games with my brother when I was in high school. Oh, Myrhia! That man is so super. He's really something!"

"Put your heart back inside your chest, Trish," Myrhia teased, laughing at Trish's expression. "He's probably old, fat, and very debauched by now."

"I doubt it. He'd only be in his late thirties." She sighed. "I wonder if he's married."

"Probably. Good-bye, you starry-eyed dreamer! I'm gone now." Myrhia was still laughing at Trish when she reached the elevator. The thought occurred to her that it might be interesting to meet the talked-about Turk Vaughan, ex-Dallas Cowboy, face to face and she was bound to do that very soon.

Since Carl would be late and plans had been altered so she would have to meet him at Élan's, she could afford to relax behind the wheel of her Volvo. Suddenly it occurred to her she might be able to afford a new, more sophisticated car soon. Now, with luck, she just might be enjoying a larger income. She settled back to enjoy the lingering euphoria the good news brought on her and unconsciously blocked out the impatient motorists and the fumes from countless exhausts along the expressway.

Her gaze traveled frequently toward the Dallas skyline. Since coming to Dallas as a child, the entire sweep of horizon had changed as the remarkable skyward growth reached ever upward. The past few years she had watched enviously as building after building rose, a proud boast to some architect's concept.

To her right was the Reunion Tower rising twenty-eight stories, stealing some of the limelight from the Southland Life Building and other old landmarks in the background. Just how soon would the Tarrington

Building hold the attention of motorists caught in slower traffic as she was at the moment? She thrilled at the thought.

To have her first large proposal accepted by the prestigious Muldrow Associates was a dream fulfilled. Her thoughts strayed to her father momentarily. Walt Lassiter had been one of the leading architects of the southwest until his death, leaving behind him the beautiful Plover Church in Tulsa as one of his outstanding successes. Although her father had been well known, she knew he never recovered from the Wrightian era. She remembered fondly he was of the old school, not subject to drastic change with the times. Now she faced the reality of her own ability. She was not a Frank Lloyd Wright or like the new rave, I.M. Pei, and possibly would never achieve her father's greatness, but she was adaptable. At least she hoped she was.

She felt a twinge of sadness that Walt Lassiter would never know about the Tarrington Building, even though her first reaction was to tell him. Even the two years since his death had not dimmed the feeling of his presence at times. Years of watching his skilled hands move across his drawing board creating hotels, churches, and fantasies that appeared like magic under his flexible fingers had fired her with desire to do the same.

"Myrhia, you've a natural talent for design," she could almost hear her father say. "Never give up on a dream."

She thought of her mother at this moment and knew she would be the first person to tell of her good luck. Socially conscious Alicia, Myrhia mused fondly, wanted to be called by her first name by her daughter. In a way, Myrhia could understand, as even now her mother was incredibly beautiful and trim at forty-eight. Her slim figure and blond hair often graced the society section of the Dallas newspaper as she flitted to one or more of her favorite charities. Her mother would never understand her daughter's need to succeed on her own.

Her thoughts had turned to Carl by the time she could drive off the busy four-lane highway onto a less crowded boulevard. It had been to her advantage having him for a friend. At his insistence she had entered the competition for a chance to design the Tarrington Building. The committee was composed of members of Carl's association and those from Vaughan Enterprises. She had been proud when Carl was made construction manager for his company, which had once been his father's. The Muldrow Company would be handling the operation of the Tarrington Building for the financiers at its completion. The heaviest investor, of course, was Dirckson Vaughan.

In many ways Carl had been a godsend the past year. Not only did he keep her informed about new projects in the area where all the heavy construction was taking place, but he was one jump ahead on the valid proposals laid before the Dallas city council. As a member of that council, he stayed abreast of building codes.

Big, friendly, and tuned with the kind of nerves that could stand heavy loads laid on by management, Carl was one man she felt who could weather the construction business without cracking under the strain. Not only was his business demanding but heartbreaking when contracts were broken, misread, changed, or coupled with union labor walkouts or delays in shipments of steel that set the projects back behind schedule. Carl remained calm through it all.

They enjoyed the same things together, but Carl's personal life was unhappy. He was separated from his wife of ten years and not willing to give her up or their six-year-old girl, Dody, whom he worshipped.

Carl was still on her mind thirty minutes later as she was parking her Volvo behind the apartment building, but there was no way she could help him with his problem. Her thoughts strayed to Trish. Her secretary's open admiration for Turk Vaughan had sparked a small interest in her, making her wonder what he would be like. She wished she could be enthusiastic about the man and allay the doubts she had formed already. She was quick to admit she was turned off ordinarily by the overbearing, womanizing type and from what she had gleaned from the gossip around Dallas, Turk Vaughan fit that category.

Would she ever find a man she could respect and be respected by both as a contemporary and a lover? Love was a priceless thing and it seemed that those who had it threw it away. *Oh, well, I'll probably never find what I'm looking for in a man,* she thought as she unlocked the door to her apartment.

She glanced around the comfortable room with objective appraisal, recalling how her closest friend, Cleo Hathaway, had called it "restful and subdued, like a quiet pond." Possibly the pale shades of dove-gray offset her favorite blues to extend that impression.

"It's like you, Myrhia—at peace with yourself." Cleo was a romantic, but her remark had pleased her.

Unfortunately she did not feel peaceful at this moment—more like a firecracker about to explode. From habit she unconsciously stepped to a small marble-topped table in front of the blue velvet sofa and struck a match to light the wick in a pressed-glass hurricane lamp. As she stood back watching the wick steady itself into a slender flame that cast a warm glow about the apartment, a sensory enjoyment washed over her. It was a room whose appointments had been chosen with care to satisfy her own needs and limited budget.

Once again she commended herself on moving from the family home in Highland Park where she had left Alicia to putter about the twelve-room home with her maid, Matty, and Brady, man of all trades. The couple had been in the family as long as she could remember and watched over Alicia like two alert eagles.

She smiled fondly, thinking of her mother's impractical, flighty ways as she picked up the receiver to tell her the good news.

"Darling, I'm so happy for you," her mother crooned. "Now maybe with that old project out of the way you can get out on the golf course more. Dear, you're looking pale lately and I think you stay in that stuffy old office too much. Do take care, Myrhia. See you! Oh, yes, darling, be sure and water the spider plant I gave you but don't overdo it. Also, you might talk to it—a little pep talk, you know. It helps the growth."

As Myrhia hung up, she wanted to laugh out loud. Her mother, she knew, meant the latter literally. Scoff as she did at times at her mother's idiosyncrasies, she had to admit the results of Alicia's green thumb were there for all to see. Her home was almost like a bower of greenery.

With a resigned shrug, she walked over to the enormous potted plant her mother had left yesterday and gave the long tendrils of vine a soft touch.

"Okay, old boy," she addressed the plant. "It's just you and me. Did you hear? I've had my first big design accepted." Her immediate reaction was disgust with herself. Would she really become silly living alone this way with no one who really cared about her success? A wave of loneliness possessed her, making her feel adrift. Only her father would have understood the importance of accomplishment. Were there no men left like Walt Lassiter, who could give love and yet be attuned to appreciation?

Why was it she had never fallen in love? She had dated often in high school and college and had been popular for a year or two at the university until her lab hours ate away at dating time. One or two architectural majors had asked her out, but there was a friction in ideas and too much competition between them to make it exciting.

Shrugging off her loneliness, she started toward the bathroom, where she intended to relax away her tension. After turning on the faucets full force, she poured more bubble beads than usual into the water, breathing deeply as she reveled in its heady fragrance of jasmine.

Slipping into the soothing warmth, she knew at once that a refreshing bath would boost her spirits. She stretched languidly, feeling the muscles in her legs and arms relaxing in the soft bubbles of foam caressing her skin.

Some minutes later she stepped from the bathtub into a fluffy bath sheet, feeling a tingle of well-being in every nerve. Tonight she would indulge herself and dress for a celebration. The choice of dress would have to be special. Slipping the padded hangers across the bar of her closet, she deliberated over her choice. For tonight's big moment, it would be the turquoise silk cocktail dress. Slipping into its soft folds, the silk billowed about her slim calves as she stepped back to admire her reflection in the mirror. The dress fit superbly over her full breasts and clung seductively to her slender waist and well-rounded hips. Although she was considered slim, she knew with her small bone structure she would have to be active as she grew older. At present the flesh that did adhere to her bones was placed in the proper places.

She had splurged on the dress at Neiman-Marcus at a time when she had felt apprehensive about submitting the design package to the committee. She remembered the frustrated feeling of futility after its submission. It was perhaps like a novelist sending a book to a publisher and hoping someone would read and understand what he was trying to say. She knew the dress was far too expensive for her budget, but it had boosted her morale at the time. Now, she thought smugly, she could afford a small luxury now and then.

After gathering her raven hair into a smooth chignon and securing it with two gold clips sparkling with turquoise stones, she took one last glimpse of herself in the mirror and decided she looked the part of a woman celebrating her first architecture victory. No matter that a moment of letdown preceded her out the door, out of the building, and to her car. Carl would not be enough tonight, although he was most supportive. She wished there was someone she really cared about in another way.

Carl came to meet her as she entered the annex at Élan's, taking both of her hands in his large ones. He looked at her for several seconds before speaking. "I don't believe I've ever seen you look so radiant. There's something mysterious about you tonight—it's those green eyes." He smiled, allowing his gaze to roam over the deep décolletage of her dress and down her slender body before retracing the course upward. He completed his inspection with a smile.

Myrhia laughed as she looked into his openly frank face, with its wide cheekbones and deep-set amber eyes that laugh wrinkles kept constantly shuttered. She could tell he was pretending he hadn't heard about the Tarrington Building yet and was allowing her the pleasure of telling him.

"Are we celebrating something special tonight?" he asked, leading her to their table. His eyes flickered knowingly, giving him away.

"As if you didn't know already! Trish told you, but I do think this calls for champagne, don't you?"

"Most certainly. Myr, I'm so proud at this moment. It couldn't happen to a nicer gal. You bet this night calls for champagne!" He looked at her quizzically, running his hand through his wiry brown hair. "But you never touch the stuff! I can see that ordinary wine won't do so...." He held up a hand. "Waiter, champagne here!"

Carl was well known and liked everywhere they went. Even on his first time in a place, his personality gave him immediate entree. As usual, the waiter, smiling broadly, approached their table. "I can see this is a special night, Mr. Muldrow," he said, casting a speculative look at Myrhia while he set an ice bucket that contained a bottle of champagne beside them. With a flourish he set about pulling the cork. "Management sent this with compliments of the house. Is it an engagement?"

Myrhia laughed at that. "The next best thing!"

Carl spoke with mock sadness, a mischievous twinkle lighting his 'amber eyes. "I've given up on that score long ago, Henri." His face brightened as he added, "But you should know that this lady is soon to be very well known around Dallas as one of its leading architects. Just keep an eye out for the Tarrington Building in the near future."

"Oh?" It seemed to Myrhia that Henri's eyebrows disappeared into his hairline as he politely backed away from them. "Congratulations, Mademoiselle!" He inclined his head still looking nonplussed.

Myrhia had to laugh as she turned back to Carl. "He probably thinks we're nuts." She felt she was basking in a glow sharing her good luck with Carl. She remembered one other time in her apartment when they had an occasion of mutual excitement after receiving the final acceptance on a shopping mall proposal. They had returned to her apartment still feeling the euphoria that can only stem from accomplishing something hard fought for and Myrhia had opened a bottle of wine and handed Carl a goblet of the bubbling brew.

"You propose a toast, Carl," she had said.

His amber eyes had narrowed. "To the most promising architect I know."

She had touched her glass to his and then lifted it to her lips. "Here's to you, Carl. The one man who doesn't think of me as a woman first and an architect last. I owe you so much." She had smiled, meeting the pleased acknowledgment in his gaze.

Now, as she let her mind drift to her friend, she felt some of his sadness that seemed to be imbedded in him since his split with his wife. Although he seldom mentioned the separation, she sensed a restlessness that stemmed from his unhappiness. If she could be of some help to him through this rift, she owed it to him, but she felt helpless to know what to do.

While Carl poured the champagne, she looked around the crowded room. She knew many of the guests on sight and a few she had come to know quite well in business. She was nodding and smiling in recognition, when out of her peripheral vision she felt something pulling her around. As she turned, her gaze locked with a pair of blue-gray agates almost hidden under thick black lashes. The rugged face beneath the eyes was dark, high cheekboned, and offset by a sensuous-looking pair of lips that were drawn tightly together. Twice in one day was too much to encounter that unsmiling face.

For some reason the stranger's look sent a shiver deep into her body, a feeling never before experienced. In the fraction of time his gaze held hers captive, Myrhia felt as if she were pinned and mounted on a butterfly mat. She was not aware of Carl's oustretched hand holding a proffered glass of champagne. Waves of pleasure mingling with unexplained pain washed over her as she returned the stranger's stare. Who was he and what right had he to stare this way?

Carl's touch on her sleeve brought her back to the moment. "Myrhia, come back to me!" he said, laughing. "I'm ready to toast the architect of the future."

She turned back almost reluctantly, forcing her mind into the present, and lifted her glass in salute.

"May the Tarrington Building start you on your much deserved career."

"Thank you, Carl." For some reason tears welled in the corner of her eyes. "You are a good, good friend."

Looking over her shoulder again as if compelled to draw the stranger into the celebration with them, Myrhia was left with a sense of loss. It had been almost physical, as if he had touched her body. Why had he made such an impact on her? Now he was gone and she did not know his name. The club room was filling with men and their dates and the noise was becoming almost cacophonic.

"Who besides Vaughan will be financing the building, Carl?" she asked, finally able to shake off the reaction to the stranger's gaze.

"All the money will be contributed by Vaughan Associates. Turk Vaughan is a wealthy promoter, you know. Money is no object where his company is concerned."

"I suppose I'll be meeting this legendary hero within the near future? From what I've been told, Carl, he is hard to get to know." She gave a wry laugh. "I'm sure I'll look forward to that."

"You'll find him different from anyone you've met. You're in for a shock of a sort. The man is an iceberg—colder than the one that sank the *Titanic*."

Carl looked around the room momentarily, a frown between his pale eyebrows. "I'm sure I saw him in here a minute or two ago. I know damn well I did!" Carl's face took on a wicked grin. "I expect he's in for a shock himself when he finds out that M. Lassiter is none other than one fine woman architect named Myrhia. I'm looking forward to the meeting."

"Oh, then, he doesn't know I'm a woman? That should be cozy!" For some reason she felt a shiver of apprehension. "What does this womanizer look like?"

"Oh, I suppose you would call him handsome. He's well over six feet tall, of course, and built like Apollo—dark, thick black hair, very strange, cold eyes—slate gray, I think." He laughed sardonically. "I'd be a fool not to admit he's good-looking. When he comes to the office, my secretaries fall all over themselves."

As he spoke, Myrhia experienced a smothering sensation around her heart as if she had been captured and impaled on a pair of slate-gray spikes. She was certain now that she had seen the great Turk Vaughan and had almost succumbed to his charm like any silly schoolgirl, but the devilish thing about it was that she hoped to see him again.

She looked up at Carl, feeling suddenly weak. "Carl, I don't think I'd better have any more champagne. Do you think we could go someplace for a bite to eat now?"

"You bet! I know how you are about champagne. We made a pretty good dent in it, anyway. I'll tell Henri how much we appreciated the gift." Carl rose and came to take her arm. "I can't get over how you glow tonight. It makes me almost sorry to have to tell you something over dinner." He was teasing her she could tell by the happy expression on his face. Now that she thought about it, the bleak look was missing from around his eyes tonight. If she hadn't been so excited about her own affairs, she might have noticed immediately there was a difference about him.

"We're celebrating at Benihana. That way we'll have plenty of time to visit while they cook our supper in front of us. I know you like the place. I called for reservations from Denton so we won't have to wait to be seated.

"Sounds great!" Out in the fresh air she regained the earlier sense of excitement. She would never have this moment to savor again and she was determined to make the most of the evening.

As Carl maneuvered his car into a parking space at the Japanese restaurant in Park Central, Myrhia had a fleeting chill of apprehension. She shrugged it off, blaming the sudden feeling on too much champagne, and stepped from the Thunderbird and walked toward the restaurant.

Carl was right to call ahead for reservations, as they were seated almost immediately in spite of the crowd waiting for tables. There were three other couples at their table already when she and Carl stepped into the well below the knee-high table. Two empty spaces remained on her right.

Carl immediately became acquainted with the other couples and soon was engaged in lively conversation, bringing Myrhia into it from time to time. Her body was halfway turned toward Carl and she was not aware of anyone on her right until she felt the movement of a body sliding awkwardly into a much too small seat beside her. Slightly irritated at the pressure on her thigh from the stranger, she turned with an impatient shrug to find she was staring into a now familiar pair of steel-gray eyes. Before she had time to react to the third encounter with this man, Carl reached across in front of her to shake the man's hand.

Smiling broadly he said, "Hey, now, this is all right! You two can meet under congenial circumstances after all. Turk, this is M. Lassiter, architect for your Tarrington Building."

If Carl had said this lady was a two-headed fox, the handsomely rugged face not twelve inches from her own couldn't have looked so shocked. Losing all her own composure, she stared into his eyes, which were becoming hooded under the heavy black lashes. His sensuously carved lips became a thin line tightly drawn across a stubborn chin.

"How quaint! A woman architect!" His stare was sending steel shafts into her own eyes as he continued to glare at her. "And what might the M. stand for?" he asked sardonically, one eyebrow rising upward.

For the first time in years Myrhia felt subdued, almost tongue-tied in his presence and was grateful for Carl's help in bridging the gap between them. He said, "Myrhia—Myrhia Lassiter, soon to become recognized as one of Dallas's best."

The black eyebrow leveled off as an unreadable expression replaced his cold stare. "You do show promise, M. Lassiter. I would be a complete fool not to recognize that."

Myrhia rallied at last. "I suppose, then, you can swallow the fact that I'm female."

A sardonic smile loosened the tight lips. "You are definitely that! Female, I mean." He let his gaze travel over the low neckline of her dress and upward to her raven hair before turning to assist an impatient redhead into the seat beside him. He addressed his glowering companion. "Here you are, Letty. You can share in this coincidence. I'd like you to meet my new architect— Myrhia Lassiter and Carl Muldrow of Muldrow Associates. They will be erecting the Tarrington Building for us."

"Oh? And which is the architect? Surely not—" It seemed to Myrhia that Letty simpered a little as she leaned coquettishly against Turk. "I didn't think you liked for women to compete with men, darling?" Myrhia thought she detected a bit of amusement in the woman's striking blue eyes.

"How the hell was I to know she was Myrhia. She signed the design proposal just 'M,'" he said irritably under his breath before turning back to Myrhia, a scowl still marring his good looks. "I have to admit, Miss Lassiter, your proposal is damned good. I chose it from all the others myself and I'll stick by my decision," he added pompously. "Seeing the name Lassiter, I assumed that the M. stood for Mark or Matthew. You see, I'm not unfamiliar with your father's work. Walt Lassiter was your father, wasn't he? Naturally, I thought you would be his son, but I see I'm quite mistaken." Again she became aware of his appraising glance raking her breasts and face insolently.

Talk about a chauvinist! How dare Turk belittle her gender! He admitted he had chosen the building plans over all the others, had admired them, liked them well enough to choose them for the final drawing. Then what the hell did he have to complain about? The fact she was a woman didn't make her less capable to design. Didn't he know that God did give women brains as well as bodies?

Turk continued to look at her with his probing gaze,

making her wish she could change places with Carl, but while the heat of her own anger was rising against him, she was also wondering what those finely chiseled lips would feel like pressed to her own. When she felt she could no longer control her mounting tension, his mouth broke into a half-smile that swept her anger away like dust into the clean air. What strange effect was he having on her, anyway?

In some ways the man looked foreign. His naturally dark olive skin was browned by Texas sun from apparent exposure, his narrow, straight nose flared slightly, highlighting the well-defined cheekbones that framed the blue-gray stare. At that moment his fascinating eyes were looking disdainfully at her. It would be hard to fathom his changing moods and she hoped she didn't have to come face to face with him often.

"As I said, I would be stupid not to recognize your talent, Miss Lassiter. For a wom—" She did not allow him to finish.

"Woman? You were about to say 'for a woman'?" she interrupted, feeling as if sparks were flying from her own eyes, and longing to wipe the smug look from his face.

"Not exactly what I had intended to say." He smiled with his lips only as his eyes were hidden by black lashes drawn like blinds. The meaningful look roved over her body again insolently. She felt the heat of passion pass between them in that moment as her own pulse quickened. His next remark broke the spell between them, leaving her adrift for a short moment.

"I was going to say, Miss Lassiter, that for a woman so obviously well endowed with all the feminine attributes, you show the talent of a master in your field."

Letty interrupted petulantly. "Turk, for heaven's

sake, can't you let up? You chose the design, didn't you? Why not accept it graciously?'' It was clear to Myrhia his companion was feeling left out of the conversation.

Still burning from his backhanded compliment, Myrhia knew she should be grateful to the woman on his right for discharging the electricity between them, but instead she resented her.

Carl, who appeared unconcerned by what had been happening between her and Turk, said at last, ''Myr, what will you order? The terriyaki—chicken or steak? The waiter will be back in a minute.'' He was concentrating on the menu. ''I'd like shrimp. How about you? And shall we try the warm saki—go all out Japanese?''

Relieved at the interruption, she nodded. ''Might as well go the whole way. I won't be able to sleep tonight anyway.''

Carl reached for her hand and held it in his, giving her a reassuring squeeze. Then she knew he had heard every bitter word that had passed between her and Turk but had probably been too nonplussed to know how to smooth over the situation. She leaned toward him gratefully, deliberately turning her back on the disturbing element on her right.

She continued to be grateful for Carl's gregarious nature as his good humor brought out the best in the other couples that shared the fun at their table. Determined not to let Turk spoil her big night, she made a special effort to be outgoing.

''Can you handle a knife that effectively, Carl?'' she said, watching the slender Japanese chef deftly slice mushrooms, shrimp, and bits of tenderloin into bite-size pieces onto the grill in the center of their table.

But she couldn't shut out the conversation between

the two on her right, much as she wished to. "This is a nice place, Turk," she overheard Letty say. "You told me to expect something different. I'll have to tell Ted all about it. He likes to hear where we've been," Letty said and it seemed to Myrhia she detected a note of sadness.

"I know, Letty." Turk's voice held a gentleness she would not have suspected before. Ted must be the woman's child and it was apparent there was a great deal of affection between this strange man and the redhead. "I hoped you'd like it. When I'm in Tokyo, I usually dine at the original Benihana. I've met the former Japanese owner; he was a wrestler. He's quite an enterprising man."

"I can see only one drawback, Turk. What if you're stuck at a communal table with undesirables?" Letty laughed softly as Turk leaned closer, whispering like a conspirator.

Myrhia felt rebuffed even though she had no way of knowing they were referring to her and leaned a little farther toward Carl for comfort and in order not to hear the intimate dialogue on her right.

Carl, who had been engrossed in watching the chef season and cook the meat and vegetables on the hibachi in front of them, turned at her movement. "He's good, isn't he? Do you think we could cook that way?"

"Oh, no, I doubt we could." She gave a little laugh. "I'm planning to get a microwave now that I have a little more income. Do you think we could cook Oriental food in one of those?"

"It's satisfying to know you'll be able to splurge a little more now, isn't it, Myr? You've really been conservative up until now."

"Maybe so, but now I might cut loose a little." She smiled at Carl's interest in her. He had been there when she needed a friend and without his support it would not have come so quickly.

When they were preparing to leave some time later, she realized the evening had passed and she had not really been aware of what had transpired, what they had eaten, or what the conversation had been about. Ordinarily Benihana was a favorite restaurant but tonight everything was unreal. For some reason the excitement over the acceptance of her design seemed detached. It was as if it had happened to someone else, and the strange feeling disturbed her.

Carl rose first, turning to help her step from the well around the table, but before he could hold out his hand, a pair of strong ones clasped her waist, lifting her effortlessly from the pit. The touch of Turk's hands through the thin material of her dress was electric, sending tingling vibrations along her nerves. As she turned to say something to him, she was stopped by the mystified expression on his face. Was it possible Turk also felt the electricity pass between them?

It was impossible to find her voice and she was grateful once again for Carl. "Thanks, Turk," he said offhandedly, tucking Myrhia's arm through his as they moved away from the table.

"*My* pleasure, Carl!"

Myrhia was puzzled by the amused grin on Carl's face as they walked over a small decorative bridge arching artistically over a tiny pool of water that was landscaped with small ferns and flowers.

There was no further communication between them until they reached the foyer and started to their cars. "I'll be in touch soon, Carl—with you and Ms. Lassiter. Very soon. In fact, sooner than you might expect," Turk said meaningfully, a frown forming between his eyes.

Why did she get the feeling the last remark was directed toward her exclusively? She made the mistake of looking directly at him and became impaled once more on his steely stare.

Letty gave them both a quizzical look as she pulled Turk from the doorway into the night. "For heaven's sake, Turk! I've never seen you act like such a boor. Why?"

His reply was lost on her as Carl put a protective arm around Myrhia's waist and they moved away. "Don't let him snow you, Myr. I should have warned you he's a killer where most women are concerned, but I think you have your head on straight. You can handle him. I'm only sorry we have to deal with him at all. I'll be there to run interference when we come face to face." He hesitated. "I'm sorry, Myrhia, my ruse backfired tonight."

She caught an inference behind his words. "Did you arrange for this meeting somehow?"

"Well, yes and no. I happened to call his office and his secretary told me he would be dining at the Benihana this evening. The rest was easy.... But it didn't turn out well for you. I'm sorry, Myr."

"Don't worry, Carl. It was an eye-opener. Now I'll know what to expect from now on." Brave words, she knew. It would take all the poise she had to confront him if they disagreed on her drawings. On the other hand she was the architect and he had chosen her design without hesitation. She would be a fighting adversary for the great Turk Vaughan.

Chapter Two

As they walked toward Carl's Thunderbird, Myrhia
caught sight of a fine, athletically trained body moving
with ease a short distance ahead of them. Letty, clinging desperately on his arm like an insecure moth to a
windowpane, was laughing at something he had said.
Something about Turk's insolent swagger made Myrhia's nerves bristle. He would never be able to affect
her the way he had tonight—never!

What the devil had happened to her the past two
hours, anyway? She had come for a celebration, her
celebration, and this pigheaded, prejudiced man, whose
only claim to her business was that he controlled the
pursestrings, had managed in one short time to sweep
away all her excitement.

"I'll be glad to get home, Carl. I'm really bushed."
She leaned against his shoulder for comfort.

Carl's arm slipped around her waist companionably.
"I know, hon, Turk has upset you. He has the same
effect on everyone, but don't let it throw you. He's a
cold, hard man but one that's good to have on our side
when we need him. You'll get along with him. You'll
see."

Myrhia wasn't so sure about that. "The big oaf! Just
because he was the best running back the Dallas Cow-

boys had for a good number of years doesn't make him big in my books, Carl! Any pin brain can play football if he has the brawn and speed to stand it and looks like an Atlas.'' Suddenly she laughed, clearing the air a bit. "I'm acting hurt and schoolgirlish! No, he won't spoil my evening. He isn't the only committee member, is he? Perhaps I'll like the others.''

"That's my girl!" There was a long pause while Carl expertly cleared the access onto Central Expressway. "I have a matter to discuss with you tonight if you can stay awake long enough.''

This was the second time this evening that he had mentioned he had something to talk over with her. "We'll have a cup of coffee. That way I'll manage to keep awake.''

They drove the rest of the way in silence to Élan's parking lot where she had left her car. "Sorry for the inconvenience, Myr. I know it's awkward having two cars. I'll follow you home. But tonight this was unavoidable.''

As Myrhia navigated her Volvo home, her thoughts went again to Turk Vaughan. She had confidence she would find the other committee members amicable, and knew the best course of action was to put the insufferable Mr. Vaughan out of her mind completely. When she reached home, the soft lights of her small apartment welcomed her, lifting her heavy mood. Here she could be anything she desired—the dreamer, the designer, the vulnerable woman seeking understanding of a need to succeed. Here she could be herself.

She turned to Carl, who had come in right behind her. "Make yourself at home while I start Mr. Coffee on his way.''

With a tremendous sigh Carl sprawled onto her

couch. "This is a restful place. I have enjoyed coming here, Myr."

From the distance away in the kitchen, she thought she heard him use the past tense. "Oh?" she called out over the sound of water racing from the tap. She finished making the coffee, setting the dial at Brew and rejoined him in the living room. "Now what was that all about? That statement had an ominous sound. Won't you be coming here anymore?"

"Not so often, I'm afraid." Several minutes passed before he spoke again, and her curiousity grew. She was about to ask him again what was on his mind when he finally spoke.

"In a way, Myr, this evening is a celebration for me too. I didn't want my good news to outshine yours in any way so I waited. I wouldn't want to detract from your exciting evening."

She looked at him directly, trying to understand the change in him, more aware than before he had been different most of the evening and if she had not been so caught up in her own excitement she would have noticed sooner.

"Well, out with it! Don't keep me in suspense any longer."

Carl drew a deep breath before speaking. "I'm going back to Belinda. We made up yesterday. That's where I've been these past few days—in Denton with her family. Dody needs us both. She's at an age where she's confused about visiting privileges and all that traumatic stuff. It isn't fair, her being upset, and to tell the truth, Myr, I've found it hell too. I still love my wife and found out she still loves me. We just got off the track somewhere, but we're going to make it this time." A smile lit up his face.

"Somehow we just didn't give each other equal

room to grow. I think working closely with you has helped me see that a woman needs to be her individual self in order to become a full partner. You have that capacity and I hope you find someone who appreciates that side of your nature—and soon. I want you to have the love of a fine man that you deserve."

She was touched by his concern for her. "Carl, you won't need to worry on that score. I may never find what you and Belinda have together." She reached over the space between them and touched his hand briefly. "You don't know how happy this makes me."

All the time she was speaking she knew the full impact of what was happening had not hit her yet. She would miss the comfortable association here in her apartment where they had shared many restful evenings over one of her quickly prepared dinners or a cocktail now and then at Élan's. However, in all honesty she couldn't selfishly wish to cling to those moments now in the face of his happiness.

"Will you and Belinda come over for dinner soon? I'd like to know her as well as I do you, Carl. And you might bring Dody. I would enjoy having a little girl around."

"They would both like you, Myr. Belinda knows I've been thrown with you often, but I explained, strangely enough, that we had never had anything but a mutual friendship. It's been damned good for me and I hope we can go on in our business relationship." His smile appeared lopsided. "You know I'm in there pulling for you all the time."

"That I do know and I treasure your friendship too." The aroma of the freshly brewed coffee alerted her and she rose to return to the kitchen.

"I don't have any wine in the apartment at the present, but let's propose a toast with coffee," she said, returning with two mugs of the steaming brew. Lifting her cup to his, she said, "To your reunion with your family!"

A look of relief crossed his open face, making her realize that he had dreaded telling her about his going back to Belinda. Was it because she had come to rely on him for her infrequent outings where an escort was desirable? Goodness, she had really been working into a rut when she relied on one man for companionship. Had she made a mistake in turning down dates with other men the past few years? The few times she had been out with anyone but Carl she had found the evening flat and lacking in either sexual attraction or stimulating conversation. There was no basis for continuing the association.

"Myr, I want you to know that I'll be close by when you face the committee for the Tarrington Building as they begin to hash over your layout. I'll be there especially to act as a buffer between you and the Dalai Lama." Carl threw back his head for a hearty laugh, clearing the slight tension between them.

"Does it occur to you, Myr, that that guy Turk just might be all bluff and bluster to cover vulnerability where women are concerned? The way he ogled you, I had the feeling you might be the one girl to knock him off his self-imposed pedestal."

"Oh, I wouldn't even want to try, Carl. Not interested!" she said, but wondered if she really meant it.

Long after Carl had left her, she lay awake thinking of the evening. It had been fraught with emotional undertones—first, her intense excitement over the Tarrington Building, then Carl's half-pleased, half-reluctant manner toward her, but the crux of her thoughts centered around Dirckson Vaughan. Why did he have the effect on her, almost like a tidal wave sweeping all of her emotions forward and then draining them back into a sea of doubt. She would have to be cautious around him. Carl need not worry on that score as she would be able to take care of herself.

The next two weeks passed uneventfully. Myrhia and Trish were busy picking up loose ends on her last project, a small shopping area not far from Lemon Park, where her office was located. It was coming along nicely, she observed, as she walked the short distance from her office toward noon one day early in the week.

The subdued design hinted of modern Spanish with a light touch of Indian influence. She held out for an illusion of the Mayan to be woven skillfully into the trim under the overhang of eaves. It was colorful, yet in good taste, and she felt quite pleased with the results.

She was standing back admiring the last portion of the center to be finished the following week, if all went on schedule, when a deep, well-modulated voice spoke behind her, startling her momentarily. Bracing herself as she recognized his manner of speaking, she turned to look up at the handsome man who had an imperious air about him.

"Your secretary told me I would find you here." The sunlight did not diminish his good looks, she thought grudgingly. In fact, the olive skin took on a glow of good health, and his casual dress of slacks and sport shirt, opened at the throat showing his strong neck and chest muscles covered with a spattering of dark hair, added to his overall sensuous look.

If her knees would stop their trembling for a moment she would be able to find her voice. "Oh?" she said faintly, gathering strength by looking away from him. "What is it you wanted to see me about?"

"First things first!" Looking at his watch, he turned back to her. "Lunch first, then we can talk. It's about a change in your design proposal."

This was something she could counter with fierce pride—a change in her design of the building. "And—just what is it you would like to change?" Her voice rose in high crescendo.

"Here, here, tiger cat! Give me a chance to speak first. Now I know I came on pretty strong the other night at the Benihana especially for our first meeting. I must say it was a shocker to find myself face to face with a siren, built like Venus, all beauty rolled into one neat package, then to find that body and face housed the ability to design my new building." He looked at her quizzically through shaded lids. "Wouldn't you say that was a shocker?"

"Tell me—would you have selected my proposed design if you had known I was female?" She managed to hold his gaze, not batting an eyelash.

"Well, I would have given it more thought. It was a surprise, that's all! Now, since I do like your proposal and am building it on nearly all counts as you specified, let's have lunch. Since we're not fifty yards away from a restaurant, how about it?"

All barriers down momentarily, she managed what she hoped was a semblance of a smile. "That will be fine."

Myrhia was glad they found a table near the window where she could look outside across the driveway passages to her own shopping center. "That's my design, by the way—the new Battle shopping corner. I know it's small, but I'm partial to the design. Do you find it attractive?" she asked, hoping he would agree.

Turk was slow in answering, which made her have doubts. "Yes, in all fairness to you, the architect, I think it's damned attractive and in excellent taste for this area. Perhaps I would have played down some of the Indian motif for the ceiling trim, but included in the overall style of the building, it fits in okay." He spoke without conviction and before she was able to reply, he continued.

"In fact, I've been going through several of your buildings in the Dallas area since our last meeting. I must say that on the whole I like them, although I find that one or two reveal the sex of the designer."

She had held back long enough, and with the last remark, she let him have it. "Where the devil do you get off criticizing anyone's designs? Are you an architect? I was under the impression you were all brawn and somehow had been fortunate to capitalize on that body to make a fortune. Isn't it possible for you to forget I'm female and stop hitting me with insults and innuendos. Would you be sitting here putting down my father or any other male architect this way?" She rose with the intention of leaving before the order arrived, but turned back having more to say. "How did you get this way? Did some woman bend that iron heart of yours into a knot?" She could feel the flush of anger in her face and hated the fact she had lost control, but still she continued. "You're the first chauvinistic client that I've had dumped on me in one overbearing dose since I became a licensed architect. But don't worry, Mr. Vaughan, I'm not easily intimidated. You'll find I'm as capable as any man in this field and determined to make a name for myself."

Myrhia avoided looking at him directly, turning to face him at last with an exasperated shrug. Much to her dismay it was her undoing as she found herself staring into a smug grin that slowly spread into a genuine smile. The blue-gray eyes seemed to be shining with a malicious gleam, as if he might be enjoying her outburst.

"You're insufferable!" She turned on her heel to walk away.

Turk moved quickly for a large man, reaching for her arm to draw her back to the table. Fortunately due to the crowded restaurant and the noise that accompanied the lunch group, not too many people had paid attention to what they probably would assume was a lovers' quarrel anyway. Not wanting to create a further scene, Myrhia turned back and resumed her seat, staring angrily out the window, seeing nothing.

"Little spitfire! You're one gorgeous firebrand, Myrhia Lassiter. By the way, I've never known another Myrhia. It is pronounced with a short *i*, isn't it? Like Miria?" His smile was genuinely warm now, matching the resonant quality of his voice. "Where did you acquire the name?"

She turned back then, feeling a small amount of embarrassment that she had lost control. She was rarely able to stay angry long and his question almost made her smile. How many times in her life had she been called upon to explain her name? Dozens or hundreds?

"Well, my father was a romantic. He had once known an Arabian girl in his early years—his salad years, he called them. She must have captured his fancy—hence, her name became his only daughter's. On rare occasions my mother teased him about his first love. I'm sure there was nothing to it, my father was barely sixteen at the time he and Grandfather Lassiter traveled in the Far East. Grandfather realized Father had talent so he put the creative juices to flowing even then, Father used to say. He exposed his son to the wonders of the world of architecture in all nations, hoping it would help him in the future."

"It must have worked, I've considered your father one of the better architects of his day—a little prosaic at times—nevertheless, steady and sound. You follow much the same pattern but are more flexible." A hint of amusement moved across his face. "I doubt you'd be flexible if you had to change much on one of your designs, would you?"

"You'll probably find that out soon enough," she quipped, toning down her reply with a smile. She didn't want to get into another argument now. Turning her full attention to her chef's salad and hot roll, Myrhia determined that she would remain cool hereafter when they had disagreements and he would not get the best of her—that she resolved.

"Now, what is this luncheon date all about? What is it you want to delete about the plans already?" she said tersely, still not completely calm. "We haven't even broken ground yet."

"I realize that and that part will take place one month from now. I want you at the ground-breaking—I thought you might want to toss the first dirt, sort of an auspicious occasion for a budding architect. Would you like that?"

She looked into his face, now guileless, wondering at his sincerity. "I'd like that very much. But you still haven't told me what you object to in the plans."

"Well, it's the fascia near the cornice around the first-floor trim. I want it abolutely plain, less ornate. After all, the beauty of the building will lie in its shape and outer facade. We don't need to guild the lily, so to speak." His eyes were hooded, preventing her knowing what lay in their agate depth.

"I'm afraid you will ruin the entry access on all sides of the building if you take away from the upper trim around the first floor. I thought the building needed that to tie it into the illusion of grandeur—after all, it will be in Turtle Creek addition and that area is tops in my book."

"It's not a serious fault and will be one we can work out—say, over cocktails and perhaps dinner this Saturday. This being Tuesday, I can't spare any more time. I've got to catch a flight to Maui and back before I see you again Saturday. I've invested in fifteen condo units that are being built five miles from Hana. Have you ever been to Hawaii, by the way?"

"Once—with my mother soon after Father's death." She looked away sadly as she remembered. "We hadn't expected to enjoy it but in spite of the loss to us both, we loved the island. We were only in Honolulu and never made it to Maui."

"Then I'll see to it we go sometime soon." Turk rose and walked to the cashier to pay the bill, as Myrhia moved into the foyer, wondering why he thought she would be going to Hawaii with him at all.

"Myrhia, I've a loophole for you. Come up with a variation of the fascia—say, several proposed changes— and we'll look them over Saturday night at Élan's. See you!"

She watched his quick stride carry him away as rapidly as he had come, leaving her standing under the passageway of the mall. Just like that! The insolent swing to his hips and shoulders irritated her almost as much as his terse manner. She had been dismissed bluntly. Who did he think he was, anyway?

When she returned to her office, she found Trish still recovering from the shock of coming face to face with her ideal of her high school crushes, when Turk had been the star of the Cowboys. "Myrhia, I thought I'd faint when he walked into the office. I've never seen a man that good-looking."

"Spare me, please!" Myrhia broke into Trish's running dialogue extolling Turk's virtues. "Spare me! I'm up to my neck in his opinions already. Why, he's nothing but a bag of wind, a pretty face, and good physique!" With that she stomped into her office, closing the door behind her and leaving Trish staring. Inside she collapsed against the door momentarily. Her first encounter with him alone had taken a lot out of her.

Let Trish have her schoolgirl crush. He was not for her. She had met other men who had more appeal on first acquaintance and certainly were not so devilishly opinionated as Turk was. He did have clout—there was no denying it—and a standoffish quality that must stem from disappointment somewhere in his life. Some woman had destroyed his trust in the female sex. Well, she certainly would not want to pick up the challenge of trying to restore his faith in women.

She sat down at her desk, leaning on her hands and elbows, trying to sort out her thoughts. As a matter of fact, she missed Carl. Other than a telephone call now and then about something that concerned the Tarrington Building, he did not call at all. She missed his good-natured presence. Nothing was so bad with Carl around. Did Belinda know how fortunate she was? This time she had better hold on to him because there were other predators who would gobble him up. He was worth ten Turks. As if she were psychic, the telephone rang, startling her.

"It's Carl Muldrow, Myrhia," Trish buzzed.

"Thanks, Trish." She heard the receiver click on Trish's desk before she pushed the blinking light from the incoming call.

"Hello, Carl! How's it going wih you?"

"Great, Myr, that's why I'm calling. Bea and I are making it better than ever—at least so far. We've been going to a marriage counselor and learning a lot about ourselves. Dody's so happy. Her little face glows from the time Belinda takes her to school and I see her in the evening." There was a pause. "But that's not the only reason I called. It's about another proposal—a convention center six miles off the Denton Highway. Would you be interested in submitting a design for a large layout—the center and cottage and hotel accommodations? I'll get all the dope together for you; buzz talk has it that the center is to be used jointly by Denton and Dallas. It is to be built just beyond Lake Dallas. A good location—in a rolling wooded area—not much to detract from the building. A good chance to expand, Myr."

"I sure want it, Carl! When can I get the dope on it—size and all?"

"Most anytime now. I'll call you next week and we'll meet for lunch. Okay?" He waited for her answer. "I'll be glad to see you again, Myr. I've really missed having our conflabs."

"Thanks, Carl! Call me again." After she hung up the telephone, she thought about the assembly proposition. It would be a real challenge. It was true that she missed Carl but not as much as she thought she would. He was the best friend she had and it was good to know they might be able to keep that relationship on that basis now. She had never had a brother and Carl served that purpose well.

It would be a long time until Saturday and her dinner with Turk. She wanted to label it a business engagement even though Élan's was not just a business meeting place between a man and a woman. Nevertheless she intended to dress conservatively and treat the date casually. Meanwhile, she wanted to see what he really could find to object to about the fascia on her rendering. She pushed the intercom buzzer for Trish.

"Trish, find the copy of the working drawings of the front view of the Tarrington Building, please."

She stepped to the coffeepot to warm up the left over from morning, thought better of it, threw it out, and started out fresh. Her mind was on the work at hand that had to be done and she absentmindedly allowed her small finger to touch the hot plate on the Mr. Coffee, causing an immediate jab of pain.

"Damn! I'm careless!" she said aloud as Trish entered.

"Is it bad?" She looked at Myrhia with sympathy. "I don't know anything that hurts worse than a burn." Trish walked to the desk, laid down the cardboard tube holding the drawings she requested, and stepped to the brightly lit window behind the desk. She pulled off a bit of the aloe plant and approached Myrhia. "That's what this plant's good for, you know. And it does work. I burned my arm on the oven a week or two ago, and this darned stuff took the sting out immediately."

Myrhia thanked her, allowing her to rub some of the juice on the injured finger. It wasn't a bad burn but the fact she was careless and allowed it to happen unnerved her. She had prided herself on her control at all times, but lately she pulled some goofs. The aloe worked almost immediately and the finger had almost stopped throbbing even though a small blister had formed on the under pad.

"Thanks, Trish. And thank you for bringing in the plans. You can leave any time you care to. It's going on five and I'll not leave just yet. I'll lock up."

"Okay, but I'll stay if there's something I can do." She watched Myrhia slip the drawings from the cardboard tube and spread them on her drawing board, which stood on one side of the room.

"I hope you won't have to change anything much.

Did Turk like the plans as they are?" Trish asked hopefully.

"I really can't tell too much about him. But he does object to the fascia here." She pointed to the stone band that would lie between the moldings. "He asked that I change it so it will be completely plain. Personally, I think it gives the building's lower part more eye appeal from ground level."

"I don't see anything wrong with the fascia as it is," Trish said, turning her head sideways to get a better look at the working drawings. "I like a building with a little artwork here and there to relieve the plain lines. Some of the modern buildings around Dallas are like the suburban homes—paper doll cutouts of the one next and the one after that. Row after row of tract buildings and it's the same way in the suburbs—like beehives. It leaves me cold." She shuddered slightly.

Myrhia turned with a smile for her secretary. "You would be a good one on an advisory board for Dallas's city council. I feel the same way—we need a touch of art now and then. I know we no longer have dentils and cornices as the old cathedrals have, but my plan was to draw attention to the entrance facade. At least that's the way I see it." She stood back, examining her work critically. "No, I'll not change it yet. I'll wait and see what the Dalai Lama has to say Saturday night. It may be his committee will like what I've done when I explain my reasons. After all, it is my design." If she was acting stubborn about the change, she didn't want to think about it.

"Saturday night? You have a date with Turk? Are you actually telling me you're going out with him?" It seemed to Myrhia her secretary was in a state of rapture when she looked at her. Poor girl! Turk didn't deserve all this sighing and heavy breathing.

"It's purely a business meeting. The great man is flying in from Maui then and, in all probability, he'll have jet lag and be as irritable as a she-bear with cubs." She laughed at that simile. "I should say a mad male bear."

"No matter how he comes on I would still like to be in your shoes." Trish walked out of the office with a look of bliss on her face, forgetting to close the door behind her.

Myrhia sank into her desk chair with a sigh, looking at the empty space vacated by Trish's retreating figure. Halfheartedly she flipped over a drawing sheet and for the next few moments doodled absentmindedly, trying to bring her mind back to the problem at hand. She was determined to come up with another presentation of the fascia that would still have style if not the same clout as the one Turk objected to. She would compromise that far but not to the extent the fascia would be devoid of any trim, unless the other members of the committee voiced objections. Then she would be forced to give in.

After several stops and starts she began to feel the pencil move over the sheet of paper as if it had a will of its own. It was always like this when she really tuned everything from her mind and concentrated hard on what she was doing. At last she came up with two designs that were geometric more than arty. Satisfied that she would have two sketches to show Turk on Saturday, she turned out the lights, locked up her office, and walked to her car, surprised to find it was nearly dusk. She had not even heard Trish leave her office.

She felt a delicious shiver of pure enjoyment as she stepped across the space to her parked car into the late spring evening. The month of April seemed to wrap its fragrant arms around her as she slowed her pace in order to revel in the atmosphere.

Throughout the plantings in the small beds around Lemon Park, mock orange, forsythia, flowering quince, and jasmine were blooming in riotous colors. The mock orange and jasmine released their poignant fragrance into the mild breeze that played about the empty parking lot. No doubt she would choose spring as her favorite season, with fall coming a close second, she was thinking as she stepped into her car to drive away. Spring in Texas was warm and full of promise.

Traffic had thinned at the later hour as she drove down Central Expressway and she couldn't help thinking the Tarrington Building, though not the most imposing, would soon be silhouetted against the fading sunset along with the other taller buildings. The dream was not diminished by the fact there would be headaches and mountains of worry before that day. She had cut her teeth on the problems of an architect, observing her father's often fanatic despair over minor details, but in the past five years she had learned to handle her clients, contractors, and builders without too much friction. Until Turk Vaughan! That was a different problem and one that would require all of her patience before it was finished.

She felt warm gratitude for Carl at this moment. It was reassuring that he would be handling the Tarrington Building on a lump-sum basis. The contractor would do the job for a fixed sum of money and it was to be her duty to see that the clients, in this case Muldrow Associates and Vaughan Enterprises, were treated fairly by keeping as close to the estimated cost as possible. She remembered how grateful she was when Carl told her this as she preferred the lump-sum deal over a cost-plus-fee basis where she would be required to supervise the purchasing of all materials used in the building. She had lucked out there.

Her telephone was ringing as she stepped into her apartment a short time later. It was her best friend, Cleo. "Just a sec, Cleo. I just walked in. Let me put down my things."

Depositing her purse and sketch board on her divan with a few other packages, she picked up the receiver once more. "Now...."

"I've been trying to get you all week but when you're in, I'm out and vice-versa. I wanted to invite you to a cocktail party Saturday night here, at my apartment." There was a pause. "I've got a new man for you to meet."

Myrhia had to smile. Cleo always had a breathless quality about her as if she might be poised for flight. They had been friends since girlhood and even now, Cleo, like Alicia, was constantly wanting to find someone that would make her blood pressure boil. Frankly, Myrhia wondered sometimes whether to laugh or cry at her friend's own life-style. It seemed to her that Cleo was in and out of affairs and trial marriages too frequently to mention. Would Cleo be able to recognize the real thing if it did come along? she wondered.

"But, Myrhia, love, you're different from me." Cleo had said over and over. "Your psyche is steady and true. When you find the right man, you'll stick for life. I wish I was made that way."

Now the voice on the end of the telephone line was waiting for her reply. "Well, what say? Can I count on you?"

"I have a date, Cleo. Actually, it's a business meeting with the man who foots the bill for the expenses in the Tarrington Building. I guess you didn't know but I got the contract for the big one at last," she announced proudly, not expecting Cleo to understand how much it meant to her any more than her mother had. She was correct in surmising her friend's reaction.

"Good! I'm delighted, pet." There was little inflection in her tone. "Is he good looking? The financier?" As usual Cleo was impressed by money.

"Some might say so, but he's just another rich client to me." She knew this was a smug answer as she was not fully convinced she had been telling Cleo the truth.

"And who might he be?"

"Turk Vaughan." Myrhia waited for the usual explosion at the mention of his name and when one did not come, she said, "Are you still there, Cleo?"

"Whew! I just picked myself up from the floor. I was too weak to answer immediately. Honest? Are you telling me the truth? Do you mean that Turk Vaughan is furnishing the money for your building and you actually have a date with him and are acting this unconcerned? My heavens, Myrhia, you've got to bring Turk to my party. My evening will be made. He'll know a lot of the others here, especially the women. He's probably been in bed with most of them either literally or figuratively. As you know, he's been around Dallas aplenty. He's Dallas's leading bachelor—or do I need to tell you?" A pregnant pause followed.

"Well, never mind, I don't expect an answer, pet. Just be here. Cut your business short. I want to see for myself if he's all that he's rated to be. By the way, you won't need the new man I had in mind. I'll take him for myself." She laughed.

Myrhia was having her own doubts about the sanity of taking Turk to Cleo's even if he could be persuaded. "I'll see, Cleo. I won't promise. It depends on what time our conference ends. It might be too late. How long do you expect your party to last?"

"Until the wee hours—you know my style. I don't often entertain but when I do I like it big!" She laughed in a trilling crescendo. "You'd better know that your escort may get away from you before the evening's over."

After she put down the receiver, Myrhia had to admit it would be interesting to see how Turk did react in a group of other attractive men. Sometimes the macho type was only that to women and would be a washout as a man's man.

Myrhia was tired as she drove home on Friday. Tomorrow she would rest, visit her mother, and do some cleaning around the apartment. She enjoyed the latter. She knew it amused her close friends that she liked to do her own cooking, cleaning, and arranging, but she felt a satisfaction in doing it. Especially she enjoyed cooking, trying different entrées and salads, shunning the frozen, packaged products that were supposed to be working woman's biggest boon, where at all possible. Sometimes these products were tasteless or dry and it was almost as easy to steam fresh broccoli or cauliflower and make a good chef's salad from leftovers than to open, thaw, or warm the other.

It was about time she had another party herself. Even though her friends did not always empathize with her desire to succeed, they just might like to celebrate this big event with her. She made a mental note to invite several some time very soon. Her specialty was a Chinese dinner that she prepared in a wok, taking pains not to overcook the vegetables but to leave them crisp and tangy.

For some reason her thoughts traveled to Turk. Would he be interested in one of her little get-togethers? She would know better after their business meeting tomorrow just how well they were getting along and if he would understand what an invitation to her apartment meant. She didn't want to give him the impression she was interested in him in any way but on a business scale. They needed to maintain a professional relationship as they continued working out the details of their project.

Why did she have the feeling he might accept readily? He had never seemed to be eager to know who she really was or where she was coming from. Strange that suddenly the picture in her mind changed abruptly to a vision of an intimate supper for two in her small but attractive dining alcove, where the glow of ruby wine highlighted by candleglow was mirrored in two penetrating blue-gray eyes. Stranger still, the idea lifted her spirits momentarily.

Chapter Three

Saturday was bright and clear when she arose. It was one of those rare days when the wind lay still and all earth seemed to blend with her body and soul. Myrhia took her second cup of coffee to her scrap of balcony, propped her feet on the railing to relax. From her sixth-floor apartment she could see the tops of the old shade trees that lined the streets several blocks away in the older residential district along Turtle Creek.

She knew that just beyond the tall fringe of live oaks, cypress, and maples the creek wandered aimlessly throughout the area. As a child she had explored its banks, reveled in each seasonal flowering, and walked the shady avenues near her home. She had even lingered in front of the large apartment complex for a glimpse of the legendary movie star, Greta Garbo, whose beauty and glamor were still talked about.

Thinking of her home, she naturally thought of Alicia. Today she and her mother would have lunch together. Every other Saturday mother and daughter either met at Anatole's or the Northwood Country Club, usually winding up on the golf course for nine holes where they were evenly matched. Today she hoped there would be no golf; she wasn't in the mood somehow.

At last she forced herself to rise, reluctant to leave the balcony, and moved around the apartment, making mental notes on what she intended to do with her free time. After deciding to do light cleaning, she whisked through her four rooms in short time. The apartment, as usual, responded graciously to her treatment, she noticed, eyeing it as objectively as possible. The sunlight filtering through the sheer draperies of pale gray batiste gave the entire living area a soft touch of silver.

The ice-blue velvet sofa had been her most exciting find. It had been purchased for comfort and adaptability. Since it was sectional, it could be moved easily to accommodate several groups for conversation. She had found it secondhand and had it covered at minimal expense since she had found the velvet at one of the factory warehouses along the highway where all the big marketing was done. Alicia had donated two only slightly used fireside chairs from her own home. They were practically new, as Alicia tired easily of the familiar and sought the new.

Now as she ran her hand over the upholstery of one of the chairs, she was pleased that she had decided on the soft rose color that bordered on pale lavender that even now, in the early morning light, picked up the dove-gray in the carpet and the ice-blue of the sofa and blended the whole together quite well. She looked around the room fondly.

She especially enjoyed the few pieces of sterling silver that had come from her mother's home. The small after-dinner coffee carafe with sugar bowl and creamer that sat on the engraved silver tray seemed made for the marble-topped cherry wood table handed down from her grandmother on her father's side.

At nighttime she enjoyed the subdued light that flowed from the two Tiffany lamps on either side of the sofa. She had found the two of them on one of her exploring jaunts in Cleo's company. They added a touch of contrast to the quiet charm of the room. She smiled now thinking that Cleo would never understand her desire to shop carefully the way she did in order to economize and be able to afford some of the better pieces of furniture in the kind of woods she preferred, mahogany and fruit wood.

"Why don't you just go and buy what you want. Alicia has told you many times to get what you want and charge it to her account. Honestly, Myrhia, you have become too darned independent. You scare me," Cleo said with a wry grin.

Myrhia had laughed enjoying their times together. "Don't worry, Cleo, I haven't changed that much. Is it possible that this new me was there all the time?"

Now Cleo would be glad to know she could afford to expand her purchases more after the project got underway. It gave her smug satisfaction to know that she didn't have to be so penny-wise in her selections.

She was feeling carefree, young, and lighthearted as she flicked away the last bit of dust and prepared to dress for her lunch with her mother. Within a short time she was ready, starting for the door, where she hesitated and turned to walk back to her bedroom. She would take time to select the dress she planned to wear for her evening with Turk. Now that she hoped they could squeeze Cleo's party into their evening, she would have to discard her first choice of something conservative for something dressy. She chose a blue-gray crepe, which she carried to her bed, adjusting the shimmering folds of the skirt across the blue bedspread to prevent wrinkles.

As the color caught her attention she realized she had never noticed before that it was the color of agate forcing an instant picture to her mind of a pair of similarly colored eyes. What was the matter with her anyway? The last thing she wanted to think of this morning was that cold blue gaze that seemed to be able to penetrate her thoughts. She didn't even like the man—then why was she selective in what she would wear?

She was still wondering and thinking she might change her mind about the evening when she met her mother at Anatole's. "You look pretty today, Myrhia," Alicia said, looking her over critically before she smiled. "I like the hair loose about your face. It softens the severity of the intense look you affect most of the time. I suppose the look is assumed purposely so you appear older in your work. But you should be glad you have a perpetually young face, that is, if you take care not to frown and worry so much. I like for my daughter to look soft and feminine."

Alicia reached across the table to squeeze Myrhia's hand. "I've been thinking about your good news, dear. I know how much the acceptance of the design meant to you. I can remember your father's pleasure so well. I'm afraid you think sometimes that I'm not appreciative of your work, but I am! It's just that I can't think of my daughter in that capacity. A son perhaps! But you know, I'm of the thirties generation and we were just beginning to emerge into the new freedom. I may be a throwback to my own mother's time." Her laugh was merry. "Misplaced in time, you know, but I do so enjoy being feminine."

Myrhia smiled, looking at the lovely unlined face before her and wondering if she would ever look so good at forty-eight. They ordered the seafood salad and ate in silence for a while, her mother finally breaking the quiet between them.

"I've been wondering about you and that nice young

man—Carl something or other? Is there anything at all stable between you?" One penciled eyebrow raised slightly.

"Now, Alicia! Carl and I were never romantically inclined. We are really good friends. Now he's back with his wife, Belinda, and his little girl. I'm delighted over that; he's never stopped loving her. He's still my good friend and will continue to advise and pass on new information concerning new projects in Dallas as he always has. We see eye to eye in our related business—that's all."

"Well, dear, take my advice for what it's worth. It isn't easy for a man and woman to be platonic anymore with the new sexual freedom. I only met Carl once, but he seemed pleasant and likable." She cocked her head to one side and the thin, pale eyebrow rose ever so slightly.

"There's something in your eyes today, Myrhia. Something different! Have you met a new man? I'm hoping soon it will happen; you know you're going on—pardon my reference to it—twenty-eight. If you plan to have any children at all, it's easier when one is younger."

'Now, Mother, don't start that again!" At times like these she often reverted back to the use of the word *Mother*, a throwback to childhood when her life had been guided by her parents. "Don't despair! What if I don't marry? I certainly don't want to marry and find I've made a mistake. Then there's the ugliness of divorce and having fatherless children like so many of my friends are doing. Ugh! One stepfather after another. Poor kids! They'll grow up more insecure than ever. I just might turn out to be a damned good old-maid architect! Then you might be proud," she said with more emphasis than she intended.

"I am proud of you now! But, my dear, I wish you wouldn't swear so often. It is unbecoming a lady of your social standing. Or have you forgotten?" A smile brightened her mother's puckered frown. "Honey, pay no attention to me. I know I'm old-fashioned even for my own generation, as I said. It's just that your father and I gave you a good education so don't fall back on vulgarities to express yourself." She sighed and picked up her ice tea glass, sipping thoughtfully. "You're not alone in this—so many of the society girls swear vehemently. I suppose it's just a fad like bobby socks! It too will pass."

She passed Alicia a warm smile. "Now that the lecture and our lunch are over, I may be too weak to play more than five holes of golf. I did feel like beating the panty-hose off you today, but now you've worn me down." Myrhia rose, picked up the check over her mother's protest, and started to the cashier.

"Today is my treat!" She waved aside further argument. "I'll soon be filthy rich—at least for someone who has barely kept above water. I've waited a long time to make it. And now I can have that old occasional chair upholstered in the velvet. I've been putting off having it done until I got some money ahead." She turned to her mother and gave her a little hug. "Want to go with me some day soon to pick out the color?"

"I do." Her mother's face shone with pride. "I'm really proud of you."

Myrhia still felt a sense of well-being as she left Alicia at the Northwood Country Club with her friends, who had gathered for two tables of bridge. The exercise from the nine holes of golf had left her body tingling with good health. She had been smiling as she kissed her mother's soft cheek and took her leave. Actually she was pleased her mother remained the same day after day, resorting to motherliness on occasion as it gave her a sense of permanence. And today was no exception.

What would Alicia say if she knew her daughter would be seeing the touted Dirckson Vaughan, man about town, fairly often for the next few months? Somehow Myrhia had the feeling her mother would opt for the arrangement even if her daughter did not. For some reason not understood, she felt buoyant and carefree as she entered her bedroom and found the dress lying as she had left it. It seemed to have a life of its own for a moment as a pair of haunting eyes flashed before her mind's vision.

For one hesitant second she felt she was making a mistake to wear it as she remembered the cold appraisal she received from beneath heavily fringed lids. With determination she slipped the silky folds over her head and down her lithe body, turning before the mirror to appraise the results. No, she would wear it! It fit better than most of her dresses, hugging her high, rounded breasts and touching lightly on her small waist and molded hips. Grudgingly she admitted she didn't look at all like M. Lassiter, architect. She should be taller, flatter, and more raw-boned maybe, to make it in her profession. That was a silly thought; many of her contemporaries, who now were presidents of their own companies, were beautiful, seductive women. *Careful, Myrhia, that you don't allow one man's overpowering personality to give you a complex,* she thought, slipping the dress over her head again.

She lay across the bed intending to rest, eyes closed, but not to sleep, but when she awoke, it was dusk and she had less than an hour to bathe and dress for the evening before her. The pleasure of a long, dawdling bath had to be denied, but she did grant herself the luxury of using her favorite bath gels, which perfumed the entire unit in jasmine.

A quick toweling gave her skin an extra glow as she applied the same fragrance in her bath powder. She brushed her hair furiously until it gleamed with lights not unlike small halos sparkling through its dark depth. A quick application of makeup and she would be dressed.

Turk arrived earlier than expected but she was ready. She had left her dark hair hanging loose about her face, turned under slightly at the ends to keep it shoulder length. It framed her heart-shaped face and accentuated the green of her eyes that were fighting a losing battle to hold on to the reflected blue of the dress.

Turk didn't speak for a second, but his eyes narrowed taking her appearance in from head to toe. "Just how could I have missed running into you in Dallas? I would never have forgotten if I had." His eyelids narrowed as if refusing to reveal what lay behind their heavy fringe.

He seemed to be waiting for her reply but for some reason she felt ill at ease. "I doubt your path crosses that of many career women, Turk. You are so bitterly opposed to the type." She hadn't intended to begin their evening with a controversial note, but he had a way of disturbing her.

"I'd adjust easily, I'm sure." He appeared unperturbed, ignoring her remark. "I'm not adverse to women in any category." A wicked gleam appeared in his eyes. "I want to tell you that you are the most beautiful girl I've escorted in many a day. Somehow, I'm a little in awe that such beauty hides a brain."

Myrhia was unable to reply, wondering whether to accept the remark favorably or take it as a left-handed dig. No reply was necessary as they were already outside and on their way to his Mercedes. She waited until they pulled away from the curbing to mention Cleo's invitation. Expecting him to say no, she was surprised his answer came easily, as if he thought he might enjoy it.

"Sounds fine. That is, if it means that much to you. We can discuss our business at dinner. Why not? If we don't come to any conclusion immediately concerning the minor change, we can meet at a later date. If we get to your friend's party by nine, that will be all right, won't it?"

Why was he being solicitous of her? It was as if he had planned to be extra nice tonight and not antagonize her. Somehow the feeling of a delayed confrontation made her edgy. Before the Tarrington Building was completed, they probably would not be on speaking terms, but for the time she would enjoy this truce.

She was becoming increasingly aware of his maleness as the fragrance of English Leather cologne filled the car. It suited him somehow. When he wasn't looking she found herself taking in the strong profile etched against the streetlights of downtown Dallas. His light gray slacks revealed long, sinewy thighs that moved in a strangely attractive way each time he pressed the accelerator or brake. Carl had long legs but never had she noticed anything unusual about his muscles when he drove. Was this man capable of putting a spell on her? Before she could sift that around in her mind, he was speaking and she had not heard what he was saying.

"Myrhia, you didn't hear me? You seem preoccupied tonight."

"I'm sorry, Turk," she stammered slightly, wondering if he would find it gratifying to know she had been studying his thighs at the moment of preoccupation.

"What was it?" she asked, half amused at herself.

"I said, do you have alternate suggestions for the fascia? If so, I hope you brought them with you."

"Oh, I did—in fact I have a couple of them. One suggestion I think you might like."

"Good, the sooner we have all the details ironed out the sooner we can give the contract for the plans to go ahead. I want to get the Tarrington Building out of the way; I'll be spending a lot of time on Maui. Things there are bogged down. Too difficult to secure building materials right now—such a boom going on—and then the high cost of shipping from the mainland."

"I'm wondering if the native Hawaiians aren't despondent over the commercialization of the islands?" Myrhia interrupted. "It's too bad. If Americans want to live in condos on top of the world, why not in the United States proper? There's more room on the mainland that on a tropical isle. Some of the buildings in Honolulu are monstrosities." She was silent for a second, just staring out of the window before continuing.

"My father told me that during World War Two when he was there with the navy that it was really a paradise. Sometimes I think we are overdoing everything we touch in America. Too much wealth, too greedy for power and we want to change everything." At first his silence unnerved her as if she had somehow annoyed him again. She was sorry she always seemed to be sounding off. Myrhia was relieved when he spoke again.

"Whew! That was a long speech! You have strong convictions, don't you? I don't know if you would approve of my newest project or not. I've tried to keep it low-key insisting that it not be over seven stories and more spread out, angling around the waterfront."

He did have some scruples, then. Some, but there was still the overriding drive for power hidden under the suave manner. "I should like to see your building, Turk. As an architect I feel a building should conform to the terrain around it. I think my favorite hotel is the Royal Hawaiian in Honolulu. It doesn't jar my nerves like the steel and chrome-plated cement structures that overpower the island."

Since there was no answer she assumed she had met with his disapproval again. Dreading the look she might find in his eyes, she did not turn her head in his direction. Suddenly arrested by something outside his window, she ventured a glance and was surprised to catch him off guard with a speculative, almost gentle expression in the gray eyes before a veil closed over them and shut her out. The thought occurred to her he was vulnerable, perhaps as vulnerable underneath the outer shell as she was.

At Élan's they ordered immediately. As it had been with Carl, Turk seemed to be held in high esteem by the waiters and guests, who had greeted him cordially in passing. When the waiter left for their drinks, Turk demanded to see her sketches, which she unrolled from a small tube in her purse. Pinning the pieces of paper between them with water glasses and cutlery, they became engrossed in the changes. Not conscious that their heads were close together as they bent over the drawings, she was intent on trying to convince him why she liked the first sketch. Myrhia was not aware of the change in his manner toward her until his hand closed over her bare shoulder. He was leaning toward her. His touch was gentle and light but the fiery path left by his trailing fingers caused her to stop talking, lest her voice betray her emotions.

She turned to face him slowly, catching his warm and seductive expression as if his eyes were devouring her. "You were saying, Myrhia?" A hint of amusement flashed momentarily in the agates. "I lost track of your last suggestion."

Aware that he was about to capture her emotions irrevocably, she felt helpless to do anything about it. Somehow she was presenting the explanation of the new sketch poorly like some mechanical automaton. His face was bent close enough for her to feel his warm breath when suddenly his lips brushed her cheek sending an ageless message to her brain. Hold on, she told herself. It would be easy to be seduced by this man. He would be a skillful adversary in more ways than just business.

She straightened, feeling his hand slip off her shoulder and down her bare back, leaving its trail of fire. She lifted the glasses from the drawing. "Perhaps this is not the proper time to discuss the details of my proposed changes, Mr. Vaughan. I'll let you take the tube with you to your committee with my suggestions in writing. Here." She handed him the tube, avoiding further contact with his eyes.

"You're beautiful yet naive, Myrhia! Or should I say Miss Lassiter, since you suddenly became formal with me." Drawn to his eyes like a drop of moisture to a larger body of water, she made a mistake of looking at him again. "What would it be like to hold that cool perfection close until it melted, I wonder?" he mused aloud.

"That you will never know." She spoke crossly but somehow her words lacked conviction. All her resolve was crumbling under his soft attacks on her. He hadn't done anything that could be considered out of hand but she felt a subtle impact of his charm. Did other women, unfortunately falling under his spell, become cast-offs like discarded merchandise? That would not happen to her.

"I hope that Cleo's party won't bore you. She does invite a hodgepodge of guests, some of the wealthiest and most unusual in Dallas. You may know a few of them—as the women are definitely not the career oriented." She let the tiny dagger have its thrust. "I'm aware you prefer the social deb type." She was fighting for her composure.

Myrhia caught a flicker of irritation in the gray eyes. In spite of her dagger thrust he replied coolly. "I'll no doubt find it amusing, but don't think for one moment this evening will let you off the hook. I came to enjoy a full evening with a certain good-looking architect, and I won't be shoved off."

As the blood began to pound in her temples, he continued. "My evening is free—just for you. I intend to find out all I can about the woman whose building plans I've chosen. It's quite a novelty to be dealing with someone so full of budding talent." His insolent gaze raked over her breasts before traveling upward to her lips. "I might say—who has budding talent in many areas." She turned away from the impudent grin.

While she waited for the warmth to leave her face, praying there was no telltale blush to give her away, she was aware she was biting her lower lip. This was no boy to be dealt with in a casual manner, but a smooth possibly dangerous man. He was all that Trish had heard he was and would bear watching. No, that was not entirely true! She would have to watch herself and not fall into his charming trap.

As they ate in comparative silence their stolen looks caused a quickening of her pulse rate and her resolve to be wary almost tumbled from time to time. She made a pretense of sipping her white wine slowly, toying with the stem of the glass as she tried to avoid eye contact. It was impossible not to be aware of his presence. The subtle fragrance of his after-shave lotion teased her nostrils, once more bringing a sensuous quality into their closeness.

She fingered a lock of hair that seemed determined to fall over her eye all too frequently. The gesture apparently caught Turk's attention as he reached across the short distance between them to tuck the incorrigible strand behind her ear, caressing her cheek with the back of his warm hand as he did so. His touch seemed charged with electricity; warm excitement coursed through her veins.

Looking up, Myrhia became aware of the enigmatic appraisal lingering in his expression. He was as much aware of her as she was of him. For some reason the moment gave her a heady feeling that was not easy to put down, and stubbornly remained the rest of the evening.

It was fortunate they both knew some of the other diners, as it gave her some diversion watching Turk's manner of greeting, which was as varied as the man's moods. Some of the guests dropped by their table to talk briefly and be introduced to her. There were several pairs of raised eyebrows, she noticed, as he introduced her as his architect. For the moment she was grateful for the interruption; it brought her emotions back to a more oriented plane, away from the disconcerting weakness she had experienced before.

Turk treated some of the visitors to their table in a cool, abstract manner that puzzled her; it did not fit into the picture she was forming of him.

"You seem to be acquainted with everyone in Dallas," she commented.

"Well, it may seem that way, but I've found I have few close friends outside of football. That was my world for so long. I feel more at home there. In business I'm not that close to people. It is only surface commitment, a cover-up in many respects. Business makes strange bedfellows, Myrhia. You'll soon learn that if you have something they want, then you are a back-slapping friend." He was unable to hide the bitterness in the statement.

"Oh?" She couldn't resist a thrust. "The great Turk Vaughan is a cynic." It was out before she could recall the sarcastic remark.

A dart of quick, biting anger showed in his eyes, only to be blotted out by a gleam of amusement that heightened his expression. The instant change was followed by a disdainful chuckle as he threw his head back and laughed, causing the nearest diners to glance their way before turning back with smiles.

"You're refreshing! I've never met anyone like you, Myrhia. This I'm going to enjoy! Where have you been all my life?"

He looked at her with a steady gaze until she turned away, but not before she felt a warmth creep into her face. "I know where you've been," he continued. "You've been growing up, I hope for me. How old are you?" He looked speculative. "Don't tell me—I can guess. You can't be much past twenty-three? Right? I'm going to enjoy our association." Since she didn't answer and couldn't have even if she tried, he continued. "If you've any interest in me whatsover, I'm thirty-eight, almost forty, single, never married, and I've found you almost too late, haven't I?"

Finding words at last, she countered. "For the record—I'm twenty-seven—but, I don't know what finding me has to do with anything, Turk. We're merely business associates for a time—nothing more."

"Don't be too sure about that, Myrhia. I can feel the

excitement beneath that cool, poised exterior. I excite you—just a little! Admit it! Now, don't I?"

"Of all the conceited, overbearing men! You win the prize! If you've finished dinner, I have—and I'd like to get to Cleo's party. Perhaps you'll find some of your cast-off girl friends there to entertain you in the style to which you obviously are accustomed." Myrhia rose angrily, her pulse pounding in her head.

She was conscious of his amusement as he rose to come to her side, but at least he didn't say anything. As he took her arm to walk between the tables, he held it possessively clamped to his side, completely spoiling her strained composure. Her rubbery legs were weakened by a racing pulse.

"You're in for a big surprise, Myrhia," Turk whispered, letting his lips brush the tip of her ear as he did so. "I'm going to be in and out of your life frequently from now on. You'll have to come to terms with your feeling toward me."

They were well away from the restaurant before she found enough breath to reply. "You're impossible!" She wanted to add dangerous but that would only add fuel to his ego. Well, she thought making a mental note to herself, she would not be alone with him from now on. The resolution was swept away when they neared the Mercedes as one strong arm pulled her to him and her lips were smothered by his mouth. His kiss was deep and probing, ravishing her mouth with his tongue. She struggled, thinking to rebel against his strength, but instead she felt a strange light-headedness possess her body as waves of explicit pleasure rocked over her. Contrary to her desire to remain aloof, she responded and returned his kisses. When he finished, he held her at arm's length, his strong hands digging mercilessly into her bare arms.

"Now, deny it! Deny you don't desire me as much as I want you." He was shaking her gently back and forth. "Say it, Myrhia!"

Denial formed on her lips, but the words she mumbled tricked her. "Yes, oh, yes! Turk, I do!"

"Ah, I thought so!" He opened the car door. "Now that we have that settled, let's go to the party."

They were halfway to Cleo's before the storm within her broke. He had outwitted her! She had actually admitted he turned her on! What the devil was the matter with her anyway? She had been kissed before over and over. It was nothing new, nothing spine-tingling. Deep inside her she knew she was lying. Nothing could be as potent as her growing attraction for this man who looked on women as toys and was skilled in the game of seduction. She would have to keep a cool head from now on, or find more than her ideas about the fascia sabotaged to suit his macho tastes.

Cleo, looking like a red-headed Lorelei, met them at the door to her apartment and greeted Myrhia with a perfunctory peck, not really seeing her, as she turned all her wiles on Turk. In response to her admiration Turk threw her the Vaughan charm full measure.

"You didn't tell me, Myrhia, that our hostess would look like a goddess." His manner was suave. Even in their short acquaintance Myrhia could tell Turk was overdoing it for her benefit. His glibness slipped past Cleo's vanity as she answered, "You look like a Grecian statue yourself."

Myrhia cringed at the byplay between the two of them. This was another mistake—bringing Turk here. Was she ever going to learn how to relate to all types of men? Perhaps it was true that she was naive in the male female game of conquest. She had been too busy to care very much. Now she had brought Turk into a group of predatory females, for that's what most of Cleo's friends were. Like Cleo herself they were constantly looking for the ultimate romance. In some ways she pitied them, as there was very little else they cared for.

Turk became swallowed up by the group immediately. He knew several of the men by their first names and if they didn't know him at once, they soon found out who the good-looking ex-Cowboy was. As a leading running back for the Dallas team, he had became the prototype of the American male. Some of the men apparently had been associated with him in business deals. She watched as they clustered about him now discussing his future building plans around the state.

Cleo clamped an arm through Myrhia's for the sole purpose of pumping her friend concerning the relationship between her and Turk. As she propelled Myrhia off to one side, she said, "Well, Well! I'm impressed. Not only are you snapping out of your cloister, but you've started at the top. Turk Vaughan! Unbelievable!" Her soulful sigh was immediately followed by an apology.

"I don't mean that it's unbelievable that you can date such a man. With your looks, heavens, you could have anyone you want. But to think—" Sentence unfinished, her eyes followed Turk's movements. "Mind if I take him away? This is as close as I've been to that man."

In spite of her rising disapproval of Cleo's flagrant frankness, she was amused. "Careful, Cleo, your lust is showing."

"I hope so—do I ever!" Cleo chuckled and walked off, leaving Myrhia to turn to the bar for solace. A hired bartender inquired what she wanted. There was nothing second rate when Cleo threw a party even though she, as her best friend, knew Cleo had squandered a week's allowance she couldn't afford.

"I'll take a screwdriver, please—light on the vodka." Taking the tall, cool drink in her hand, she sauntered toward the windows, which were thrown open to the spring evening. Cleo's balcony, like her own, was a scrap of afterthought, but it did command a view of Dallas at night. Myriad lights shone from the tall buildings like necklaces on phantom dowagers fiercely standing in the midst of opulence.

It had been a mistake to bring Turk here. Their evening had not been successful from the beginning. His kisses had unnerved her, weakening her while uncovering a sweet longing she had denied even to herself. Now she was miserable and on the defensive as if she had to prove herself again. Romance and work didn't mix. It was unfortunate that the money for the Tarrington Building lay in the hands of a man like Turk Vaughan instead of some older octogenarian who needed an outlet for his investments. It would be easier to conduct business with a man like that.

"Here you are!" Turk's voice was low and seductive as he came up behind her taking her in his arms possessively. "Why do you avoid me?"

"I wasn't aware I was. It seemed to me you were well occupied and among friends. I just needed a breath of fresh air."

She tried to pull away but his arms held her as his lips sought the lobe of her ear, tracing a pattern of warmth and prompting an immediate explosion of excitement in her body.

"Don't Turk!" she said crossly.

"I know you like it. I can feel the electricity between us. Why do you fight it so?"

"I'm sure if there is any feeling it's on your part. I

feel nothing." Her lie would have been convincing if her voice hadn't trembled.

"You two lovebirds out there, come in here! There are several people who want to meet you." Cleo stood behind them laughing. There was amusement in her voice and Myrhia wondered how long she had been standing behind them or what she had overheard.

"Some of the guests are interested in the fact that you two are working together on a project. They can't believe that Myrhia is an architect."

Turk was smiling as he turned to face their hostess. Not releasing his hold on Myrhia's waist, he said, "She's a damned good architect! Perhaps a little arty in some ways from a man's point of view concerning minor things, but nevertheless my committee was unanimous in choosing her design proposal over fifty others that were also good."

Myrhia felt trapped. She was the target of all eyes at that moment and she didn't like it. The thoughts of the guests were obvious as she overheard one of the women's whispered comments.

"It would be a boon to be an aspiring architect with that man in your corner. With him attentive to you, who needs talent?" A spatter of laughter followed the spiteful remark. Most all the guests glared at the speaker who glanced about her, suddenly realizing she was out of order. With a wan smile she looked at Myrhia apologetically.

"Sorry—I had no business saying that. I'm sure you must be a good architect."

Myrhia, who had been fighting to control her irritation with herself for bringing Turk here in the first place, was struggling for poise. "That's all right, think nothing of it. I assure you I've run the gamut of criticism and skepticism during the five years I studied at

Texas University. Most of my colleagues were male, but they came to respect the work of the few women in class. I'm a good architect and you will no doubt find I am not wholly dependent on one man to sponsor my rise. I intend to make a name for myself in any event."

"Touché!" came his husky whisper. Addressing the others, he said, "You'll find the Tarrington Building rising against the Dallas skyline by the end of next year. I predict it will be one of our most spectacular. For the record—this lady is damned good!"

Myrhia glanced at Turk in disbelief. There was no guile hidden beneath the warm look turned on her. He meant what he said. In a wash of gratitude she felt consoled in the face of these strangers.

"Thanks, Turk. For the moment I believe you mean it."

"I do," he whispered. "Any time you want to get out of here, I'll go willingly."

"Now. I'm ready too." She was smiling as she walked toward Cleo to say their good-byes.

"You can't leave yet!" Cleo's anguished cry was because the evening prize was snatched from under her nose.

They were halfway to North Dallas when Turk took her hand. "I don't want to end the evening this early. We just might go over those plans without interruption at your place. What say?"

"Sounds fine. I'll make us some coffee."

Turk seemed to blend with the colors of her apartment. From her vantage point in the kitchenette, she could see him rocking back and forth on his heels, hands behind him, looking the living room over. When she walked back carrying two china cups of coffee on a tray and set it down on the coffee table, he said, "Quite

nice! I like your taste more and more. Would you consider decorating the condos in Maui at a later date? I'd
like to get your opinion."

Flattered, she said she would. "I'd like a try at it,
Turk."

He made a step toward her just as she started to hand
him his cup. Taking the saucer from her hands, he set it
back down on the table and pulled her to him. Although she had been priming herself to resist further
lovemaking, her resolutions were melted. Her senses
had come vibrantly alive, tingling in a frightening,
whirling new experience.

"I want to make love to you, M. Lassiter. Will you
be my undoing?" He was molding her spine with his
strong fingers, working his way upward to the bare-
ness of her back. She had to stop him somehow or
she would be hopelessly trapped in a one-sided affair. She started to protest but his lips found hers,
cutting off all remonstrance, as she was vanquished
by his sensuous lips demanding a response from her
own. He was taking his leisurely time with her, playing her emotions like a harpist plucks the strings to
produce his music.

"Wait, Turk!" she cried softly, suddenly self-
conscious of her own mounting desire. "I'm not sure
of you—"

He released her slightly holding her away from him
as he looked deep into her eyes. "What does that
mean?"

The small reprieve gave Myrhia courage. "I don't
know you, Turk. I want more from the man I give my
love to. I want understanding."

"Then, my darling, let's get about that understanding." With a soft laugh he pulled her close once more.
"You know you want me too."

Placing both hands on his chest, she tried shoving him away. "It isn't enough—I want—"

Not waiting for her to finish her sentence, he pushed her back on the couch and crouched beside her, pinning her arms over her head. "We'll see if it's enough or not. Let me be the judge." He explored her throat, her shoulders, and the soft hollow between her breasts where the folds of her neckline had fallen back leaving a mound of soft flesh. "You're too beautiful not to have love over and over again."

His eyes were alive with passion as his lips moved to hers in possession, gently encouraging her own to respond. Myrhia's body flamed with response as his hands, releasing her own, worked their way downward from her taut breasts to her rigid thighs that slowly came alive under his sensuous caress. Myrhia felt as if her body would explode as waves of pleasure raced through her nerves. A moment more and retreat would be impossible. Summoning her failing strength, she managed to slip her legs over the couch to the floor and push him back. Angered at her body's betrayal, she lashed out at Turk, unable to cope with the mounting desire she felt.

"Dammit, Turk! I'll not be added to your stable of women." She started forward but a strong hand on her ankle held her back.

"Hold it, spitfire! Don't be afraid! I can feel you tremble with desire, darling." Turk rose slowly, his hands tormenting her flesh as they worked their way up her slim legs and rounded hips, using her as a prop to steady himself. Her flesh did tremble as the heat of his sensuous hands penetrated the sheer material of her dress.

Grasping her shoulders as if in a vise, he looked down into her face. "Don't fight it! What's between us is inevitable. Don't you know?" Strong arms circled her waist as his lips caught in her hair, moving downward to her shoulder.

Weak with a longing she had never experienced before, she cried softly, "I think you'd better go, Turk. I have a big day planned for tomorrow." The lie was just a ruse and she was aware he could see right through it.

"All right, I'll ignore the subterfuge for now. But tomorrow is a day of rest, or don't you observe the Sabbath?" His voice was muffled against her earlobe, straining her resolve to the breaking point.

"I'll go." Turk's laugh cut through her as he released her too abruptly to stride toward the door, where he turned. "I found out what I wanted to know about you. I might add—it's just as I suspected." His steel gaze pierced her, leaving her perplexed by his meaning.

She struggled to regain her composure. "Just what does that crack mean? Just what did you suspect about me? Care to tell me?" Her defensive anger gave her strength to face him.

"I wouldn't dare—not at this time, M. Lassiter!" His sardonic smile was the last thing she saw as he closed the door behind him.

The snap of the door unleashed her anger. How would she ever complete a business association with him now? Damn Turk! Just what had he meant he had found out about her? Did he think she was totally unworthy of his attempted seduction? He certainly didn't think he could bowl her over quickly, did he? He would find out she could be a coolly impersonal businesswoman from now on and that is what she intended to be from this moment. Her guard was up!

Chapter Four

Myrhia awakened with a dull headache from a sleepless night. It had been close to dawn when she had finally fallen into the deep, unconscious sleep that usually sparked impetus for the new day. Not so this morning. Shut away in her mind was the nagging reminder she was becoming involved with Turk against her will. His powerful effect on her not only left her weak and vulnerable but with a growing dissatisfaction with things as they were.

Carl's relationship had been a restful one, as both of them had acknowledged it was only friendship. If this new association with Turk could be casual, an interlude, with no damage to either at the passing, it would be exciting and acceptable. It wasn't possible, she admitted honestly. Already she felt a quickening of pulse and excited anticipation whenever she thought of him. With a groan she pulled herself out of bed and walked zombielike to the kitchen for coffee. The many things she had planned to do today had slipped her mind and for the first time in years, she felt lonely. Her apartment, usually a haven of contentment, no longer filled the niche of a retreat as it loomed larger than it really was and appeared to be filled with emptiness.

While the coffee brewed, she adjusted the stereo to suit her, hoping the soft music would smooth the wrinkles from her thoughts. It would be pleasant for Carl to be present, sprawled comfortably on her divan half-asleep as he often was in the past, but she couldn't begrudge him his new happiness with Belinda. He seemed to be walking in a satisfied glow lately.

Work was a panacea for her ailments. She took a mug of steaming coffee to her small workroom just off her kitchen and scanned the new sketch pinned on her drawing board. It was a raw outline of a filling station, a commission she had promised to have finished by the end of the month but had set aside to complete the Tarrington place.

Myrhia worked halfheartedly for an hour, forcing her mind to think of work-related matters. The new auditorium project would be another challenge. She had Carl to thank for many of her bigger chances, and it was comforting to know he would continue channeling work her way.

The filling station idea was shaping up nicely, she thought as she laid down her pencil and picked up the half-empty cup of cold coffee. Not until she stepped into the kitchen for a refill did she notice the rain beating on the windowpane. It had been a long time since she had walked in the rain and it just might be what she needed to clear the cobwebs from her mind.

Throwing on her raincoat and rain boots and grabbing an umbrella, she started at a determined pace toward the elevator. As she turned a corner of the hallway, she bumped into an immovable object—all male and smelling of rain and remembered fragrance of after-shave lotion.

"Such haste!" Turk took advantage of her collision to hold her against his wet slicker for a moment. "May

I ask just where you're running off to on this wet day?'' Myrhia couldn't answer for a moment as his lips pressed against her forehead and trailed like an electric wire to find her lips. His kiss was sweet and soft with a hint of things that might follow.

"I was going to walk some of the kinks out of my body and mind. It's been quite a while since I've had the opportunity to walk in the rain," she answered, surprised at her sudden happiness.

He looked down at her, the beginning of a smile playing about his sensuous mouth. "That's one more thing we share in common. I've come to ask you to do just that—walk in the rain with me."

As they adjusted their steps to pace along together she felt an uplift of spirits. If she dared to believe he did enjoy her company in such simple pursuits as this, it might be their relationship would extend beyond an interlude.

She was unconsciously taking the lead in their walk, she noticed, finding her steps were leading them along Turtle Creek and down to one of the many paths along the creekbed. She took his hand impulsively and led him a little way toward a wooden bridge spanning a waterfall that emptied from a small lake.

"This is Exall Lake. The migratory birds come through each spring and fall for a brief respite before flying farther south or north depending on the season."

"You must have come here often as a child, Myrhia. Am I right?" He spoke softly, his voice low and husky as if he too were caught in timeless beauty for a moment. As he took a step closer to her, it was only natural to lift her face for his kiss. A feeling of contentment washed over her as his strong arms closed around her waist and his soft lips captured her own.

Myrhia stood in the circle of his arms feeling secure and contented, her head against his wide shoulder.

Pulling away slightly, she glanced up into his face to find gentle speculation in his expression.

"To answer your question: Yes, I did come here often as a child. This was my private thinking spot—all along the creekbed there beyond the falls. My home is only a few blocks away from here."

"What kind of thoughts could a kid have?" he asked softly.

"Oh," she said, recalling memories out of her past. "I used to build castles of the small rocks down there below the waterfall." She glanced over the railing of the bridge, feeling once again the childhood imagery. "Sometimes my imagination peopled my castles with knights and ladies who came and went over the castle drawbridge. I always visualized my castles reaching high into the air."

Suddenly embarrassed for revealing her childish memories, she glanced up into his eyes expecting to find amusement, but was surprised to find warm perception mirrored there instead.

His arms tightened their hold on her waist as he drew her to him once more. In that moment a heavy downpour of rain pelted the new green leaves above their heads before the drops fell over them.

"Oops!" She laughed, pulling away from his embrace to open her umbrella. "Oh, grief! It's stuck!" she cried, wrestling with the obstinate slide.

"Here, let an expert do it," Turk said, reaching for the umbrella. On his second attempt it opened into a blue circle above their heads. "You weren't holding your tongue right," he quipped, the dark-fringed lids narrowing over a gleam of amusement as he bent his tall frame toward her in order to share in the umbrella's protection.

"You mean hold my tongue like this?" she said, biting down on the tip of her tongue as she smiled up at him. She felt ridiculously young and carefree and marveled at Turk's own abandon.

"Here, cuddle up," he said, pulling her close under the umbrella and leading her down from the bridge to a bench beside the creek. "This is cozy, isn't it?" He laughed while raindrops played a delicate staccato on the umbrella over their heads.

She laughed with him, having to admit it was. It was possible the spring rain was making her a little mad, intoxicated with the mood of the moment. What had happened to her, to them? With a sigh of contentment she turned her head to find him looking at her. The look was tender, full of sensuality, yet almost gentle.

"You're the most intriguing woman I've ever met, Myrhia," he whispered, tracing her cheek with his index finger, then downward to her chin and over her parted lips.

His touch triggered a shiver of delight along her nerves that caused her to lay her head on his wide shoulder. It was involuntary, she knew but oh, it did feel so right.

His free arm closed around her waist as they sat together while rain fell around them, each lost in thought—yet drawn together by the need to share the moment.

At last they rose to walk along the path again, hand in hand, not speaking but communicating through that strange perception two people sometimes have. She wondered why they had become close in these moments as her feet led them into the older residential part of Turtle Creek area. She was flying unerringly like a homing pigeon to the old home of her girlhood.

Coming in sight of the sprawling red brick mansion, Myrhia experienced a tug of nostalgia for the way it had once been when her father was waiting inside, perhaps his pipe in hand, poring over some exciting new idea, his thinning head of hair bent over his drawing board as he assessed his plan. Her feet lagged, slowing to a standstill as they reached the center of the long block under the canopy of sixty-year-old elms.

What would her father think of this man at her side, whose entire life had been spent in different pursuits from his own? Would he approve of Turk for a son-in-law? In that instant she knew he would, but why would she presume as much? Turk did not appear to be the single-minded type who would want permanency like the Carls of the world.

"Why have we stopped?" Turk's eyes seemed softly aware of her. "Any particular reason?" He looked up and down the lovely old street. "I used to dream about this—these old mansions where I could imagine people lived out their lives in gracious yet heedless unconcern for those less fortunate. I've known some of the scions of these old Texas families since proball. They were born to it and have never had to fight for a place in the sun." A note of bitterness crept into his voice.

Myrhia looked up at him trying to fathom the meaning behind his words. Had he lived a hard, struggling existence, counting on his prowess in athletics and handsome good looks to put him across? Would it make a difference in their relationship if he knew she was from this old, established background? She would have to find out, as there would be no possible way they could ever relate to each other if they didn't know each other's background.

Alicia's car was neither in the garage nor parked under the porte cochere. She started walking up the curving driveway with Turk following, his wonder toward her behavior transmitting itself to her back.

"What are you up to, Myrhia?" he asked, half amused.

"I want you to see something. Come on, Turk. I'm welcome here."

She could read the puzzled expression on his face as she produced the key to the heavy oak door and they stepped into the wide hallway. She looked around her half expecting to see either Matty or Brady step from the butler's pantry beyond the spacious dining room to see who had come in. Then she remembered it was Sunday, the one special day Alicia gave the couple to do with as they pleased. They were in all probability visiting a married daughter who lived in nearby Plano.

Turk came up behind her and put his arm around her shoulders. "Is this your home? Somehow I didn't have you pegged in this type environment—yet I should have known from your father's reputation."

Releasing her he walked about the hallway looking up the long curving stairway and into the living room off to one side of the spacious entrance.

Myrhia watched silently, wondering what he was thinking. She was seeing it again through his eyes, the rich, parquet floor of the hall with its Persian rugs— Father's penchant for the Orient was evident throughout the rooms—the stairway angling downward to spread gracefully like a lady's skirt at the bottom of the tread.

"It is a lovely old home, Myrhia." There was hesitancy in his voice but as his eyes found hers, she felt warmed by their expression. "I can see where you've come from and why you are what you are. Does it occur to you seeing all this makes you an enigma? You've had it all the time—comfortable wealth, position in society—yet you turned your back on it for a career. That in itself is incredible but you chose a new challenge for women. What makes you tick, Myrhia?'' He started toward her but stopped as his gaze rested on an oil painting hanging on the mahogany-paneled wall.

"That's a Russell, isn't it? He appeals to me the most of all the Western artists. I found one when I was at the Gilcrease Museum in Tulsa and made a bid for it. It was out of someone's private collection.''

"Do you paint, Turk?'' Something about the intensity of his gaze as he surveyed the painting hinted that he might.

"No, I'm devoid of talent!'' It occurred to Myrhia his answer was glib, too spontaneous, as if he were covering an emotion he wanted to deny. "I leave the artistic impulses to the weaker types.''

She chose to ignore the gibe, wanting to believe it was a cover-up for a true appreciation for art forms. "Just how do you class a Remington? He's anything but a weakling.''

"Well, in my books the artistic temperament follows a form of weakness,'' he persisted stubbornly.

A slow anger was upsetting the sweet closeness that had grown between them. "You mean weak character or physical weakness? They are not one and the same, you know. Some of the strongest characters I know are slight of frame,'' she said tersely. "I fail to understand how physical strength and a big body mean much.''

"I guess we're from different worlds, Myrhia. It would be easier for me to accept you as a society butterfly than a hard-hitting career woman.''

"Ho!'' Myrhia snorted turning away from him in disgust. "My first intuition about you was correct. You are a snob besides being a chauvinist. I thought you might be different if I let you know me just a little.'' She gestured to include the luxurious surroundings.

"Can't you see—this was too easy. I wanted to make

it my way. I turned my back on the easy, cut and dried life of a stereotyped girl of affluence because it would have stifled any creative desire I had."

She turned back to face him, her body trembling with controlled anger. He stood there looking so damned attractive, a half-smirk on those devastating lips and the lids half closed over his eyes. "I see you prefer the society type—the wealthy, jet-setter playgirl who cares only for her own importance, not what she can contribute to the world to make it better or to people who want to get close to her." Myrhia was growing angrier by the minute, wanting to wipe away the smug look that had fastened itself to his well-defined lips.

Turk's agate eyes narrowed under the heavy lashes as he took a step toward her.

"No, you don't! Keep away from me, Turk! It would never work between us and I don't want to become involved with you. I wouldn't be able to turn away. I should have known you would be a snob."

"Just how much do you know about me?" His strong arms pulled her close as his lips wiped off all the hateful response she had planned to hurl at him. "You wouldn't be interested in finding out a few things about my past, would you?"

She started to say no, but her emotions had become twisted with each spine-tingling kiss that wiped away more and more of her anger. A reflected flash of sunlight on a car windshield washed over the wall of the hallway as Alicia's car pulled under the porte cochere. She was grateful for both—the sun breaking through the clouds and her mother's well-timed appearance. Things were getting out of hand and the interruption would slow them.

"Here's Mother!" She looked up at Turk whose

arms slowly released her but not before Alicia appeared taking in the parting embrace with raised eyebrows.

"Oh, Myrhia—dear! I had no idea you were here. I didn't see a car—" She looked back toward the drive as if expecting one to materialize now.

"No we walked over." Under her breath she whispered to Turk, "Be prepared to be smothered by her effusiveness. Don't let her presume too much by what she just saw."

"Can it be too much?" came the ambiguous reply, followed by a shimmer of amusement. "I hope she is more perceptive than her daughter."

Alicia advanced toward them. "My! What a beautiful young man! I do think your taste is improving, Myrhia." She switched on a small lamp near the wide doorway and stepped closer to Turk, who was smiling at her. Before Myrhia could introduce the two of them, her mother's keen eye recognized Turk and brightened with the knowledge. "You're— It isn't possible, is it? Dirckson Vaughan!" She advanced on Turk like a friendly chickadee. "You played eighteen holes for our Charity Benefit at the Northwood Country Club. Last spring, wasn't it?" She tipped her head to one side and clasped her hands together, happy that she had cataloged him so quickly.

"Right, Mrs. Lassiter!" Turk, who Myrhia could see was totally charmed with her mother, threw back his head with a laugh. "You have a good memory."

"You are not one to forget easily. I believe you are called Turk, right?" She turned to Myrhia. "Dear, I'm pleased you have acquired good sense at last. You need to be dating and relaxing more. I've been after this child for so long," she addressed Turk again. "May I call you Turk?"

"Of course," Turk managed to sandwich into the conversation before she continued.

"As I was saying, I want Myrhia to get out more. She stays in that office hunched over a drawing board too much. I want her to have fun while she's young." To Myrhia she said, "Don't just stand there. There's a bottle of wine cooling in the refrigerator. Come into the living room, Turk. My daughter is sometimes lacking the proper protocol."

"We just arrived and she was showing me the house." Turk smiled and the eyes reflected amusement in the situation.

"What a day this has been! I'm happy it's stopped raining." Alicia became aware of their raincoats for the first time. "Walking—and in the rain! Well, Turk, you must be prepared for eccentricities in my daughter. No one, but Myrhia, would want to walk in the rain."

When Alicia was part of a group, conversation seldom lagged. As she chatted amiably, Myrhia noticed the rays of the late afternoon sun slanted through the beveled glass of the double front doors to create rainbows on the mahogany wainscoting of the hallway. Soon the sun would make its stately descent in the west, clothing the late afternoon in long, tall shadows under the elms.

Turk appeared at ease with Alicia, but then he was accustomed to the women in her stratum of society. They were the ones who fawned over him, invited him to charity sports events and as a guest celebrity for all telethons. He was certainly no stranger to feminine admiration.

It was time to leave before Alicia talked them into staying for one of her hastily prepared little suppers she loved so much to prepare. With Matty out of the kitchen, her mother felt self-righteous when she whipped up an omelet or French toast and little sausages. It was always good but nothing that required undo attention as the usual rapid flow conversation was not omitted from her bustling preparations.

"I've some work to do before morning, Alicia. We must be going." Myrhia rose leaning over her mother to give her a good-bye hug. "I'll see you next weekend for lunch. Same time?"

"Of course, dear, but I do wish you'd stay. It's been so long since you've brought such charming company to the old home. I've enjoyed your visit, Turk." Her head tilted sideways as she looked at him. "The name suits you exactly. You have a mysterious look about your face—a far Eastern look—in those devastating eyes. I don't know how Myrhia keeps from throwing herself at you. It would be hard for me to resist if I were younger."

Turk laughed heartily, sending Myrhia a challenging look. It was obvious he was enchanted with her mother. "Tell that to your daughter again and again, Mrs. Lassiter." His smile was disarming.

"I do hope you can call me Alicia. I want us to become good friends. Myrhia, dear, bring him back soon."

Myrhia was relieved when they were finally at the door and leaving. Turk stepped out first after leaning down to kiss her mother's cheek. He was really overdoing it, she thought. Alicia's eyes sparkled with delight as she reached for Myrhia and pulled her face close to whisper, "Don't you dare let that beautiful man go!"

Feeling her face flaming, Myrhia turned to join Turk whose bland expression belied the merriment she could see behind his narrowed eyelids. He had heard the whisper. They were both insufferable! It had been a mistake bringing him here knowing her mother's penchant for matchmaking and her weakness for the tall, dark men who in all probability reminded her of her husband.

As that thought crossed her mind, Myrhia experienced a sense of dull relief. Turk's very slight resemblance to her father accounted for her own attraction to him from the start. He was the same height and build and had similar coloring. It was a relief to know this because it explained so much. She wasn't falling in love with him, it was that he reminded her of her father and somehow he had become a surrogate replacement at a time when she missed her father so much. Now she could ease away from the relationship with Turk knowing it was only loneliness for male companionship that prompted her feeling for this big piece of masculinity.

"I repeat—she's a delightful bit of womanhood." Turk took hold of her hand to pull her about. "I've been talking to you about your mother for several minutes. Where's your mind?"

"I don't know. I guess...I was wool-gathering. I do that too often." Why was she rattled this way, almost stuttering? She never had trouble speaking out.

"In answer to your statement: Don't take mother on whole cloth. She's a dear but she's a romantic and thinks all girls—daughters especially—should be married and involved in housekeeping chores and babies at my age."

"And just what is so darned wrong about that?" His direct question required an answer.

"Nothing, I suppose, if a girl is geared to that kind of life. I've seen too many of my friends make the wrong move. I don't want a failure in my life."

"It sure doesn't follow that you will make the wrong move. Besides, how do you know that these friends are trying to stick with their marriages? Doesn't that have to be worked at just like anything else?"

"You're right, but perhaps they don't know they're not trying. Besides, how do I know I would be any different, I wonder?" They were nearing her apartment again. Myrhia hesitated before asking, "Would you care to come up—I'll make us a sandwich or something."

She felt his hesitation as she waited for an answer. There was a disarming softness about his mouth as he continued to look at her, a question on his face. "Do you want me to? Or are you being the well-brought-up lady from Highland Park?"

"I would like for you to. I wouldn't have invited you if I hadn't meant it."

"I believe that's true." His eyes were mocking. Turk glanced at his handsome gold wristwatch, no doubt awarded for football honor. "Would you think me rude if I left by eight? I'm sorry but I did have a previous commitment."

For a moment she toyed with the idea of saying she'd make it another time. Chances were that he had a date and couldn't possibly break it at the last minute. On second thought she said, "If you care to come, that's fine—but we can make it at a more convenient time if you prefer."

"No!" The small word sounded enormous for some reason. "I want to get to know the architect of my new building in every respect."

With that statement hanging between them, they entered the elevator and rode in silence to her floor. Inside the apartment Turk didn't waste time making himself at home. He turned on her table lamp, switched on the television to catch the final inning of a baseball game, and flopped on the couch. "Can't you sit down a moment? Here, beside me." He patted the spot next to him. "Okay." She felt lighthearted suddenly. It was comfortable to have him here, the apartment seemed less lonely. "I'll get something for us to drink and nibble on, and then we'll plan a light supper. Do you like crepes with ham and cheese—perhaps asparagus?"

He reached for her hand and held it securely as he turned her to face him. "I like that very much, but aren't you going to a good deal of trouble for Sunday night supper?"

"Not really. I make the crepes in advance and freeze them ready to be filled and warmed as I need them." The charge of current running up her arm and flowing into the rest of her body tantalized her. If she stood this way holding his hand and looking down at that seductive mouth much longer she would fall into his lap. It was an effort to look away but she pulled her hand free and fled, mumbling an excuse about the drinks.

When she found her voice, she called from the kitchen, "Wine?"

"I'd like that. I'll help you." He rose—or sprang nimbly to his feet would be a better description. Myrhia was never sure as his movements were controlled and fluid, yet there was an illusion of swiftness about him.

He joined her in the kitchen as she was stretching to reach into the cabinet for the wine goblets. His hands circled her waist sending a tingling sensation along her spine. "I can almost close my fingers together around your waist with my two hands. You're built just right—proportioned to suit the most discriminating male."

She turned awkwardly, holding the goblets between them. "And are you a discriminating male?" She was trying to keep it light between them in spite of her increased flow of adrenaline.

"Quite!" he teased, taking the glasses from her and setting them down on the counter as he pulled her to him with one arm behind her and cupped her chin in his other hand. She fought a silent battle not to look into his eyes, but once held there in those agates of seawater, she could not turn away. Her mind spun in confusion while his strong hands on her back dug into her flesh with hot, sensuous fingers. Turk bent his head, his lips closing softly on her own. His kiss, teasing at first, lingered while excitement mounted in her own matching his. "Myrhia, beautiful—you are so lovely."

His kisses became more demanding, forcing her lips apart as his tongue explored hers and sent a whirling dervish of excitement through her. When she thought she could no longer stand in spite of his arm supporting her, he pulled away slowly, reluctantly. "Has anyone ever made real love to you before?" Again he secured her face with his hand making it impossible to look anywhere but in the eyes so close to her own.

"I know the score!" she muttered childishly, pulling away from his embrace as best she could.

"I doubt it! I honestly doubt you know what heights you're capable of and I'm going to be the one who teaches you."

Even the vision of what his words conjured in her mind sent ripples of anticipation along her nerve ends. If she submitted now, she would never be rid of the power Turk had over her. She had to fight for her right to decide these things for herself.

"I think I should have something to say about that. After all, it's my body—my feeling, my choice. I'm free to choose what and whom I want." It was necessary to make her words emphatic to strengthen her waning decision. His male nearness disturbed her and she had to force her legs to move a few feet away on the pretext of going for the wine.

"Will you open it?" she asked, not daring to look back at him.

"I will, but don't think by turning off beginning desire that you can turn my thoughts off as well. I know what I want. I know you want me and I'll not rest until you tell me that to my face."

She whirled on him, at last finding a small measure of spirit. "Oh! So you think that because you're the great football star acclaimed by thousands that any girl will let you slip into her bed willy-nilly? You may think you're the gift of the gods to all females but I assure you, Turk, I'm not turned on by you or anyone like you!"

"Oh, no? We'll see about that!" One stride brought him to her side as the arms of steel closed around her again. This time she was held tight to his male hardness, feeling the ripple of muscles beneath his clothing. Just as she felt he would break her in two, he released her. "We've plenty of time. After all, part of the thrill of conquest is in the chase."

"Oh, you!" Her hands were trembling when she turned to the counter to try opening the wine bottle. "Damn!" she said as it slipped from her hand.

"Here." Long fingers closed over hers as he removed the bottle from her hands. "Don't tremble so, beautiful. I won't take you by force. I promise when that day comes, you will desire me as you never have desired another man."

"Oh, you are a conceit—" The sentence remained unfinished as the telephone shrilled into the room. She couldn't remember when she had been so grateful to hear it ring, and she fled the kitchen, leaving Turk opening the wine.

"Myr, Carl here!" Again she felt a wave of gratitude for his call. It gave her something concrete to do that would bring back reality.

"Yes, Carl," she said louder than necessary so Turk could hear. "I've missed hearing from you. Is everything going all right?"

"With Belinda, yes, quite good! How about you? Are you getting out some?" When she didn't answer, he continued. "I called to ask if you had any ideas about the convention center. How about lunch tomorrow? Say Lemon Park—twelve thirty? We'll talk then. Buzz talk has it that this will be a ninety million dollar venture. By the way my company wanted me to get the auditorium plans very soon."

"They're almost finished. And, Carl, about lunch"— with malicious intent she allowed her voice to become intimately seductive— "I'll look forward to it." From her peripheral vision, Turk's expression indicated he was listening to her conversation. Some devil inside her prompted her to put excessive warmth into her last remark. As she turned from the telephone, all visible signs of interest were erased from Turk's smug countenance.

Handing her a goblet of wine, he said, "Is there anything I can be doing on the crepes?" he asked matter-of-factly.

She would have to go some to keep ahead of him in this game of wills. He often had the upper hand in most situations that usually ended in his casual amusement with her. Myrhia, angry with herself, turned back to the crepes and attacked the ham mercilessly with the chopper. While her anger cooled, Turk made himself useful setting the small table in her dining room. He even found her one candlestick with the burned candle and centered it on the table.

He moved easily about the table humming snatches of "Lara's Theme" from *Doctor Zhivago* from time to time. It occurred to Myrhia the tension building up inside her was due to apprehension Turk would try to seduce her and she might not be able to resist his strong masculine appeal. On the other hand it was wonderful this way, the two of them sharing an evening and, for once, compatible. It would be perfect if she could be certain he felt the same.

Myrhia became engrossed in her preparations, thinking she was glad she had allowed herself the luxury of the new microwave for such quick meals as this. This way she would be able to prepare their light supper without having to wait on the older oven to heat. She was unaware that Turk was lolling against the kitchen door, arms folded over his expanse of chest, one long leg crossed lazily over the other with his head tilted against the doorjamb, until she turned to lift crepes into the microwave.

When she became aware of him out of her peripheral vision, she turned to find a warm smile softening the lines of his face.

"You're one hell of a looker, Myrhia Lassiter! Why did you have to be so stubborn and independent?"

Damn! Once again he was referring to her career. Oh, it was subtle, but she knew deep inside him he resented her profession. His remark completely spoiled the moment she had been enjoying a few seconds ago. Her anger flared briefly but before she could frame a suitable reply, he chuckled.

"Now, now, let's not start that again. I can live with the fact you're a career woman. It's just taking me some little time to accept the idea of a woman architect coming in such a neat package, that's all!"

Angrily turning away from him, paring knife poised in one hand and a tomato in the other, she began chopping furiously as bits and pieces of onion and tomato flew into the salad bowl. "Who asked you to accept my profession anyway?"

"Knives are sharp, sweet! So are your claws, I see!"
He replied maddeningly through a deep throaty laugh.
"I love it when you explode this way."

His laugh was contagious and she found she was
laughing with him in spite of her angry retort. It was
hard to remain aloof in his presence. Her laughter filled
the kitchen area and before long she required a handkerchief to stem the tide of tears that ran down her
cheeks, partly from the laughter and partly from the
onion she was attacking for their salad.

"Here, let me dry your eyes." He took out his handkerchief and dabbed at her eyes. "You should laugh
more often. You're lovely that way."

The levity cleared the air between them throughout
the supper, which Turk ate ravenously, consuming his
own four crepes and two of hers.

"You're quite a gourmet cook. Do you really like
it?" There was disbelief in his question.

"Love it! It's a way to relax. I cook when I'm puz-
zling over a design or stymied by figures that don't jibe
with what floor plan I'm working on. It's a form of
therapy."

He leaned back totally relaxed, an unreadable gleam
in the depth of his eyes. In the single candleglow the
blue had turned to gray. From behind their smoky
depths he looked at her for a long time before speaking.
She made a move to rise and clear the table but his
quick movement to capture her hand stopped her.

"Is it Carl Muldrow?"

"What do you mean?" Myrhia was truly surprised
by the question.

"Is he the one who shares your heart? He's married,
you know." There was a touch of sadness in his voice.

"I'm aware of that." Her reply was terse. Much as
she wanted to, she couldn't lie to Turk. She had wanted

him to believe there was something between her and Carl only a moment ago when he had telephoned but now, with the soft flicker of the candlelight playing in and out of the shadows on his face, she told the truth.

"No, Carl and I are very good friends—that's all." Now since meeting Turk she admitted to herself there had never been anyone who interested her. She had been frequently thrown with eligible men—some who might have interested her enough for a follow-up date or two, but never for long. Carl's friendship had staved off loneliness, making her less vulnerable to risk her heart in a dangerous game where she might come out the loser. Now here she was again, perilously perched on the edge of falling for this overbearing man who would never have doubts as to his own prowess with women. And she no longer could count on Carl's intervention as a shield.

"So, I'm to understand you're free of any entanglements at this time?" Turk stated, releasing her hand abruptly.

She looked at him, feeling a frown pucker her brow. "You speak as if I'm a calendar of events—now your slate is clear—take a vacation—go shopping—start a new romance—clean house—or fly to the moon. As if you're arranging a schedule for me. This week Myrhia's free of social, amorous entanglements." Her sarcasm was curt and she hoped to the point.

"Sarcasm doesn't become you at all," he said tersely. "I think for now I'll help you clean up and leave." He glanced at his wristwatch once more. "It's seven and I do have to make a quick change to be somewhere by eight."

"You needn't stay for the cleaning up. I can manage on my own." It was dismissal and she hoped he would leave quickly. She felt rebuffed somehow and couldn't bear to have him touch her again knowing he was perhaps leaving for someone else—a romantic evening, no doubt.

"Good-bye, for now." Turk rose abruptly, looking deep into her eyes before starting to the living room. As he reached the door, he turned with his disarming smile. "I don't know when I've enjoyed an evening as much."

He was gone. Myrhia stared at the closed door, feeling as if she had been soundly reprimanded. All the time she had been hoping he would leave without touching her again, she contrarily had been longing for his arms around her and his lips on hers. Now he had gone without so much as a parting endearment and perversely she felt annoyed. What had happened to the cool, poised, sophisticated architect named Myrhia Lassiter?

Chapter Five

On rising next morning, Myrhia stepped to the mirror, grimaced at her reflection, disappointed that there was not some miracle that could erase the lines from around her eyes from lack of sleep. She longed to look coolly controlled to offset the growing dissatisfaction with herself and the fact she was finding it hard to concentrate on anything lately. Remnants of dreams flowed in and out of her mind—insolent, provocative dreams in which Turk had caught her to him, held her against his virile body, and kissed her until she had no will of her own and clung to him breathlessly.

Shrugging her slender shoulders, she slipped into her housecoat and scuffs and padded into the kitchen where Turk's invisible presence still hovered and filled her with a sense of loss. She wanted to despise him, blame him for her feeling of ineptitude, yet she was unable to do so.

What an unspeakable, highhanded way he had of coming into her life, disdainful of her talent as an architect on one hand, yet choosing her building design over all the others, which proved he liked her work, kissing her as if he meant it, tricking her into saying she desired him, and playing on her emotions to prove his power over her. Yet all the time he was subtly disclaiming her efforts to make it in the professional field.

She was more angry with herself. What could have happened to the Lassiter common sense the past few days? Men had never interfered with her concentration, but Turk was interfering not only with her mental alertness but her well-being as well.

She tried making her usual two cups of morning coffee in the coffee maker only to find she had made six cups and would have to pour out the rest as she hated to leave stale coffee all day in the pot. The frozen orange juice slipped as she was opening the can and splattered over the counter before she could grab it and prevent the toaster receiving a generous blob of the sticky orange concentrate. Inanimate objects often picked inopportune times to prove their superiority over humans and this morning the entire kitchen ensemble seemed to be letting her have it.

Gulping down juice and two cups of coffee while standing at the sink, she wiped up the spilled juice, poured out the remaining coffee, and tried the bedroom again.

A second glance in the mirror showed a solemn young woman, black hair flowing like a silken fan about her face and shoulders, full lips compressed in a severe line of determination and eyes fiery with resolve. This was better, she thought as she lifted the thick raven mass and began brushing it into a smooth, dignified chignon. She would present a proper image as a businesswoman from now on, no more admitted weakness toward her natural femininity.

She selected a lightweight pearl-gray suit contrasting it with a red silk blouse. The red might give her the courage to forget her wild night's dreams and face the day ahead. She shuddered slightly. Turk would destroy her if she wasn't on guard from now on. Surveying herself from all angles, she was satisfied but hesitated at the last minute. One touch of femininity couldn't be denied. She chose the tiny gold ear loops and matching gold stick pin for her blouse. Red pumps and red bag completed her appearance.

Walking with her head erect and her shoulders thrown back gave her added determination by the time she reached the elevator. She was in a better frame of mind as she drove through the early rush of traffic and pulled into the parking ramp under her building. She was even cheery with the attendant in the lot and greeted him with a bright "Good morning, Harvey!" as his heavy eyelids lifted in an appreciative gleam of approval.

Myrhia was feeling better by the minute as she rode the elevator to her floor. She had really been angry with herself. What could possibly have happened to her common sense these past few days? She would not tolerate Turk doing this to her. She needed her sleep and he would not invade her dreams again. As she entered her office and breezed past Trish's smile with a cheery good morning, she hoped her face was noncommittal and relaxed. She had a busy week ahead of her and much to look forward to.

No sooner than she settled at her desk and was riffling through her daily mail than Trish appeared in the door opening.

"Myrhia, you have a number to call. I couldn't get the name of the person but the secretary insisted that it was important."

"Oh?" Myrhia reached for the memo in her secretary's hand and began dialing the number.

"Dirckson Vaughan and Associates!" came a starched query. "Who's calling?"

A lump solidified in her throat. She resisted an urge to hang up. Speaking thinly over the obstruction, she said as matter-of-factly as she could, "M. Lassiter returning Mr. Vaughan's call."

"Just a minute, please." She wasn't sure but she thought it was followed by a giggle.

"Good morning, beautiful! I trust you slept well." His banter apparently was entertaining his secretary as another lilting giggle burst over the wire. "That's enough, Letty!" she heard him say, though his voice sounded muffled as if he had put a hand over the receiver. The memory of a pretty girl who accompanied him to the Benihana flashed before her. He dates his own secretary. How convenient! She must remember to tell him so.

"Sorry for the interruption." His tone held amusement. "I'm calling in regard to the fascia. I've decided to go along with the plainer of your two sketches. I think you'll agree with me in the long run—no folderol is needed. The beauty of the structure will lie in its outer facade."

"That's fine with me." She was not going to argue over the small matter now. "I'll change the master plan. It won't be difficult. Is that all?" She was having difficulty keeping her voice on an even level.

"Why do I get the feeling I'm about to be cut off?" He laughed. "Well, in case you wonder about my whereabout for the next two months, my secretary will know where to reach me in Hawaii." A long silence followed. "By the way, I'm sorry I won't be here for the ground-breaking ceremony, but Vaughan Associates will give you a good show anyway. I guarantee that. It will be impressive, I hope. I'm anxious for the building to be underway as soon as possible."

"I'm sure everything will go on schedule. Have a nice trip!" Myrhia struggled to keep from betraying her disappointment that he would not be here for the launching of the new project, at the same time wondering why she was not relieved he would not be in Dallas.

There was a lengthy pause from his end of the line, giving her time to adjust to his announcement. Unconsciously she had been counting on his sharing the big moment with her.

"I leave within the hour, Myrhia. I'll get together with you on return. I have something else to discuss concerning the building. I'm somewhat bothered by the idea of precast concrete for the exterior. I'm leaning more to the all glass curtain wall," he said offhandedly. "But then we'll discuss that when I return from Hawaii."

"You're what?" Her explosion carried around the door to Trish's office, causing her to poke her head around the doorjamb, a perplexed frown on her face.

Myrhia was too angry to care who listened to her conversation. "Do you mean that you selected my design knowing it calls for vision panels and precast concrete blocks and now—*now*—you want to change it?" Fury dissolved the lump in her throat, making her words spew in terse, controlled bites. "You will not do this to my building, Mr. Vaughan! I'll never allow it!"

She purposely let the receiver drop into its cradle, hoping it broke his eardrum at the other end of the line. Glancing at Trish, whose incredulous look was almost comical, she said, still biting her lips in anger, "That man!"

"That was Turk Vaughan, wasn't it, Myrhia? Does he want you to change something else? Why?"

Myrhia rose from her desk and began pacing about the small office. "Because he's an opinionated, gauche, overbearing know-it-all without one bit of artistic talent. He thinks he has a right to dictate everything and control everyone. Well"—she whirled on Trish not able to stop her tirade—"he'll find he's met his match. I'll not give an inch. One concession of mine has been given already and that's all I'll change. Even if I have to go to the other members of the committee one by one and convince them I'm the designer and I'm the one they voted for."

"I sure understand how you feel, Myrhia," Trish said meekly as she tiptoed from Myrhia's office back to her own desk.

"Trish!" Myrhia stepped to the door. "I'm sorry you have to hear me sound off this way but that man is a pain."

"I see your point," Trish said, quietly closing the door between them.

Myrhia sank down in her chair, staring at the sky outside her window. Turk Vaughan couldn't do this to her. She would not allow him to spoil the appearance of her first big building. Panels of precast cement were part of the beauty of the structure and it would make the building distinctive.

Rising from her desk, she moved thoughtfully to the window and scanned the skyline, mentally counting four buildings with shining walls of curtain glass close to where the Tarrington would stand.

"I refuse to have my building commonplace!" She said aloud to the empty office. She wanted her building to be diversified and she would not conform to a change. Just as in the suburbs, she could not find it in her heart to design tract homes with each floor plan identical to the one next door. She had too much of Walt Lassiter's talent to capitulate to mediocrity.

As she continued to stare out the window, the memory of the Sunday walk in the rain and the bittersweet closeness they shared later in her apartment over a hasty meal rose now to haunt her. Turk had seemed sincere, almost loving, as if he too might be feeling something deeper than infatuation. She was honest in admitting to herself the evening had meant something more to her too. Now she was hurting inside at the thought he might have set about to soften her up. Was he pretending to enjoy the walk? Had he tossed out overtures of lovemaking to make her more flexible about her building? It was tearing her apart to think that.

The idea he might hold out for curtain glass walls made her almost sick with apprehension. She needed to ask Carl if some mention had been made to change her initial drawings. It wasn't doing her any good mulling it over and over in her mind this way. She would call Carl and find out if he knew anything.

Myrhia stepped to the telephone to dial Carl's office only to be told he would be out of the office for the rest of the day and unable to make their lunch appointment.

"Damn it all!" she said, setting the receiver back in its cradle. "I need to get this off my chest." With a sigh of dejection she picked up her purse to make ready to leave the office, the problem still unsolved.

It seemed forever till the ground-breaking ceremony finally took place. At first the May day appeared overcast but by the time the small crowd assembled on the building site, the clouds had broken overhead and a shaft of sunlight fell onto the block-wide area as if highlighting a major event. That was how it seemed to Myrhia, who wore a new suit for the occasion. Trish had been invited to accompany her and Carl to the site.

Everything went smoothly. Mayor Wallis and several members of the Dallas city council were on hand for the soil turning. Besides the city legislators there were several from Vaughan Enterprises and Muldrow Associates to share in the event.

Carl beamed on her throughout the mayor's brief speech and insisted Myrhia accept the Mayor's offer to make a turn at earth scooping herself—for good luck.

"It isn't often that such an attractive architect appears on the Dallas scene, Ms. Lassiter." Mayor Wallis bent his portly frame in her direction, holding out the shining shovel. "I would deem it a pleasure if you would toss a scoop of dirt yourself."

Myrhia accepted, feeling a knot of excitement welling up inside her, almost smothering her. So this was the way it was? This was the way her father must have felt time after time, this sense of expectancy that the building would stand as a tribute to the designer. She was awed by the occasion and humbled beyond a doubt. If only— She stifled the thought quickly. She had been about to wish that Turk was here to share in it, but after their last conversation about another change, she felt it best he was not present to pour cold water on her excitement.

She only half heard the words of congratulations and praise during the final moments of the ceremony as her excitement was at an all-time high. Carl and Trish smiled at her continually, making her grateful to have them for friends who could share the moment that meant this much to her.

Carl accompanied her and Trish back to her office, where he produced a magnum of champagne he had hidden in the backseat of his car for the occasion. There was much laughter and toasting and Myrhia was on her second paper cup full of the bubbly wine when the telephone rang. Trish answered, handing the receiver to Myrhia, a gleam of interest shining in her face.

"It's Hawaii! I imagine it's Mr. Vaughan calling to congratulate you." She smiled knowingly at Carl.

"Not to congratulate me, I'm sure," Mryhia said, moving to the other office and closing the door behind her.

"Hello?"

"Hello, beautiful architect! How did the ground breaking go? I'm damned sorry I wasn't there to hold your hand during the ceremony." The resonant voice brought a pair of sensuous lips to her mind and she felt her legs tremble slightly. She never could drink much champagne. "Are you there, darling?"

"Yes, I'm here. It was an impressive ceremony, Turk. Several of the council members congratulated me too. The mayor was very nice—he made me feel a part of the new Dallas look. He'd looked at the overall rendering and found the building beautiful, he said. Turk, I was really thrilled," she said simply, all guard down. "It was—"

"He'd like it even more with vision panels," Turk said, interrupting her.

Too angry to reply at first, she swallowed a gulp of air. "Turk, you can infuriate me more than anyone I know. No, I will not change my design! I told you that already and that's my final word! She slammed down the receiver but was not quick enough to blot out the sound of masculine laughter from the other end of the line.

"Oh, that man!" she said under her breath as she returned to Trish's office where Carl and Trish were finishing their second cup of champagne.

Trish's eyes clouded momentarily. "Don't let him spoil your day." She grinned, holding up her cup to touch Carl's. "To you, Myrhia, the best of luck!"

Through the following weeks of summer Myrhia was swamped with work thanks to recommendations from former clients who had used her designs for their buildings. With the auditorium plans half ready and the new proposal for a shopping mall, it seemed she was at the drawing board constantly for almost two months. She needed a break from the work, something to take her mind off drawing for a while. A small dinner party was the answer. She would call Cleo and several friends to invite them to one of her wok dinners. Perhaps Carl and Belinda could manage to come if they could find a sitter for Dody.

Myrhia put Trish to work inviting eight of her friends for the last Saturday night in August. She would not have much time for shopping or cleaning her apartment, but these friends were from a long way back and, with the exception of Carl's wife, had been to her apartment frequently when it was shiningly clean. It didn't really occur to Myrhia that she had deliberately avoided inviting a man for herself to round out the party until Trish spoke out.

"Do you mind telling me which man is your current interest, Myrhia, or is it any of my business?" Trish asked, cocking her head sideways in a look of speculation. "I know you could tell me to buzz off, but I am concerned. My boyfriend said to tell you any woman who looks so good should lay her sights for a superman."

In spite of a slight annoyance that Trish had brought up the subject, she had to smile. Trish was never going to be a grown-up woman. There would always be something of the ingenue in her makeup.

"There's no reason to be paired off in couples at this party, Trish. They are all just good friends—and in answer to your question, there's no one in the group that I'm romantically interested in, no one who raises my blood pressure." She tried to laugh but had to admit it had a hollow ring to it. "I just don't have time for men."

She turned away from her secretary's appraisal, hoping the thought of a pair of steely blue-gray eyes that momentarily flashed across her vision had not left a telltale trace across her face. She shoved his image back into the shadow of her mind, wishing with all her heart she could lock him there forever. He only meant trouble and she wanted none of it. She hated to admit she had deliberately left the guest list uneven hoping he would return in time to join them. It was unthinkable that it was already late summer and she had kept a mental calendar during the time he had been gone. Of course, that was easily explained as they were thrown together for a few months as business associates while the building was going up, nothing more. It was only natural that he would be in her mind often, whether she liked it or not.

Saturday arrived in a burst of heat. Fortunately her apartment was air conditioned but better still, by evening, a Gulf breeze moved up through Texas cooling the city of Dallas. She opened her balcony doors, allowing the fresh air to spread throughout her small apartment.

By the time the guests arrived preparations were complete, even the tray of hors d'oeuvres. There were puffs filled with hot shrimp salad, tiny cheese biscuits with a touch of cayenne, and small bites of chicken livers marinated in soy sauce and bruised scallions and fried quickly in peanut oil.

Cleo and her newest craze, Barry something or other, arrived first. Her friend, after giving Myrhia a quick peck of affection on the cheek, moved toward the snack tray. Leah and Herbie came next followed by Carl and Belinda.

As Carl entered moving to her side with Belinda on his arm, he gave Myrhia a hug with his free arm before introducing her to his wife.

"Myr, I'm glad you two could meet at last. I want you to know each other."

Myrhia turned to the round-faced woman at his side. "I'm happy to know you, Belinda. I feel I should anyway."

"Me too." Belinda's shy smile touched Myrhia. "I'm a bit intimidated, Myrhia. Carl is always touting your praises. He doesn't expect me suddenly to become a designer, but I believe he hopes I can learn to cook the way you do by association." She laughed, giving Carl a warm smile. "I'm just not a gourmet cook."

"You suit me," Carl said loyally, pulling her close and kissing her lightly on the forehead.

Myrhia smiled. "My style cooking would soon become cloying to the average male, I'm afraid. Most men would grow tired of party fare night after night." Carl shot her a look of gratitude before moving off with Belinda on his arm.

While the hors d'oeuvres kept her guests entertained and Herbie tending bar, she moved to the kitchen for the final preparations. For some reason a feeling of detachment followed her from the presence of the couples who seemed paired off happily. It was as if she had become an observer. Slowly a feeling of loneliness replaced the detachment. She was moving automatically about the small kitchen, ready to put the vegetables into the wok for a quick stir-fry when Carl walked into the kitchen.

"Myr." His hazel eyes scanned her face, frowning slightly as he spoke. "Is everything going all right with you? You seem to be uptight."

"I don't know what you mean." Her answer was more emphatic than necessary but she hoped Carl would not pursue the matter further. It would be impossible to fool him for long, as he had known her moods well these past few years. She turned away from him, picked up the mallet, and began to pound the already bruised ginger root with force.

"There's a meeting with the commission on the Tarrington Building Thursday or Friday of next week—not sure what day. Muldrow Associates' office. The day depends on Vaughan's return from Hawaii. I thought he was due back sometime this week." He paused as if waiting for her to clue him in on Turk's arrival. When she didn't, he continued. "I'll let you know as soon as I hear myself." Again the perceptive look caused her to glance away but not soon enough. He had heard her quick intake of breath at the mention of Turk's return.

"Myr, is Turk Vaughan getting to you?" Carl had come to the point immediately.

"No, why should he?" She spoke crossly. "I see very little of him. He's conspicuous by absence." After she had spoken bluntly she knew it was a mistake again as Carl jumped her once more.

"I thought so! That guy could upset his own mother, if he had one. He has about as much diplomacy as a herd of buffalo. Hell, he'd run over anything in his path to get what he wants."

She remained quiet, thinking it was a good thing she hadn't been able to reach Carl that day in her office when she was so furious with Turk. Carl was perceptive anyway and would know the reason for her tenseness soon enough. Besides, the matter of the building's exterior was her responsibility.

"Carl, spare me further discussion where he's concerned, will you?" She tossed the conversation off lightly. "How about being a good guy and popping those cut-up bits of chicken into the wok on top of the ginger root and garlic. I want the chicken to brown and heat all the way through. It's already cooked." She managed a smile, hoping it was convincing enough that Carl would not see she was upset at the mention of Turk.

"Will do!" Carl set about following her orders. "Just remember, Myr, I'm ready to run interference for you if you need it."

"Thanks!" She reached for his hand and gave it a squeeze.

Myrhia was grateful the subject was dropped for a time. What Carl didn't know and what she hated to admit to herself was that the thought of Turk had sent tingling tremors throughout her body. Was it possible she wanted to see him if for no other reason than to do battle again?

Belinda wandered into the kitchen to help and soon the buffet was ready, with steaming rice, condiments of raisins and chopped nuts to add to the main dish, Chinese Chicken Almond Ding.

As the guests moved toward the bar, which was a makeshift buffet, the telephone shrilled into the chatter. Myrhia felt her heart do a skip. It wasn't Alicia: she knew the party was in progress, as Myrhia had canceled their afternoon golf date to prepare the dinner. Instinctively she knew it was Turk but she was powerless to cross the room and answer it.

It continued to ring before she could move toward it. "Want me to answer? I'm closest," Cleo called across the room.

"Please do," Myrhia answered, feeling a tight knot of fear she was going to be disappointed in the caller after all.

"Yes, just a moment." Cleo turned with a knowing smile. "I think you'd better take this call in your bedroom, Myrhia," she said under her breath as Myrhia reached for the receiver. "I think it's that macho Cowboy."

"Okay." Myrhia walked zombielike to her bedroom, fighting down her rising pulse rate at every step, and closed the door before lifting the receiver. She waited for Cleo's click showing she had hung up at the other extension before she managed a weak "Hello."

"Am I interrupting something? Sounds like a party's in full swing." The deep resonance of his voice touched a responding chord somewhere in her body making it hard to answer him.

"Just a few friends for a small dinner party—six guests." Why had she said that? He could add and subtract and would in all probability wonder at the odd number.

"Not matched pairs?" came his terse answer.

"Not exactly. Where are you, by the way?" she asked, trying to remain cool.

"Not far away—in fact I'm calling from downstairs in your apartment building. I hoped you would be free to have dinner with me. I just got in around four and—I hate to admit it—I had a short nap—jet lag, I guess. I intended to call sooner. Sorry, I didn't know. I'll be in touch. I have a lot of things to talk over with you."

"Why not come on up? I'm just now serving and there's plenty for one more." She was trying not to reveal her excitement, but his call was having a disconcerting effect on her. "You'll know most everyone from Cleo's party, anyway."

He was hesitating and she was praying he would accept. "I promise you won't be poisoned." She managed a laugh that broke the tension.

"Be right up!" The line was severed between them. By the time she set down the receiver and walked back

into the living room to inform her guests he was
punching her buzzer.

"We've another guest—Turk Vaughan. You remember," she said as matter-of-factly as possible to the
faces that were turned toward her, avoiding Carl's and
Cleo's—the latter especially, as she was wearing an I-
told-you-so expression.

It was amazing what his entrance did for the group,
she noticed, as he stepped inside and nodded to everyone. The women began to sit a little straighter, find
some stray lock of hair that needed attention. Even Belinda seemed interested in him. The men were less de-
monstrative, but Myrhia could sense their reactions.
Some eyed him with admiration taking in his tightly
knit body that seemed, even to Myrhia, to be in excellent shape without an extra ounce of superfluous fat. In
fact it was hard for her to look away from him as she
stepped to the doorway to make him welcome. His eyes
caught and held hers in a long, intimate look that was
disconcerting.

Fighting for control of her emotions, she stopped
just in front of him. "I'm glad you could come before
everything was devoured, Turk. Come on, I'll see that
these ravenous guests don't have seconds until you and
I have firsts.

Carl set down his tray of food and came to greet
Turk. "Glad you could make it, Turk. Myrhia and I
were setting up the meeting with the commission for
the end of next week. Now we can finalize it. Would
Friday be all right?"

"As far as I know I'll be back in time." Turk said,
still turned toward Carl, "I'm sorry I missed the
ground-breaking, but Myrhia told me it went well."

"It did," Carl said, turning away to go to Belinda.

Myrhia sent Carl a silent message of thanks. By bringing business into their conversation he had smoothed over a situation that might have been emotional between her and Turk. In spite of Turk's offhand manner, she sensed his growing awareness of her. Was it possible he had missed her just a little as a person and not just as a business associate? The thought gave her spirits a happy boost.

Turk helped himself to what was left of the hors d'oeuvres and filled his plate with Chicken Almond Ding. For now the silence between them was companionable as they sat side by side listening to the others. From time to time Turk entered into the conversation, especially when it drifted to the Dallas Cowboys.

"The team just doesn't have the motivation this year!" Herbie said, looking at Turk for confirmation.

"I doubt we'll take it this time. Hate to lose the title match like that," Carl added. "We don't have a good running back."

"Oh, I don't know about that, Carl," Turk drawled, slipping back into the world he loved so well, "Greg Powers is a powerhouse this year. Wait and see. He needed last year as a seasoner. We'll win—you'll see."

"Can we quote you on that?" Cleo interjected. "You should know."

"Yep! You can quote me." Turk laughed and smiled at Myrhia.

Sinking back comfortably against the cushions of her couch, she watched his hands articulate his conversation about different plays he had experienced with the team. From time to time his eyes darted to her, including her in the conversation. Each time their eyes locked, a warm flame seemed to ignite her senses. He was a dynamic personality in many ways and she felt as if she were being absorbed into his aura.

The party was breaking up. Carl and Belinda were the

last to go and were almost out the door when Carl turned back. "I almost forgot, Myr. Here's the dope on the convention center competition."

He handed Myrhia two sheets of folded paper. "That contains the information on the area, acreage, and purpose. It's heavy competition but one you're certainly up to." He said the last pointedly, looking directly at Turk. "Five hundred acres of woodlands will be included. Since it's to be multipurpose, it'll need to be considered from all angles."

"Great! Carl, this is great!" She looked up from scanning the material briefly. "I appreciate your getting me the scoop." As usual she felt a surge of nervous excitement at the prospect of new competition. "Thanks, Carl." She laid a hand on her friend's arm as he and Belinda left.

"I have no doubt you'll be able to do it, Myr," he said over his shoulder. "I'll be out of town a couple of days. Be back by the middle of the week. How about lunch Wednesday noon—at Lemon Park?"

"Fine. I'll be there." She smiled at Belinda, grateful she understood these meetings were in the line of business. "Good night, you two. Belinda, come again soon." As she turned from the doorway she moved inadvertently into Turk's arms, feeling them automatically close around her, pulling her against his strong body.

"Neither do I have doubts about your ability, darling." His husky voice was muffled in her hair. She pulled away slightly to look up into his face, surprised to find his expression warm and gentle. For the moment his compliment pumped new hope into her wavering confidence in their business relationship. Perhaps Turk was ready to concede over the facade and the vision panels.

Her imagination began to soar when the pressure

of his hands increased, erasing all thought of buildings, facades, or panels as his fingertips moved upward to brush back the hair at the curve of her shoulder. His lips found the soft spot below her ear teasing her senses; her hands moved upward into his thick hair marveling at its silken texture under her fingers.

He laughed, deep in his throat, as he bent his head to brush his lips across her cheek until they came to rest on her own, where they demanded a response. She was powerless to resist as waves of pleasure swept over her. She could feel her body yielding to the pressure of his virile strength as she became weightless, almost mindless, in the ecstasy of the moment.

Turk's kisses, gentle at first, became more forceful, waking every sensual spot in her body until she became limp with desire. She had never responded to passion before in this way. It was becoming all-consuming, almost frightening, and she was reveling in its primitive fierceness.

"Myrhia, Myrhia," he said her name over and over, holding her pressed against him as if he would never let her go. "You were never out of my thoughts these past weeks. Is it possible you missed me too?" His whispered endearments teased her further. "You were like an ache that would never leave me. Say you missed me—say it!" His lips came down on hers, making any reply impossible for the moment.

When she was able to find breath enough to whisper softly, she said, "I did, Turk. I did miss you. I tried not to think of you, I tried to hate you, to put you out of my mind, but I couldn't help—" She was not allowed to finish as his lips closed over hers once more. Lifting her with ease, he carried her to the velvet sofa and sank down holding her in his arms.

"I hope to heaven you mean it," he said huskily, clamping his strong arms around her like a vise and crushing her to him. She was barely able to breathe as she gave up to the ecstasy of his embrace and laid her head against his muscular shoulder.

They sat together lost in a timeless rapture neither aware of the passing of the hour. It was like nothing she had ever before experienced, being held close, comforted and safe. Now and then his hands explored the curves of her body, cupping her breasts gently or running his fingers lightly over the hollow of her throat and deep into the cleavage between her breasts.

"You are so beautiful, darling," he whispered hoarsely as he turned her on his lap to find her lips.

His tongue was sweetly exploring, seeking her own, arousing an ardor too strong to resist. His free hand came up to touch her cheek, move downward to trace across her upper lip. "Myrhia, you are my torment."

She was unaware of the soft lights in her apartment, unaware of everything but the beating of someone's heart. Whether it was hers or Turk's she could never be certain as they seemed to be throbbing as one. Their lips touched gently sometimes, fiercely at others, while their fingers explored the planes of the other's face. The touch of his hands on her flesh was like fire and she wondered if her own were working like magic on him.

Suddenly Turk lifted her from his lap and sat her down beside him, pushing her back against the couch. His strong body moved over her sending waves of pleasure throughout her nerves.

"Damn it all! I want you! I've never wanted a woman this way before." He pulled her to him fiercely, holding her against his chest while his lips plundered hers, almost bruising in their demands. "It's maddening we can't be together. I promise you—I promise you we will be together soon and nothing will keep me away after that!"

A slight shiver rippled over her at the vehemence of his words. His eyes flamed with passion and desire as his hands grasped her shoulders as if he would pull her body into his own. His mouth came down on hers, forcing hers to open once again. All restraint was gone between them and she gave up, admitting her own need of this man. Her body arched to meet his as the telephone rang, shattering the moment into shards of unrequited passion.

"That's probably for me!" Turk rose angrily, yanking up the receiver at the same time looking at his watch. "Hello. Okay, be right down!" he said tersely, letting the receiver fall heavily.

"I've got to go. I'm flying back to Maui tonight. That was my limousine driver calling from your lobby. I told him to pick me up at eleven." Turk took one giant stride toward her, lifting her to her feet as if she were a rag doll.

Disappointment crowded out her pleasure as she felt her legs buckle under her, causing her to sink onto the edge of the coffee table for support. "You can't go, Turk. Why? Why did you come back at all?"

In spite of the pain she could read in his eyes, they were gentle as he leaned forward cupping her face in his hands. "Don't you know? Don't you really know why I came, darling?"

The husky tone of his voice was all the assurance she needed to understand his meaning. "You actually came home because of—"

She was not allowed to finish but she knew the answer in her heart. He drew her gently to her feet, supporting her body with his strong arms, and kissed her lips. This time the kiss was sweet but far stronger in its sweetness than the probing fierceness of their passionate ones.

"Good-bye, my darling—until Friday."

He released her slowly, the deep blue-gray eyes filled with pain and longing. With a groan of agony he turned away, standing for a moment with his back to her, as if reconsidering his need to leave, then moved reluctantly.

Unable to follow him to the door, she watched him stride away with his easy grace. As he touched the doorknob he turned back. "I had to sign some papers that Letty had waiting for me. I'm taking her back to Maui with me this time. I'll be needing a secretary." With that he was gone.

Myrhia stood a while longer, braced against the coffee table, as the impact of Turk's last statement made its way through her nervous system to her brain, hatefully shoving out the rapture of their last moments together. Letty was going with him. He would need a secretary this time. Anger, hot and menacing, prodded her from the spot. "Oh, what a fool I am! What a stupid fool!"

Trembling, she strode purposely to the door, furiously slamming the lock into place. "There, Mr. Turk Vaughan! You will never get the best of me again! I will not be manipulated."

He could just go find another architect and renege on his contract for all she cared. She would never capitulate on changing her design. Never! If that was what he had in mind, then he could go to the devil.

With those bitter words ringing in her ears, she made ready for a sleepless night, one that would be fraught with sensuous dreams of his hands moving over her body, his lips claiming hers, probing and compelling her surrender.

In spite of a subconscious wish Sunday would not dawn, it came. Myrhia dragged herself from her rumpled bed and slippered to the disarray left behind in the kitchen. For once she was glad of the mess. It would give purpose to at least an hour of her time.

In spite of the rattle of dishes, the sounds did nothing to erase the rapid pulsing of her heart. She couldn't go on like this all day. She had things that needed to be done. Her time was precious and couldn't be wasted on Turk. How could she have allowed him to seduce her heart this way? But for the telephone call, her body would have been seduced as well. He spoke of need, of desire and missing her—yet, he could turn blithely at the doorway of her apartment and calmly inform her he was taking Letty back to Maui with him. He must take her for a bigger fool than she had almost become.

Still feeling limp and exhausted, she wandered into her small workroom. There were tag ends of previous work left on her drawing board. Her filling station design, ready at last, had been delivered to the company Friday by messenger. She was glad of that. By eleven she was calmer. Work usually was a panacea for most of her problems, although this problem was unprecedented. She had never before had to fight off the memory of a man whose gaze could melt her will this way.

At eleven the telephone rang and she was grateful for its sound. The apartment had become increasingly small and filled with memories of the night before. The caller was Dick Watson. "Miss Lassiter, sorry to disturb your Sunday morning but I have to be out of town tomorrow. Just wanted to tell you the design proposal for the filling stations was accepted. Our company will be building them in the Big Bend country. Your check will be in the mail sometime next week. By the way, I'm recommending you to a friend in Louisiana."

As she put down the receiver she wasn't certain she had even thanked him. She had been so grateful for his call and the boost it had given to her spirits. It would be a pleasure to work with his Big Star Company and she would be able to comply with any changes necessary. Setbacks with the big wheels like Turk Vaughan could be offset by praise from the other smaller companies.

The first part of the week was more or less uneventful, giving Myrhia time to work on the auditorium and make tentative sketches for the convention center proposal. There was no news from Turk or the Vaughan Associates and as far as she knew the meeting with the Tarrington commission would be as scheduled on Friday.

If anyone had told her it would be impossible not to dwell on the fact Turk was probably enjoying his days in Hawaii with his red-headed secretary and not be furious and hurt by it, she would have told them they were crazy. She had every intention of putting the two of them out of her mind, but the memory of his lovemaking and the rapture she experienced in his arms left an indelible mark. Not even the love of designing could erase those moments of ecstasy from her mind.

She awoke Wednesday morning, glad to have something ahead of her to break the monotony of her days. Not that lunch with Carl was such a big deal, but at least his friendship was stable enough to absorb some of her problems with Turk.

Myrhia left early to do her shopping before meeting Carl at Lemon Park. As she strolled thoughtfully along the shopping mall sidewalk, she glanced into the windows. A flash of magenta caught her attention, causing her to stop in front of a small exclusive dress shop. The softly draped cocktail dress was too pretty to pass by without trying it on. A quick glance at her watch told her she still had time before meeting Carl.

The dress was in her size and an exact fit. The color brightened her complexion, something she needed lately as she noticed a gray strained look about her eyes. It was a romantic dress made for moonlit nights and candleglow. She felt a momentary lift of spirits as she stepped from the shop clutching her purchase under her arm.

As she stepped into the restaurant, Carl motioned to her from across the room. "I see you've been shopping," he said by way of opening the conversation.

"Nothing like a new dress to perk up a woman's libido. I may never have a chance to wear it, but the color took my fancy," she said as she sat across from him at the glass-topped table.

"You had a great party the other night. Belinda enjoyed it and said to tell you she was happy to meet you at last." Carl looked at her quizzically. "But even she noticed you were tense for some reason."

"I wasn't aware that I was any way but normal," Myrhia said with a trace of irritation. "I'm surprised that Belinda could pass judgment on a first meeting that way."

"Sorry, Myr, you know I didn't mean that critically and neither did Belinda. She really likes you and wants to see you more often." He looked up as the waitress stepped to their table for their order.

"Just make mine a quiche and salad, Carl," she said, turning to stare out of the window.

"Two, please—and coffee." Carl dismissed the waitress before addressing Myrhia again. "Is your mother all right, Myr? You haven't mentioned her lately."

"She's fine! Why?" She turned back to him, a frown forming. "What made you ask that?"

"Oh, I don't know. It's just that I'm trying to get you to open up and talk. It's been a long time since you've discussed your problems with me. That's all."

Myrhia was forced to smile in spite of her feeling. Carl had always been perceptive where she was concerned. Perhaps it would be easier to come right out and tell her good friend that she was hooked on a man who could tear her life to pieces with little concern to him. The problem might diminish in importance if she told Carl.

Taking a deep breath, she plunged in. "It's Turk! I would be lying if I said he didn't upset me. But it's not the way you think, Carl. I can handle him in a business way even if I have to pull a few tricks myself. But it's more than that. He's getting to me emotionally. I think I want to hate him more each time I'm away from him, but yet when I'm with—" She couldn't finish, not even to tell this brotherly man who had listened to all her woes for years. It was like baring her naked body to the world.

Carl remained silent for a while. Finally he reached for her hand and gave it a friendly squeeze. "Are you by chance falling in love, Myr?"

"Of course not!" The emphasis on the words only made a mockery out of her statement.

"I hope you're not. Dammit! I don't want that man to hurt you. I think I'd take a poke at him if he does."

She looked into his open face, seeing concern behind the amber eyes. "Don't worry about me. I'm certainly old enough not to be taken in by his charm, which I understand is appreciated by many women in Dallas." She forced a nervous laugh. "I'll make it where he's concerned." Then she grinned, feeling better for having shared as much as she had with Carl. Besides, there were some things she dared not reveal to this good friend. Little private moments that only her heart was handling badly, but had to be dealt with alone.

"My real gripe with him is about his wanting to change the outer facade of the building. He wants curtain glass instead of the precast concrete my plans call for. You know that will make an entirely different appearance in the building, Carl, and I just can't take it. Anyway that big oaf doesn't know one thing about architecture."

"You're right. Don't let him get to you. I've never seen that side of Turk before, but I feel you can handle him. You've differed with other promoters, I recall, but none of them have made you this belligerent." Suddenly Carl laughed out loud.

"Remember the time that guy Tolbert took you to task about the shopping center in Midland? He wanted it to represent some kind of flying albatross and kept after you to create the feeling of a bird. You grew exasperated and designed a huge bird head, complete with staring eyes and beak, and dumped the design in his lap." Carl continued to chuckle. "I'll never forget the look of horror on his face as you walked out on him." Carl's laughter was contagious, causing her to explode in merriment. It was the therapy she had needed for a long time and she rocked with laughter, throwing all restraint to the winds.

"It was a shocker, wasn't it?" she said when she could speak again. "That bird—had he known it—resembled my mental impression of him."

For the next half hour they enjoyed their quiche, from time to time making small talk about unimportant matters. She came away from her lunch with Carl feeling better, she admitted to herself. Myrhia felt a spring in her step when she entered the office sometime later. Perhaps there was something to the old adage that having a shoulder to cry on had a therapeutic effect. It had been that way with Carl.

The afternoon spent at the drawing board went smoothly. Trish was in and out watching the rough sketches of the auditorium proposal materialize under her nimble fingers, only to be crumpled over and over and tossed into the trash basket. The sixth or seventh try—she had lost count—held merit at last.

"Well, what do you think?" she asked Trish, who had come in again to share a soda with her.

"I like it." Trish peered over her shoulder, then stepped back, moving around to look at the sketch from various angles. "Yep! It looks good."

"Sure it looks like what it's supposed to be? An auditorium?" Myrhia asked, stepping back from the board to get a better perspective on it herself.

"That's what I'd take it to be," Trish said, sipping her drink.

"It's supposed to be a multipurpose auditorium. For musicals, stage plays, sports events, and big church gatherings. So I was told. It's difficult to do—make the building cover all that and still look good," she said by way of explanation.

"I think it's all right, Myrhia. As you say, there isn't much you can do to make an auditorium glamorous." Trish started from the room. "Why would they want one building to be used for all that, anyway? Unless it's for economy's sake," she said, looking pleased with herself for her observation.

Myrhia turned back to her drawing board with a critical appraisal. This rough sketch, when improved and refined, would possibly be acceptable to the committee. The more she looked at her sketch, the more certain she was. She hoped they could see the three facets she had deliberately included in the design. The fact that Trish had not seen its multipurpose didn't worry her now. She was confident she had touched the media she desired. Now, if she could do as well on the convention center.

It was late when she left her office. Trish had gone long before. As Myrhia stepped from the buiding into the street, she noticed tall shadows were appearing on the pavement and there was a hint of a long, somnolent fall in the warm humidity. She couldn't believe the months were slipping away from her and it was already the first of September.

She would rest this evening, take an early dawdling bath, and eat a light supper. Perhaps a small salad and a glass of white wine on her balcony would make her feel rewarded for doing something right the first time. It wasn't often a design went together as easily as the auditorium building had.

As she entered her apartment the telephone rang, but when she picked up the receiver, she heard it click at the other end. She had probably picked it up on its last ring. Perversely she thought of Turk. He wouldn't be calling her, as he was well entertained in all probability. Perhaps he was just coming in from a round of golf or a light luncheon beside the blue Pacific with, of course, a redhead. Why did she torture herself this way? Attempting to shove Turk out of her mind, she began to hum a tune and to her angry surprise, realized she was humming the tune from *Dr. Zhivago*—"Lara's Theme." Turk had been softly whistling that melody the first time he had come to her apartment after their intimate walk in the rain. It had been a beautiful afternoon and now it hurt to remember.

Shaking off the mood, she decided to bathe first and then, if the caller had not tried again, she would dial Cleo or her mother. It might be one of the two calling, since it was very unlikely it was a client or anyone pertaining to her office. She groaned aloud. Who was she kidding? What made her keep thinking it might be Turk? As Myrhia sank into the tub of warm water, the fragrance of her jasmine bubble bath sent a pleasant sensation into her nostrils. Nothing was as restful to her at the end of the day as a luxurious bath to ease away all frustrations. She became so relaxed she almost fell asleep, but then the telephone rang again.

Muttering to herself, she rose and wrapped a towel hastily about her body before padding wet footed and dripping to the bedroom telephone.

"Hello!"

"One moment, please. Hold for Lahaina, Maui. I have a call for Myrhia Lassiter."

Turk! In spite of her resolve concerning him, excitement welled up in her. She was shivering for some stupid reason in the warm room.

"Speaking."

"Miss Lassiter—" She recognized the feminine voice. Letty had a musical, breathless quality in speaking. "I'm calling for Turk. He wanted you to know he will be in Dallas tomorrow evening, Thursday, and will take you out for dinner. Just a minute, please." During the pause that followed all Myrhia could hear was the furious pounding of someone's heart—her own. "Yes, he said to expect him at eight o'clock. Good-bye, Miss Lassiter. Aloha." Her soft laugh followed before the click of the receiver cut off further conversation.

Myrhia stared at the dead receiver seconds longer, as if it were a living thing. "Oh!" She slammed it back into its cradle, knocking over the small white rattan table and telephone. "Damn," she muttered, bending to pick up the telephone and straighten the table.

She was unaware how angry she was until her skin began to sting from the hard rubbing she was giving it with the towel. Turk had his nerve to do this to her. He had probably been standing not two feet away from the telephone and had Letty call to torment her. Well, it was a childish, stupid thing for him to do and he could not expect her to honor a date made in that manner. She had no intention of being here at eight o'clock on Thursday. That was certain. She would not see him until she had to face him at the meeting, which was to be scheduled on Friday. This was a deliberate slap in the face and she would not be treated in this manner.

Chapter Six

By morning Myrhia was still determined she would not be home when Turk came for his date, but contrary to her well-laid plans, circumstances late Thursday afternoon caused her delay in getting away from the office. A problem with one of the contractors, who called from Midland to complain that he had not received the shipment of window framing detained her until almost five. By the time she could assure him that the matter would be taken care of first thing in the morning, she was later still.

She scratched off a hurried note for Trish to check out the problem of the framing first thing in the morning and laid it on her secretary's desk, locked her office, and headed for her apartment.

The traffic, which was always terrible, seemed unusually so. It had snarled to a creeping movement as she turned onto Central Expressway. She was still determined not to be home when Turk arrived, but she didn't have much time to dawdle. She wanted to prove to him once and for all he could not treat her like a yo-yo, pushing and pulling her emotions this way.

The meeting with the commission for the Tarrington Building was set at two o'clock tomorrow, Friday, and

Carl no doubt would come by for her. She was certain she would not need him to give her confidence as she felt everything was under control. After tonight, when Turk found himself stood up, he would no doubt get the message theirs was to be only a business association. From now on he could keep his distance.

By the time she reached her apartment she was forced to hurry through her bathing and dressing, but she seemed to be lagging behind. She could expect Turk around eight, which would mean she should be out of there by seven thirty at the latest. She stepped from the tub, dried herself quickly, and splashed on some of her favorite bath cologne, which left her body cool. After slipping into her silk panties and bra, she pulled a flesh-colored knit sweater over her head and was just about to snatch a pair of worn jeans from a hook in her closet when she heard the door buzzer. She gave a quick glance at her bedside clock, reassured it was only seven fifteen. Turk wouldn't be here this early, he would never be that eager to see her.

Pulling the jeans on hastily, she unpinned the knot on top of her head and let the heavy mass of dark hair fall to her shoulders, taking time only to run her hands through its silken strands.

"Who is it? she called as she padded barefoot to the door.

"Turk. Have you forgotten? We have a date."

"Oh, no!" she moaned softly to herself. She had delayed too long. "You presume too much, Turk. I didn't accept or even say I would be here. As I remember, you used an intermediary to make the arrangements for our date. That made it quite impersonal." She leaned against the door, feeling her knees slowly buckle beneath her. He was so close to her now and all week she had been trying to put him out of her mind.

"Myrhia, you'd better open the door or I'll smash it in! How will you explain that to your neighbors?"

"You wouldn't dare!" she countered, knowing that was a loaded statement.

"Oh? Just try me."

With a sigh she opened the door a crack to the length of the safety chain. Myrhia knew she had made a mistake after a glimpse of his smiling face. He had never looked so handsome; it took her breath to look at him. His light gray suit was worn with a pale blue shirt and tie that contrasted to his dark skin, bringing out the blue in his eyes. Those eyes, at that moment, appeared to be melting with tenderness as he peered through the crack at her.

"Well, darling? Are you going to open the door?" he whispered.

Slowly she slid the chain bolt and opened the door, stepping back as she did so. A puzzled expression flashed over his face as his look traveled over her body, taking in the snug-fitting jeans and knit sweater that was clinging seductively to her breasts, revealing the cleavage between their soft peaks. A rueful smile swept the corners of his sensuous lips as his lids narrowed dangerously over the grayness.

"Quite revealing! I've never seen you so provocative. You're one woman who can get away with tight jeans." His smile widened. "The bare feet are especially attractive, as I can imagine the rest of you might be without the outer casings." A sardonic twinkle appeared in his eyes. "You look plenty cute but I don't think that is exactly the outfit you should be wearing for our first dinner date."

"I had no intention of—" Before she finished her sentence she was trapped, powerless to run, as his lips closed over her own parted ones, shutting off any verbal retort. Fire sparked along the nerves in her body as her passion rose to meet his. Her guard crumbled as her need for him grew.

Turk pulled away slightly to look into her face, muttering huskily, "You're so lovely and desirable. It's hell being away from you." Once again he pulled her close, his lips brushing a vulnerable spot below her ear, leaving her breathless. "I'll never get enough of you!"

"Please, Turk!" she pleaded, finding the strength to move away from him a short distance. "You make me lose all control when you do this to me." After the admission she wished she could recall it as his smile widened when he reached for her again.

"That's what I want to hear. Darling, don't fight it— or us. We both know it's there. You've just admitted I have an effect on you. God knows, you have one on me." His eyes grew pale, almost pure gray, as he pressed her to his hard body and his lips again wove a sensuous magic over her.

"I desire you above all the women I've ever known," he murmured into her hair while his hand fastened itself into the luxurious mass of raven silk, pulling her head back, making it impossible not to look up at him. The handsome face not two inches from her own would have been her undoing at that moment if he had not released her.

"You're a disconcerting minx! Making me forget everything. I left something in the hallway for you and they'll wilt if I don't do something about them in a hurry." He went to the door and turned back with a devilish gleam in his eyes. "Now's your chance to run, honey. I'll wait for you to change into something more feminine. You won't be able to get out of this date so don't plan on it." With a laugh he disappeared behind the partially opened door.

Myrhia bolted, taking advantage of the moment to slip into her bedroom. Trembling all over, she leaned back against the closed door until she had strength to move again. What had happened to her and to her resolutions not to go out with him? Instead of making a definite stand, she had capitulated, even enjoying every moment. Involuntarily she ran her finger over her lips, feeling the lingering sensation his lips left on hers. Hadn't she known all along she would be going?

Drawing a deep breath, she slowly moved toward her closet. She wouldn't dare stay holed up in the bedroom, refusing to come out. It would be silly, and besides, there was no lock on the door. Not that it would matter—she had the feeling no lock would keep Turk out if he wanted in.

Quiet settled over the living area of her apartment as her ears strained to hear his movements. Once she thought she heard a cabinet door open and close and water running from the kitchen tap. With trembling fingers she slipped the new magenta chiffon off a padded hanger and held it briefly to her face as if its silken texture might somehow soothe her agitation with herself. It was probably imagination but the cool material did bring some measure of comfort.

Laying the dress across the bed, she moved to the dresser to give her face a quick touch of makeup, accenting her eyes with green shadow to make them appear darker. Her black hair, when brushed, shone like a raven's wing, her father's usual comment when as a child she complained about not being blond like her mother. Tonight the hair would have to hang loose, since there was no way her trembling fingers could create a stylish upsweep. Oh, well, so much for hasty resolutions to be prim and demure in Turk's presence. She had never been demure and admittedly now she was a woman in love, filled with desire and passion who would need all the strength she could command to hold out against this man.

As the soft texture of the dress slid over her head to ripple down her body in shimmering folds, she faced herself honestly. The real reason she had bought the dress was with Turk in mind, in spite of the fact she had tried to convince herself she would not keep the date. Perhaps the magenta chiffon had pumped needed confidence into her, she thought as she surveyed herself once more in the mirror. Fortified with this feeling, she admitted she liked the effect of the gently provocative points in the skirt that called attention to her slim, well-shaped legs. Her dark hair framed her heart-shaped face and the color of the dress heightened her light olive skin. Suddenly she felt reckless, as if starting on a new adventure. Pausing just long enough to dab perfume on her wrists, the hollow of her throat, and below the décolletage neckline, she breathed deeply its ambrosial fragrance before rejoining Turk.

He looked up as she stepped from her bedroom, a smile lighting his eyes as a low masculine whistle of appreciation diffused over the room.

As she moved nearer to Turk, Myrhia became aware of a soft radiance coming from the marble-topped coffee table. Her attention riveted on a large bowl of pink anthuriums artfully arranged in one of her cut-glass vases. Their shiny pink petals were turned like faces toward her, their long yellow stamins protruding pertly from the center of the flower.

Myrhia caught her breath at their beauty as she turned to the man responsible. "They're lovely, Turk."

"You're lovely." A huskiness developed in his throat as he came to meet her, mirrored admiration in his eyes. Taking both hands in his, he turned her around slowly, looking her over. "Each time I see you I wonder at the perfection." The kiss that followed was gentle, a caress that was almost reverent in its feeling.

Shaken, yet touched, she pulled away from him and directed their attention to the flowers. "I've never seen a pink anthurium before. They're different and so pretty." She was surprised that he remembered her at all. She stepped closer to the flowers to touch a shiny plasticlike petal. "These particular flowers have always looked unreal. Did you bring them back from Maui?"

"Yes, they're called Maui pink. A friend, Dr. Izumi, grows these in his hothouse. I told him a beautiful girl waited in Dallas for me—one who was as exquisite as these flowers."

"You're usually not given to flattery, Turk. I'd better take care." She hoped her look was guarded as she intended it to be. "You look quite handsome yourself this evening," she said. "I like your new suit."

"Thanks, but does it scream its newness that way?" He stepped toward her, moving with his usual animal grace. She could feel her body tense as she waited for his touch, knowing all the time her restraint would crumble. Through half-closed lids she could see a smile forming in the corner of his mouth as her lips parted ever so slightly for the expected kiss.

Instead Turk pulled her to him in a warm hug. "You keep looking that way, darling, and you'll end up with more than you're expecting. You're seductive enough as it is." He pulled back to look into her face. "Not now, sweetheart. We'll have to save that for later." The kiss touched her forehead instead. Chaste as it was, she still trembled, as if an electric wire telegraphed itself to her brain. She fought off her overpowering emotion; she was becoming too easily manipulated by him.

"Now, darling what say, we go? I've made reservations for eight thirty at Anatole's. Does that suit you?"

Concealing her chagrin with herself, she answered, "Fine. It's one of my favorite places." She stepped ahead of him, walking erectly, her shoulders straight and her head held high to conceal the tremulous excitement she was still feeling in his presence.

Throughout the drive to the restaurant in the Reunion Tower she had time to sort her thoughts and examine her reaction to him during the last few minutes spent in her apartment. This emotional involvement with him was foreign to her nature. At least she had never experienced anything quite like it before.

As the Mercedes hummed through the traffic, she observed Turk. He was acting extremely casual since their heavy moments together. Was it easy for him to turn off his feelings? She was finding it increasingly hard herself. Perhaps Turk had decided on a cool truce between skirmishes, a temporary lull. Either way it gave her time to regain some of her composure. By the time they had entered the elevator that carried them upward to Anatole's on the twenty-eighth floor of the Reunion Tower, her spirits had been lifted too.

There was always something breathtaking about the view of the sprawling metropolis of Dallas by night and tonight was no exception. She felt her imagination spurring her thoughts into a reflective pattern. As an architect she admired the work of the designer of this spectacular high-rise tower. How would it feel to create a monument of acclaim such as this?

As soon as they were seated, the waiter appeared. "Good evening, Mr. Vaughan. Would you like something from the bar?"

Turk looked up at Myrhia. "White wine, as usual?"

"Fine, Turk," she said, pleased that he was aware of her choice.

"Then it's white wine for the lady and a dry martini for me, Paul," he said, dismissing the waiter with a smile.

As far as her eyes could see, lights glimmered from all directions, the panorama changing slowly as the restaurant made one revolution every hour.

"What are your thoughts, Myrhia? Your eyes are shining mysteriously."

Turning back to him slowly, she looked into his face to find a half-smile on his lips.

"I was waiting for the turn of the restaurant so I could have a view of Turtle Creek." She smiled back at him.

"I think I'm beginning to understand what it means to be an architect, darling." He reached for her hand as she toyed with a spoon. "I assure you the Tarrington Building will command attention, Myrhia, standing tall and spectacular among the others in that area. The completed structure will require another celebration, don't you think? A private one?"

She nodded, unable to speak for the moment. He was actually sensing her own feeling about the building, and his sincerity was touching.

"I repeat my question. Shall we have a private celebration?" He squeezed her hand intimately, causing a flush of warmth to cover her face. "What deep thoughts lurk behind those electric green eyes of yours? Is it possible I might share those secrets?"

She smiled in return feeling a growing oneness with him as if somehow they were one entity at last. "You already share those thoughts. I was thinking how thrilling it will be to see it completed and I was wondering how the architect for the Tower felt when he first sat here having a sip of wine. He had offered the human spirit the chance to rise beyond the flight of birds." She laughed, suddenly self-conscious, afraid he might think her too dramatic or maudlin.

Instead his expression softened as he lifted her hand to his lips. "I'm beginning to understand your need to create. You are real and very... precious, Myrhia."

She looked away, too overcome with emotion to reply for a moment. "I love the city by night," she said lamely to fill in the silence between them.

"So do I. There's something seductive about it—almost like a woman." The pressure on her hand tightened, forcing her to look at him. She was surprised to see the warm look on his face with just a hint of wistfulness. Under his cool outward appearance she often found an occasional gentleness that could be more unnerving than his stronger traits. He was not so worldly and blasé that he could not be hurt. Perhaps some other woman had done that already and made him cautious in showing permanent interest in anyone.

In the silence that followed, while they sipped their drinks, she began to feel a closeness to this strong man sitting across from her wrapped in his own thoughts.

It was Turk who broke the silence between them. "I was thinking how very different our backgrounds are, Myrhia. Do you know my father could barely read beyond the fifth-grade level? But he made it in the oil fields in Texas. He earned and saved enough money to take care of the two of us. His hard work and brawn kept a roof over our heads as we moved from one job to another. I guess I was sixteen before I had a chance to stay in school a full year before moving again and then I did get to finish high school in Midland."

"Did you play football all through high school?"

"Yes. It was the one way I could get acquainted with

the other guys." He looked up as the waiter approached with their menus.

"Be back in a few minutes, Mr. Vaughan, to take your order." He handed them each a menu and walked away.

Turk nodded, glancing over the menu. "I no longer had a father by the time I was ready for college. He fell from an oil rig and died almost instantly. I've regretted always that I was never able to make life easier for him."

"You haven't mentioned your mother, Turk. Is she—"

A look of pain knifed through his eyes. "No more about me," he said abruptly. "It's your turn." With a slightly bantering tone she suspected was forced, he said, "I see before me a sophisticated girl who has definite ideas in her lovely head. One with brains and talent and a strong will—a frightening combination, I'll admit." He took hold of her hand again. "Shall we order now?"

Myrhia had been unaware the waiter was hovering behind them. She picked up the outsized menu and without hesitation decided on crab Louis, a Caesar's salad, and steamed broccoli. Turk ordered steak and salad for himself. Turning to their waiter, he said, "Perhaps a flagon of wine to go with the crab and steak. Make it French." The waiter nodded, retreating quickly.

Turk reached for her hand again. "Well, continue. I want to know all there is to know about you. It's important that I know everything. I will be away from you part of the time our building is in progress—the Maui condos are bogged down by labor disputes and lack of supplies. I've got to get back again right away."

The latter remark dimmed her growing elation that

he was interested in knowing about her. "There's not much to tell about me really." Her eyes became entangled in his gaze as she looked into his face. She felt she was being absorbed into their ever-changing color. They moved like seawater—now gray, now blue, and tonight, contrasted against his new Hawaiian tan, they appeared almost luminous.

"I guess I was a lonely little girl. My father was away often and I related to him more than Alicia. She can be flighty to the point of neglect of the ones who love her. She's not insensitive, just unaware of another's needs. She wanted a daughter to enjoy things in the society world with her. Perhaps if I'd been a son, she could have accepted me as an architect."

While speaking frankly this way to Turk, she realized there was a hurt in acknowledging her relationship with Alicia. She gave a wry laugh. "Okay, your turn again." She spoke flippantly, trying to offset a growing embarrassment at talking about herself—something she seldom did.

"I'm not interesting enough to be in your league, darling. I didn't have the social advantages you had. Summertime I worked in the oil fields from sixteen on. Dad lied about my age at first, since I was a big kid. I guess having me working around him was one way he could keep me out of trouble. Kept an eye on me, so to speak. I loved him. He never remarried after—" Once again a blank fell into their conversation. Myrhia could see it related to his mother and it pained him to remember.

Turk leaned back in his chair, releasing her hand as he did so, "You know the whole sordid rest—football scholarship, degree from Texas University, and proball for fourteen years after a year's stint in Vietnam."

Myrhia sipped her wine thoughtfully, enjoying putting the pieces of his background together as the puzzle seemed to be falling in place. "What was your college major?"

"Don't laugh! I majored in geology." He smiled. "At the time it was a mistake to go into anything like that, I soon found out. The oil market was down and you know the trend. With the oil business at a standstill, I fell back on my first love, football. I was lucky to make the Dallas Cowboys. I guess I was at my best out there on that football field." He looked out the window for a long time as if reliving the experience. "After my injury I got into developing, but you know, Myrhia, now with the new burst of oil exploration in Texas and Oklahoma I just might dust off the old brain and dabble a little in oil myself."

For some reason she gave in to an impulse to touch his hand as it slipped up and down his wineglass stem. At her touch his eyes warmed toward her. "I have a feeling, Turk, that you could be successful at anything." The compliment sprang spontaneously from her lips. It occurred to Myrhia this was the first normal conversation they had enjoyed without sparring. "What was your football injury? Do you mind telling me?"

He turned her hand upward and thoughtfully stroked the soft flesh of her palm with his thumb, sending pleasurable impulses to her heart. After a moment he lifted his wineglass to her in a toast.

"Here's to one lady I find it easy to talk with and who just might be sincere." His smile became disarming. "As for my knee, I shattered the right kneecap, have a metal piece, causing a slight stiffness—nothing more. Not serious!"

She could see the conversation about his injury was over for now, and she had been permitted to see a bit of the inside of the man. Somehow she felt closer and the knowledge sent a wild exaltation to her brain that this was a real beginning for them.

After their dinner arrived, they ate in what was possibly their first compatible silence since meeting several months ago. Myrhia was nearing the last bite of her crab Louis when their waiter approached the table with a telephone in his hand. Plugging it into a nearby jack, he handed the telephone to Turk.

"You have a call, Mr. Vaughan. The young woman said it was urgent." The waiter cast as apologetic glance at Myrhia before walking away.

Turk wore an expression of surprise as he picked up the receiver. "Hello. Yes? Letty? My God! When? I'll be right there." He replaced the receiver in haste, laid down his napkin, and at the same time rose from the table.

"I'm sorry, Myrhia. Dammit, I'm sorry, but I've got to take you home. Something has come up, something I have to do—at once!"

In spite of his stricken look she felt a stab of disappointment that was followed by yet another emotion that she hated to admit. Jealousy! Letty certainly wielded power over her boss as his secretary. What kind of relationship did they really have? It was not an impersonal one for certain. She could imagine the pretty redhead filled several categories quite well.

He reached for her hand to hold it for a moment before pulling back her chair, but she jerked away in exasperation. This was too much to have their one peaceful dinner spoiled by that woman.

While her angry thoughts whirled about, she rose stiffly from her chair. "You needn't concern yourself with me. I can get myself home in a cab." If she expected him to protest, she was surprised he answered with a note of relief in his voice.

"Good, if you don't mind too much. I hate to do that to you, Myrhia, but it's an emergency and I don't have much time." He looked contrite all of a sudden. "I do want you to understand."

Turk was not aware she was seething under her pretended composure. At the snap of her pretty fingers Letty could call him anytime from a romantic engagement. She kept tabs on his whereabouts. Very efficient!

"I assure you, Turk, it's immaterial how I go home. I've lots to do tomorrow and a good night's rest will prepare me for the committee meeting or as you call it—preconstruction conference. No doubt it will take a good deal of fortitude on my part to appear at all." The dig did not go unnoticed.

A frown creased his forehead. "It might. I know you don't like criticism of your plans. I've found you don't take it kindly, but we'd better go into that later tonight— at your apartment. I won't be too late." He was waiting, impatient for her answer and anxious to be gone.

"Not tonight, Turk. I'm bushed. Sorry our evening was spoiled. I felt I was beginning to really understand the great Turk—football legend—but now I doubt if I ever will. I suppose it's awfully hard for you macho types to keep all the women in your stable happy at the same time," she added flippantly as they waited for the elevator.

It was a nasty crack and she should have been prepared for his reaction. His strong fingers dug into her bare arm as he shoved her ahead of him into the elevator. "Can't resist a fight, can you, tiger?" Turk's black-fringed lids narrowed over the cold steel of his eyes as he backed her against the elevator wall, his lips crushing hers cruelly, his hands moving fiercely over her body. Waves of desire flamed over her as his hands came to rest on the soft rise of breast, now exposed as her neckline had plunged lower from his rough handling. His strong thumbs stroked the taut breasts, rousing them to firmness beneath the chiffon of her dress.

"I don't know which way I like you better. Sweet, docile, and yielding or angry and spiteful." He let her go slowly as the elevator neared the ground floor. "I find both sides of your personality enchanting." His devilish smile didn't improve her disposition.

As the elevator door opened, Turk took her arm and led her rapidly to the outside curb, where he hailed a cruising taxicab. He directed the driver to her apartment address and as she stepped into the cab, he pulled her back.

"No, you don't! It's bad enough to let you go this way, but I want something more." His warm mouth closed over hers, claiming what he had no right to.

"Dammit, Myrhia, I can't shake you loose from me." He released her abruptly, leaving her drained of all emotion.

She stumbled as she stepped unaided into the backseat of the taxicab. From his rearview mirror the cab driver smiled, looking away quickly pretending he had not noticed the little scene.

"Nice night," he said matter-of-factly. He'd probably seen dozens of lovers' quarrels—not that she and Turk were that or ever would be.

Chapter Seven

The implications of the evening became more evident to Myrhia throughout her sleepless night. Turk had purposely set about to soften her resolve in order to get his way at the preconstruction meeting. She would have to learn to deal with these strange feelings she had in his presence or she would not be able to cope with her project. It occurred to her it probably was more than the minor change already made to the fascia that he wanted to bring up at the conference. Meeting a man of steel like Turk at the beginning of her budding opportunity to design skyscrapers was a proving ground for her future. If she could come out halfway victorious on the Tarrington Building, then nothing else she ever attempted would be half as hard.

She should be grateful to Letty for saving her from disaster. If the secretary hadn't called when she did, the evening might have been different—soft lights, wine, and who knows what later. In spite of the logic of her thoughts she felt cheated. By morning, after a few hours sleep, she was better fortified to face the meeting. If a suggested change to the outer facade of the building was mentioned, she would not give in. Carl would stand with her on the original plan. She was certain of that.

Myrhia dressed carefully, determined to be conservative yet womanly in her appearance. Choosing a tailored blouse of bright kelly green to wear with her tweed pantsuit, she stepped in front of her full-length mirror to see if she looked businesslike and capable. Satisfied with the result of neatly combed dark hair swept into a chignon, she felt her confidence returning. Today would be crucial, a test of her ability to talk with the big developers. Several of the executives in Carl's company were on the committee but she had no idea how many Vaughan Associates would be sending.

Two o'clock came too quickly. Myrhia had not eaten lunch, telling herself she was not hungry and choosing to remain office bound to work out another angle on the auditorium plan. Trish, concerned for her employer, brought her a doughnut and coffee and insisted that Myrhia eat it.

While she was waiting for Carl to come by the office for her, the telephone rang. It was Turk. "Myrhia, I'll be by shortly. I want to take you to the meeting. I've got to talk to you."

"Sorry, Turk, I'm ready to leave with Carl Muldrow. He'll be here any minute." She wanted to ask about Letty but knew the bitterness she felt would color her attitude at the meeting.

She was aware of his hesitancy. "Sorry about last night, but it was unavoidable. I'll explain later."

"It isn't necessary. Besides, the taxi driver was quite attractive." As soon as she put the receiver down, she knew she had made him angry. It was foolish of her to aggravate him just before she knew he was going to demand a change of material for the outer wall of the building. Now she had added more fuel to his fire by antagonizing him further.

As Carl walked through the door of her office, she

felt a wave of gratitude for his constancy. He had never resented her ability in her profession but apparently enjoyed vicariously something he would like to be doing himself. She felt at ease as they walked off the elevator on the fifteenth floor of the Muldrow Building and into the carpeted director's room where four pairs of male eyes focused on her approach. They were not unfriendly eyes. Quickly scanning the group, she was relieved that Turk had not arrived yet. His gaze would not have been friendly, she was certain.

Carl introduced her to the four members of the committee from his own company. Two of the men were in their late forties and the other two were white-haired, distinguished-looking men with open, guileless expressions.

One of the older men, Robert Mitchell, she learned was executive vice-president of Muldrow Associates. As Myrhia moved to take the chair next to him, he turned to her. "Miss Lassiter, your father was my good friend. I know he would have been proud of you. It's quite evident you have his talent. I always envied his ability to envision something and place it on paper, hoping it would become a reality."

She turned to Mr. Mitchell, pleased by his compliment. "Thank you. I can't begin to tell you how thrilled I am that your committee selected my proposal. It is an honor."

The ice was broken and conversation began to flow about the long table. It was a comfortable room for one of its kind. The rich mahogany paneling matched the long conference table that could seat as many as twenty or more. Rich russet carpet was offset by the deep brown leather upholstery on the chairs. Dark tan draperies with a bold Indian print were pulled back from the wide windows to admit sunlight, giving the room a cheerful glow.

If she could count on Turk's actions being just slightly normal, she would be able to relax, but she couldn't tell how he would react in any situation. It would be impossible to outguess him. Carl glanced at his wristwatch. "It's two o'clock and time for the big man to stage his grand entrance," he said, a wry twist to his smile.

As if on signal Turk arrived, followed by three men. "What did I tell you?" Carl whispered.

For some reason Carl's remark triggered a negative reaction as Turk, more self assured than any man should be, advanced across the room toward those seated at the table. He wore a look of confidence like an armor about him and his disarming smile was well received by the men at the table.

Turk avoided Myrhia's eyes when his gaze swept over her as if she no longer existed, when only sixteen hours ago his warm lips had been pressed to her own, a feeling she was recalling too easily now as he came closer walking with his catlike tread over the deep-pile carpet.

"Gentlemen," he began, taking a seat at the head of the table as chairman of the committee. After a cursory nod to the other men, he turned steel-gray eyes toward her while her pulse raced out of control.

"I know you've had time to study Ms. Lassiter's plans for the Tarrington Building. I'm glad we're underway and the first floor is already shaping up. Sorry I missed the ground-breaking but as you know, I've been out of town and will be frequently for the next few months. I trust we can have the topping-off party by February or before March at least."

Turk turned to Carl. "As usual your association will see to the leasing, Carl." Carl nodded assent. "Good, then it's up to us to discuss with our architect what proposed changes we'd like to make in her overall plans before the final erection."

She might have been a total stranger from his impersonal remarks toward her. Myrhia's anger was mounting rapidly under his cool appraisal of her in front of these men. He had kissed her, held her close, and now.... This cold treatment would not be forgiven. She was the one who should be angry over last night's abrupt termination of the evening. Not Turk.

He looked around the group, going from man to man. No suggested changes were forthcoming as they talked it over among themselves.

"Well, I take it we have decided on building the structure as the original plans specify." His eyes sought Myrhia's for a moment. Had he reconsidered changing the facade? Then her hopes were dashed as he said, "I have one change I would like to request of the committee. I've talked this over with our young architect here. I don't go along with the precast concrete and the vision panels for the outside. Ms. Lassiter and I have come to an agreement that we will have the all glass curtain wall."

Male eyes turned her way awaiting confirmation. A tremor passed over her in her struggles to remain calm. Turk was railroading this over her and he knew it. She glanced at Carl, finding the courage to speak her mind.

"You had my answer to that last week, Mr. Vaughan." She spoke tersely, not taking her eyes from his face. "I told you at the time I had no intention of making my building like all the others that have been erected in Dallas lately. I'm not opposed to the curtain wall, but I don't believe the style of my design would call for that kind of facade." She stopped to smile around the table at the other members of the committee. It was deliberately disarming on her part and only Turk reacted negatively. "Gentlemen, I would prefer not to change the exterior of my building at all. I've made one concession to Mr. Vaughan already—a minor one, I know—as I agreed to design another fascia under the first-floor cornice."

There was a buzz of conversation following her announcement as all eyes focused back and forth between her and Turk. Robert Mitchell spoke out in the group, commanding all to silence as he did so.

"I think our architect knows what she wants. I for one trust her judgment. I admired her father and I'm sure the daughter has the same eye for beauty. I'm certain we won't be sorry."

"Thank you, Mr. Mitchell," Myrhia said gratefully.

The Muldrow group nodded approval but Turk's group held back in deference to his opinion. It was evident to Myrhia they might have been briefed beforehand. Turk's steely agates sought her eyes, entrapping them, holding her prisoner.

"I refuse to be persuaded by the inexperience of our young architect against my better judgment. I know she's talented but she lacks years of knowing what's important in a finished structure." A hint of a smile formed on his sensuous lips as Myrhia fought for control.

Rumblings of disagreement ricocheted around the room. Furious with Turk, who gave the impression he was doing this to torment her, she choked back the words in her own behalf until she was certain she would explode at any minute.

"Turk, the young woman is right. There's a lot of that glass stuff all over Dallas. So much reflection could become monotonous on the skyline." She sent a look of gratitude to Robert Mitchell again.

"I don't see it that way!" Turk snapped.

"I propose we bring it to a vote." Mr. Mitchell spoke with an authoritative manner. "Turk, I move to accept the design as Miss Lassiter submitted it."

"I'll call for a vote, gentlemen, if I may be allowed to step down as chairman of the committee and cast my vote." Turk's chin was set in a stubborn line.

It was agreeable to all and the move was restated and seconded and the vote taken by a show of hands. With Turk's three men going along with him, it was four on four without Carl's decisive vote.

As Carl raised his hand, his eyes locked with Turk's. The two men remained that way until one of Muldrow's men cleared his throat, breaking the spell. Without doubt there wouldn't be a man in the room that didn't know now there was more to this disagreement than what was on the surface. Carl's voice had clinched the project.

With a shrug of his massive shoulders Turk rose, apparently unconcerned he had been voted down. "That's all, gentlemen, and Ms. Lassiter."

He strode past Myrhia's chair as she rose to leave and, leaning close, whispered, "Round one!" Grinning wickedly, he walked away as if they were total strangers. She would like to get her hands on that smug face for a moment; she'd scratch that smirk off.

"I'd like to strangle him," she muttered.

"Don't let him get under your skin, Myrhia." Carl's face was brick-red. "For some reason I've a hunch he only raised that problem to upset you. The other three— the Vaughan committee members—liked the precast concrete. Obviously they had to agree with Turk—no one would dare oppose the great man," Carl said sarcastically, taking Myrhia's hand as they walked from the director's room.

It was a bitter victory, Myrhia was thinking as she said good-bye to Carl at the curb and rode the elevator to her office floor. Had he brought up the controversy to aggravate her? Either way Turk had succeeded in spoiling the afternoon. Before she stepped into her office, she announced to Trish she would be leaving early and she could do likewise.

"The meeting went all right. The building plan will not be altered from the original—not even the facade," she said offhandedly in answer to the unspoken question in Trish's eyes.

"I'm glad for that."

Myrhia walked to her large window that framed the busy scene below. This was another truce with Turk. Only he knew when he would begin to bombard her again with proposed changes. Was he like this with all architects and contractors? He must have built up a reputation for being a hard man to deal with—yet why did she feel he didn't give a damn really about the exterior of the Tarrington Building? He had liked the plans the way they were when he thought the design was submitted by M. Lassiter, one male.

It was good to find out these things about him before it was too late and she could not turn away. She sighed and moved away from the window, preparatory to leaving the office.

"She's going home, Mr. Vaughan. I don't think she's seeing anyone at all this afternoon." Trish's voice caught her attention from outside in the hallway. There were a few more words that were unintelligible before Trish said, "At least let me announce you."

"That won't be necessary. I see you had started home yourself. I don't want to detain you. I'll announce myself."

Her office door opened abruptly as Turk strode in

shutting the door behind him. He stood alerted as if listening for Trish to leave. After a few seconds of silence they heard her steps lead toward the elevator.

"I want some straight answers from you, *Ms*. Lassiter," he said almost menacingly. Myrhia had never noticed before how Turk could fill a room with his presence. He was nearly overpowering in her small cluttered office.

"And why do I owe you straight answers?" She spoke coolly in spite of the sensation his presence caused.

"I think you know, Myrhia. How involved are you with a married man?"

"Are you referring to Carl? You would call him my boyfriend?" She tried to laugh. "Well perhaps he is. I don't know what difference it would make to you. Carl is my best friend—something I doubt you'd ever be to anyone unless they could serve a purpose."

She could feel the anger in him as he moved closer. "I had something I wanted to discuss with you on the way to the meeting but you seem to be inconstant where your men friends are concerned. I thought you were interested—just a bit—in me but I see you play the field." He was only three feet away now and the steel-gray eyes burned into her own.

Not daring to look at them longer, Myrhia turned away. "I think you have the roles reversed, don't you? Aren't you the one that walked out on our date last night? It isn't often I have to taxi home from what I was expecting to be a romantic evening. If you had this late date with Letty planned all the time, we could have eaten a quick supper at some fast food place."

"Dammit, Myrhia, I told you that was unavoidable. It was and if you'll stop getting so all-fired huffy, I'll try to explain. You're acting like a jealous schoolgirl."

"And I suppose you weren't jealous of Carl?" As much as she wanted to fly at him and tear into his cold, highhanded manner, her intuition told her not to turn around. She could not only feel the heat of his anger directed at her back but there was something more. It was his magnetism she was fighting. It would be too easy to back into those strong arms and feel them close about her, blotting out all discord between them. True, he might want to crush her but at least there would be no more angry words between them. She was fighting for strength now to build a barrier between them.

"When has it been good manners to let your date find a way home by herself while you admit to going to another girl's arms—who knows, perhaps her bed?" she said, trying to sound angrier than she really felt.

A strong hand closed on her shoulder as Turk turned her slowly. "Don't say something you'll regret when you learn the truth. I'm here to explain about Letty, thinking you deserved an explanation for my behavior last night, but I see you're not ready to hear me." He released her momentarily. "You're the most exasperating girl I've ever met."

His voice broke abruptly as he reached for her once more, pulling her soft body close to his own hard one. "I'm sorry that our evening was ruined, so sorry. I was more disappointed than you last night and when I saw you and Carl so chummy today, I wanted to make you hurt too. Circumstances we can't seem to control are interfering with us and I'm afraid I'll lose you."

"You can't lose something you've never had in the first place," she said primly, knowing all the time what she said was untrue.

"I'll have to think about that one, but now you'll have to sit down and let me explain about Letty."

She had to make one last try for independence before the incredible yielding sensation took possession of her body as it was slowly moving from her legs upward. "I really don't want to hear it and I do have to be leaving. I have a—a date." She had hesitated too long in saying it.

A look of cunning crossed his face at that remark, indicating he could see through her lie. "This early in the afternoon? Oh, my he is an anxious one, isn't he?" Sarcasm dripped from his words.

"Oh, well, it's no business of yours anyway, is it?" She managed to pull away and reach for her handbag. She took two steps toward the doorway, calling back over her shoulder, "When you've finished pacing around my office, will you kindly lock the door behind you?" She barely reached the doorknob when Turk's arms enfolded her, turned her around, as his lips came down on hers.

"Cut this out! We've got to stop badgering each other," he groaned between kisses. "I'm having enough trouble fighting off a desire to make love to you at this very minute. When you're soft, sweet, and pliable it's hell staying away from you, but when you act as if you hate me, I'm not going to be able to stand it much longer." He was muttering into her hair, his warm breath sending signals of surrender to her brain. The long fingers of his hands were molding her body to him, playing up and down her back like a musician fingering the piano chords.

This time when his lips found hers and began their gentle probing, they aroused a spontaneous response. Against her will her hands slid upward over his strong shoulders to the back of his neck, where they locked into his thick hair.

Slowly he pulled away, still looking at her, his eyes still glazed with passion. "Isn't this proof enough of what we have between us? What more do you want, darling?" he whispered softly, pulling her close to his massive chest once more. She could feel his muscles tense as he too fought for control of his emotions.

"It's not enough for me, Turk. I want understanding and I don't get that from you, do I?" She had to fall back on the disagreement only an hour ago with the Tarrington commission to give her fuel to resist him when he was like this.

"You're wrong, you know. I'll admit it has been difficult from the first to accept you as a career woman. I recognize talent like yours is rare and precious, but it also frightens the devil out of me. I have to fight back some way, it seems. I don't want to lose you because of it. I saw what happened to my father when—" He cut the sentence abruptly but not before she saw the pain that crossed his face.

Turk stepped to the window where he stood a moment, staring unseeingly before him. With a sigh and shrug of his wide shoulders he turned back to her. "Never mind about that. My mother is a different story. I came to explain about Letty Chappel. Ted, her husband, and I served in Vietnam together—same outfit for a year. We fought side by side throughout the jungles. We were both wounded—a land-mine explosion—but Ted got the brunt of it. Mine was a shrapnel bit to my rib cage, nothing serious. Ted was disabled by the time the medics picked him up. After six months in an army hospital he was dismissed—blind and forever condemned to a wheelchair."

It was evident to Myrhia the memory, though long ago, was still painful, but what was so strange at that moment was the related pain she was feeling for him and his friend. She was beginning to understand and empathize with him in a way she had never thought possible before. At that moment for all his size he looked vulnerable.

"I think I know the rest, Turk. If it hurts you to talk about it, I understand. Letty needs you from time to time." She walked a little way toward him resisting an urge to pull his head down and kiss him but something in his manner held her off.

"No, let me finish, Myrhia. I need to make you understand now. You're right. Letty needs me from time to time when she has trouble controlling him. I seem to be the only one who can reach out to him and make him understand. You see, she wants to keep him at home so he can enjoy his boys—they're teen-agers now—but once in a while he goes off mentally and is too upset to take his medication. Letty has a male nurse for Ted throughout the day. He's usually docile and gentle. She needs the job I offered just to get away from her drab life and her problems." He stopped talking and looked long into her eyes. "This has been hard to understand, hasn't it?"

She watched him move restlessly around the office, stopping to pick up a pencil, examine the latest drawing on her board with unseeing eyes, finger a paperclip. She didn't want to interrupt now that he was able to talk to her about these things, so she remained quiet.

"You'll like Letty. She's cheerful and courageous. They're two of my oldest friends. I met Ted at Texas U. and I was best man at their wedding so long ago. They married young. The worst part of it all is that Ted didn't need to volunteer for Vietnam—he already had two kids—but he felt it was his duty."

Turk turned away from her, hiding the deep pain, and for a moment she knew she had lost him to a time when she was not a part of his life.

"Well, enough of that." His head went up and he

straightened his shoulders. "Letty said to tell you she was sorry to spoil our dinner and would like to make it up to you and me by inviting us over one night when Ted is at his best. Would you go?" She couldn't be sure but thought Turk seemed afraid she would refuse the invitation.

"That would be nice. Were you able to help her with Ted last night?" She was relieved she could answer affirmatively to Letty's invitation to dinner.

"After a while, but he'd fallen out of his chair and we had a hard time getting him quiet. He was irrational again and the boys were really frightened when I got there. They're thirteen and fourteen, good boys, but Ted's too big to handle and when he's violent, it's impossible to do anything with him for a while."

Myrhia remained thoughtful for a few minutes before speaking. "That's so sad. Turk, I'd like to be Letty's friend." She reached for his hand, intending to pull him over and kiss his cheek, but found instead she was smothered in his arms while he buried his face in her hair.

"My beautiful darling. Letty could use a friend like you." He held her away from him while the magnetic eyes searched her face. "I have a feeling that you and I'll come to terms after all. You don't know how much I need you."

There was no time to mull over what he meant by "coming to terms" with each other with his lips seeking and probing hers, sending waves of delight along her nerve ends. Her office began to spin around, seemingly bathed in gold as the slanting rays of sunset crept around the corners of Lemon Park and wound a leafy pathway through the native live oaks and creek elms to find them clasped together.

Chapter Eight

It was some time before they broke apart. As Myrhia pulled away from the comfort of Turk's arms, she was disturbed by the strong emotions she had experienced. Is this what love was all about—the complete subjugation of her mind and heart as it joined another's? If so, then she had never been in love before. She glanced up into Turk's face, wondering if it was possible to see in his expression some of what she was feeling at the moment.

From a soft gleam in his eyes she believed he was and it warmed her, making her feel alive and loved. He couldn't pretend this way; no one could be that clever an actor, heightened as their emotions had run these past few minutes.

In spite of the tremulous throbbing in her veins, a shiver of doubt raised its head as she tried vainly to recall his declaration of love. It was just a small thing, but one she had imbedded in her heart years ago—love was the key to sexual attraction. Turk had mentioned over and over his need, his desire, his wanting her, and she had responded with the same primal feelings. With his lips trailing a fiery path down her cheek, neck, and soft rise of her breast, where her blouse seemed to part at will, she had been powerless to resist.

She forced her mind to think of something sobering at the moment, something that would give her impetus to leave him before she was completely swept up in this new excitement. Letty would serve as the impetus needed. Perhaps Letty's regard for Turk was not the same as his for her and she just might wish to become more than a friend. This thought gave her the strength to break away from him now.

"I must get home, Turk. I've work piled high enough to choke a mule." With a sigh she reached for her handbag and started toward the drawing board, beginning to roll up several large sheets of drawing paper. "I must finish the first sketches of the convention center tonight. The design proposals have to be in by the middle of September and I'm far behind in the overall plans—so far it's an idea only."

She turned to find him standing behind her, his eyes focused on one of her finished renderings she had taken pains to finish as a painting to be hung when she was a struggling novice and had the extra time to indulge her artistic temperament.

"You're a damned good artist, you know it?" He was studying her face with his sharp appraisal. Myrhia had become aware of a gentle softening toward her work lately. Was he sincere? Had that awareness been there all the time—perhaps hidden beneath a thick veneer of male ego? A feathery hope settled briefly in her heart that she and Turk would meet on conciliatory grounds from now on—at least where her profession was involved.

"Sometime I'd like to show you some of my other artwork. It's in my apartment workroom. I keep the paintings—those sketches made just for fun and for my own amusement—in a portfolio. If you're interested at all, I'll show them sometime." Suddenly she became shy, wondering why she had offered to show this art-work to him. She had never offered to let Carl or Alicia see them, for that matter. His eyes continued to trace the contours of her face, making her feel as if he had somehow caressed her cheeks.

A smile broke into his seriousness. "What's wrong with right now?" Grinning amiably, he reached for the roll of sketches she had just tucked under her arm. "I promise I'll not interfere with your work if you allow me to hang around the apartment for a while. I just might whip up a bite of supper for the two of us while you slave away."

Feeling it might be a mistake to take him up on the offer, she ended up saying yes anyway. There would be no way she could work with a clear mind as long as this disturbing presence was stalking her apartment. Didn't he know that?

"Oh, all right," she said, half irritated at herself for being spineless. Where he was concerned she was get-ting to be like a jellyfish. "But—I do need an hour to myself," she added by way of compensating for her weakness.

"I promise you'll have it. While you have that hour of uninterruption, I'll scour the neighborhood wine cel-lars and grocery stores to come up with a pièce de résistance. I'm not too bad in the kitchen, or in the living room, or"—devilish gleam glided across his blue-gray eyes—"am I too bad in the bedroom, I've been told."

Myrhia laughed in spite of herself. "Oh, and you're so modest too."

When they entered her apartment, Turk's presence seemed to chase the loneliness from the shadows. Lately she had become more aware of the emptiness. She was constantly experiencing new emotions when with him. Sometimes there was tenseness, often anger, as they groped for an understanding of each other; frequent tender moments when she knew there was nothing more beautiful in the world than wanting him to make love to her, hold her, whisper endearments; and then there were these times when the fun of just being with him doing the simplest, most mundane things was best of all.

The companionable mood stretched between them as she continued working in her small studio room off the kitchen. Contrary to her expectation, she became lost in her sketching, only half aware of Turk's coming and going in and out of the apartment. She listened with one ear tuned to the sounds of silver and china rattling in the kitchen, short steps back and forth from stove to sink to dining room and back.

It was a comfortable confusion of homey sounds and strangely she found her ideas jelled into a concrete plan for the convention center. The pencil flowed effortlessly over the large white drawing paper before her as she sketched the grounds around the main buildings, planning a rough layout for all the five hundred acres that would be Forest Grove.

Unknown to her, Turk had come up quietly. "When can we move into one of the bungalows, darling?" His arm closed around her waist, pulling her back against his hard body, just as she completed the last rough drawing of a small bridge that connected the center itself with the assembly quarters.

"I can see that's going to be a romantic spot. Intimately romantic!" Turk gave her waist a squeeze, making her feel warm all over. "Is this a new proposal?"

"Yes, it's the one Carl mentioned at my party. Remember? I don't feel I have much chance at it; the competition is keen." She leaned back against his broad shoulder feeling his strong muscles flex slightly.

"I remember, it's the one Carl was certain you would be able to get." His arms tightened as she sighed, leaning against him more heavily. All creative tension flowed from her body into a comfortable lethargy as she continued to rest in his arms. "Do you remember I assured you I felt you would win out on the assembly proposal, too?"

She had to smile at that. Was it possible Turk held some resentment over Carl's admiration for her work and he, himself, just might be capitulating a little and admitting to himself that M. Lassiter could compete in the field?

Ignoring her imaginings, she said, "I'm trying for a resort atmosphere, where the delegates can feel they've taken a vacation as well as attended a conference."

Turk studied the drawings without comment. After a few minutes he said, "I think I might be able to feel the mood of the place. It's good, darling."

Feeling an incredulous delight in his comment, small though it was, she sensed his sincerity and turned slowly in his arms to look up into his face. A teasing smile crossed his face, wiping away any trace of seriousness.

"I came to tell Mademoiselle that her dinner awaits." After making a low bow, he took her arm to escort her from her studio into a candlelit dining alcove. He stepped to the kitchen, returned with a clean towel draped over one arm, an ice bucket holding a bottle of red wine, and two of her best cut-glass goblets.

"Does Mademoiselle prefer wine with her dinner?" His exaggerated bow forced a ripple of laughter from her.

Falling into his playful mood, she nodded haughtily.

"If you please, Henri. My escort is detained but I'd like to get soused before he arrives. Makes me more irresistible," she teased, unprepared for the flame of desire that flashed briefly across his face nor the soft lips that traced a pattern of fire over her cheek.

"I think Mademoiselle will have to be content with me until her escort arrives. And, I assure you, your desirability will be deeply appreciated by the chef." With an outrageous wink Turk popped the cork on the wine and poured it into the two goblets, where it glimmered ruby-red in the candleglow.

Removing the towel, he sat across from her and lifted his wineglass toward her. "To my darling—for now, for tomorrow, and forever. May all her dreams come true."

The sincerity of the toast brought tears to Myrhia's eyes as she looked long into his, somehow feeling entrapped there. "I'll drink to that and wish the same for you, Turk."

"I'm beginning to believe my dreams have a damned good chance of just that." His eyelids narrowed dangerously over the agates beneath concealing the beginning of an awakened desire she caught glittering in their depth.

He rose slowly, setting his goblet aside, and moved again to the kitchen for their main course. Myrhia exclaimed as he set her plate before her. The chicken Kiev was arranged artistically on her Spode plates, acquired from Alicia's collection, with small new potatoes drenched in butter and parsley flakes lying side by side with broccoli spears crowned with a generous swoop of Hollandaise sauce. A rosy spiced apple added a touch of color to the plate. With his second return he set her olive wood salad bowl down on the small tea cart where he began tossing the oil and vinegar into the greens with expertise. She was again impressed by his grace of movement for a large man. The long fingers tapered at the end looked more like the hands of an artist or perhaps a musician as they deftly spaded the wooden forks through the mixed greens.

"This is delicious, Turk!" Myrhia said after several minutes of total enjoyment. "You're a man of many talents."

He smiled. "I can't take credit for the Kiev. I persuaded the chef at Élan's to part with two of his. The rest I threw together."

"I'm impressed. In all due respect to my own sex, I believe that when men like to cook they become gourmets, outshining most of us women."

"That's a straightforward remark, darling. I'll admit I like to putter about the kitchen but not on a house-husband scale. I'll admit that to you but there are not many of my close friends who know this."

Their dessert was a surprise too. Myrhia had heard the whir of the mixer only abstractly as she worked in her studio, and now she saw the results in the form of a mystery pie topped with whipping cream and a bright red cherry.

"I've had this several times at Anatole's but never known how to make it. Will you teach me? It's light and just enough sweet after a heavy meal."

"It's easy and I'll divulge my secret someday, but for now I've other ideas I want to share." As his warm look caught hers she felt her excitement rising too. The candle flame fluttered a moment as if to warn her before it was snuffed between his fingers but the afterglow lasted long enough for her to read a message in his eyes that was timeless as the seasons. He pulled her to her feet.

"Don't you think we've both worked enough for one day and are entitled to a little relaxation?" The implication of his remark sent a shiver of excitement through her as they moved to the living room.

"Would you go to a football game with me three weeks from Sunday? I have to be out of town off and on so I want to make sure you'd like to go. The Dallas Cowboys play the big one—the New York Giants." His voice rose slightly with excitement showing her how much his football team meant to him. Before she answered, he said, "Do you like football? I have never asked you, have I?"

He seemed so eager for her answer. "I used to like football, Turk. When I was in college I went to all the games I had time for, but I haven't kept up since. Yes, I'd like to go with you. Sounds like fun." It occurred to Myrhia in that moment that most everything she did with him was fun.

"Good! Then it's a date for the last Sunday in September."

It seemed she had made him happy with her answer as he grinned devilishly. "I'm warning you in advance. I want your company all day and evening and...." Turk gave her a quick hug, then gently pushed her to the couch where she lay in a half-reclining position. He proceeded to stretch his large frame next to hers. She marveled at how well their bodies fit together, even through several layers of clothing.

They remained wrapped in complete unity for sometime before his sensuous lips began exploring her own. His kisses, gentle at first, fired with intensity as her own lips responded wildly. Her tongue traced his well-defined lips, experiencing a small tickle as the tip came in contact with a beginning growth of new whiskers on his upper lip. His mouth pressed to hers and his hands, almost without her awareness, were moving skillfully— almost too skillfully, she remembered later—to unbutton and remove her blouse, but she was powerless to do anything about it as her own hands were doing similar things to his shirt front. As she fumbled with the last button, her fingertips explored his powerful chest, eliciting soft moans of pleasure from him.

They tasted and touched each other gently, caressing and enjoying the ecstasy of sharing until it seemed to Myrhia her heart would burst with the joy of holding him so close to her.

"Myrhia, darling, do you know how wonderful you are? I can feel it in your response. You need me as I do you. Let me love you."

She reached up with her fingertips and ran her fingers over his eyelids, shutting out the momentary gleam of his passion. He moaned softly, reaching for her hand to kiss the open palm, sending tingles of anticipation throughout her body.

"It is wonderful, Turk. It's something I've dreamed about." She studied him quietly, thinking what magic his hands and lips could work on her when he gently rolled with her to the carpet. Waves of pleasure coursed over her as his hands began their electric journey down her shoulders to the rise of her breasts.

She responded by touching him, running her fingers through the curling hair on his chest, feeling the soft flat contour of his breasts. They clung together, touching, kissing, and feeling until she heard his sharp intake of breath.

"Let me make love to you," he whispered hoarsely. "Don't you feel what I'm feeling, darling? Tell me it's all right."

Why did she hesitate? For what? He hadn't said what she wanted to hear—the three words that would make it all right. A doubt arose somewhere in the back of her mind, just enough to make her hold back.

"I feel the desire too. I want you; I would be lying to say I didn't. But there has to be more for me. Turk, don't you see? There must be more!" she repeated, gaining strength with each repetition. "I want more than sex." She waited for a protest and was surprised at his reaction.

His hands moved away from her body slowly, leaving her flesh crying out for fulfillment even as she had protested before. He did not speak the words "I love you." Instead he sat up slowly, a look of bewilderment replacing the desire in his eyes. He looked down once more at her semibared breasts, reached angrily for her blouse, and tossed it at her as he rose. "Put it on, Myrhia. I don't know what further proof you want of me!"

"If you don't know, then this is wrong between us." She rose self-consciously, clutching her blouse to hide her quivering flesh.

"I'll never understand, Myrhia. You're a strong-minded woman but you are punishing us both. It's not a weakness to admit your body's cravings. It's natural between two people who find their body chemistry is compatible."

Anger flared to her defense. "So! It's body chemistry! It's for this we come together—to satisfy our flesh? How can you be so clinical?" She stifled a sob, walking away from him, unable to look into his face. "You'd better go—if you don't, we'll both be losers."

Turk took a step toward her, reached out for her, then let his hands drop to his sides. Tucking his shirttail into his trousers, he picked up his coat from the back of the couch, then strode toward the doorway. He turned back with his hand still on the knob.

"You'll be mine—if not tonight, then soon. I'm quite sure of it. I usually get what I want. Don't you know by now?"

The door slammed behind him, rattling the pictures on the walls and leaving her sick with apprehension that she had just pulled the final curtain and this would be the last time he would come to her. He surely would not want to keep their date for the football game now. There was only desolate loneliness ahead for her now, but she couldn't have done otherwise. If he had only said he loved her, then it would have been sweeter than anything she could ever imagine. Even now she felt the warmth of his hands on her breasts and shoulders. She threw herself on the couch, which so recently held their love, while sobs racked her body. A faint scent of masculine after-shave lingered on the cushions, tearing her apart.

"Turk, oh, Turk, why didn't you say you loved me?" she whispered to the empty room.

Chapter Nine

If anyone had told Myrhia she could walk, talk normally, and conduct her business during the next weeks without seeing Turk, she would have told them it was impossible. She did manage during the daylight hours to put him from her mind, but nights were a different story. Then he seemed to lurk within the shadows of her apartment; the fragrance of his after-shave would manifest itself at the oddest times in her imagination.

Somehow the pain subsided and she managed to conduct her business. She met the auditorium committee and came away feeling that she had won them over with her design. Her arduous work on the Forest Grove convention center now was under consideration. Carl had heard through buzz talk that hers was one of the top four still before the selection committee. She would know for certain by the end of October. It had been a hard summer with her increased work load added to her new emotional problems.

It was late September already and for several days only terse notes had been channeled her way indirectly through Vaughan Associates from the man she wanted to forget. Carl had expressed concern for her only a day or so before as they met for a quick lunch at a nearby restaurant.

"Myr, you're not yourself lately. Are you ill or working too hard?" His concern almost brought tears to her eyes. What was the matter with her anyway that she had become so emotional lately? She had never been one to cry but now tears seemed just below the surface and could be triggered at any sympathetic remark from a friend.

"Perhaps I've just been pushing too hard. I may have to hire an architect to work under my supervision if my business gets any heavier. It's almost more than Trish and I can handle alone. I don't want to turn down any chances and if I do get the convention center, I'll be busy night and day. I want to do a super job on that one. I have visions of it being a romantic spot."

Why had she said that? It brought Turk's burning gaze to mind and the way he had held her that last night as he looked at the rough sketches of the convention center and made the statement. She had let him go out of her life. Why hadn't she taken the initiative and told him she loved him and see if he responded in kind? Some men were unable to express a commitment. Was Turk one of them? He reveled in his physical strength but the more emotional facets of his character sometimes surfaced but were soon covered by a curtain of masculinity. No doubt he was vulnerable but weren't they all?

She was trying to tell herself she had shoved the invitation to the football game out of her mind as she poured her third cup of coffee and walked to the balcony for the fifth time to see what a glorious Sunday it was going to be. September days could tantalize her senses and it was certainly that kind of a Texas day. It was turning cooler—almost as if the world had hushed for a brief interim to enjoy its own loveliness. If she could just put him out of her mind, she might take a long walk and absorb some of the beauty of the day. But she didn't dare leave the telephone. Deep inside her heart she knew she was waiting for his call.

When the telephone rang she not only jumped from the start it gave her but her fingers trembled as she picked up the receiver.

"Hello, Myrhia. It's Turk." In spite of a brusqueness his voice sounded wonderful to her. He had remembered. "Are you still receptive to our date?"

She hesitated, not really certain what he wanted her to say. "Yes, if you still are planning on it," she said as casually as possible with her pulse rate tripling in the last few minutes. After all, there was no reason he could be expected to keep the date after their fierce parting. He would have no problem in finding someone else more easily receptive to his charm. Immediately she formed a bitter dislike for this imaginary woman in her mind. She had to face the fact she wanted desperately to be with him herself.

"Good," he said almost cautiously. Was it possible he was remembering the tenseness between them at their last parting? "I'll be around early. The game is called for one thirty, but you know how heavy the traffic is on football days. They already have a sellout." There was a slight pause. "Oh, hell! Myrhia, I'll be over within the hour. I want to see you. After all, we did plan to spend a day together, didn't we?" A hearty chuckle broke the slight strain between them. "Am I welcome? Our last date didn't end very well, did it?" Another pause while she could hear his steady breathing. "I don't want another repeat of that. I just want to be near you—on your terms."

"Oh?" She laughed, suddenly feeling lighthearted again. If he only knew the turmoil in her mind and heart since he last held her in his arms, he would know how close she had come to giving in to him willingly. "I'll be glad to see you too. How about lunch? Should I fix us some?"

"No, that will all be taken care of at the game. I'm anxious for you to see the Sky Box. I had it redecorated. Hope you like it." She detected a growing enthusiasm in his voice. "If you don't, you have my permission to redo it completely."

She had heard of Sky Boxes purchased by wealthy men but had never known anyone who owned one. "I'm sure I will like it. I'm really looking forward to the game. It should be interesting."

Although his tone of voice had warmed considerably since he first called her, she had been unconsciously waiting for some word of endearment, something that would bring him closer.

"See you shortly" was his brief reply before hanging up.

Still somewhat disappointed, she sank into a nearby chair, holding to the dead receiver. At least he had said he wanted to be with her, but she had wanted more from him. Unless she could come to terms with this new emotion growing in her heart since meeting Turk, she would never find peace. She could no longer lie to herself. She was in love with Turk and frightened at the outcome. If only she knew he felt the same, she could deal with it no matter what happened.

Myrhia rose with a sigh. At least his call had filled some of the empty spots in her apartment even though a tiny doubt lingered that he had not wanted to keep the date.

It had certainly been a long time since her last football game at the University of Texas. Her memory focused backward on her senior year and a tackle on the Texas team. What had happened to Dick? she wondered. Once she had toyed with the idea of accepting his proposal, but it had been easier not to accept with her dream of a career before her. Thinking back now, she remembered he did not leave her weak and breathless at any time during their amorous moments the way a certain rugged individual could do with one electric glance in her direction.

Walking thoughtfully toward her bedroom, she halfway anticipated the day before her and halfway dreaded it. An hour later, however, she was outwardly calm and dressed in jeans and a teal-blue blouse, her heavy hair pulled back into a ponytail. She felt comfortable but far from relaxed by the time the door buzzer sounded.

It was the first time she had ever seen Turk in cowboy attire—jeans, dark rich blue shirt with silver studs for buttons. His gray cowboy hat was in his hand. He popped it on his head playfully so Myrhia could see the entire outfit. Then with a wide sweep, he lifted it from his head and did a stiff bow. "Mo'ning, pardner!"

"Mo'ning," she replied in kind, finding his smile drove any doubts away that he had not wanted to confirm their date. He looked like one of the fashion ads for western attire—tall, wide-shouldered, with a rakish air about him. It was a relief to find he was in a good mood, which, of course, was because of the game and had nothing whatsoever to do with her.

In cowboy boots of tooled gray leather, he towered above her even more. She had forgotten to put on her own boots, so she excused herself and returned to the bedroom to dig them out of the corner of her closet. Turk poked his head around the doorframe to see what she was doing.

"Need any help?" He grinned wickedly.

"I haven't had these things on in a year," she said, sitting on the side of her bed and struggling with the first boot. "They're a little stiff."

He came toward her as she wrestled with the right

boot and knelt at her feet. "Here," he said, taking the boot from her, "let an old cowboy assist a damsel in distress."

He rolled the leg of her jeans slowly and deliberately, caressing the calf wantonly. A look of purest guile crossed his face before he lifted her leg to shove it into the boot as once again his hands moved over the tight boot sliding up her leg from time to time. All the while exciting tremors raced up and down her leg at his touch, and a devilish smile crossed his lips. "They're quite pretty, darling. Just lovely!" he said wryly, rising to his feet and pulling her up. "That's some better. In your boots you at least reach my shoulder now."

He lifted her face with his free hand, slowly forcing her to look at him. "You look wonderful, you know." His mouth came down on hers in a gentle kiss as she closed her eyes involuntarily for another. He glanced at his watch. "It's about time for the car to pick us up."

There was no time to ask him what he meant by that as they walked to the door. She had assumed he had driven his Mercedes, but when they stepped from the foyer of her apartment and a long black Cadillac pulled from the parking area to stop in front of the entrance, she understood.

"Good timing, Paul," Turk said to the uniformed chauffeur at the wheel.

Myrhia sank back against the velvet-cushioned upholstery with a sigh. Things were starting off in elegant style. This was a far cry from the old college routine of riding six deep in someone's car and walking a half mile after they got there and climbing over feet and legs to find their section in the Austin stadium.

As the chauffeur moved in and out of the increasingly heavy traffic she could see the necessity of leaving early. Sometime later the big limousine pulled into the parking grounds and like a homing pigeon moved to a private area just for chauffeur-driven cars. She and Turk stepped from the limousine, joining a group of others who arrived in the same luxurious manner and moved to the stadium elevator together.

Turk seemed to know all of them and introduced her casually to them. They, in turn, looked her over, accepting her no doubt as just another of his many girl friends.

The elevator stopped on the top floor of the stadium, making her surprise complete. "Well, what do you know?" she said aloud half to Turk and half to herself as they stepped into his Sky Box.

It was terraced in wide semicircles downward to the window that framed the entire front of the room. It was larger than she had expected and the rich, dark blue carpet enhanced the gray leather upholstery of the chairs that were placed at intervals on each graduated landing. Gray and blue, of course, she remembered were the team's colors. To one side was a wet bar and to the other a table set up for buffet service. Turk tucked her arm inside his own and moved downward to have a word with the two bartenders, dressed in white coats and black bow ties.

"I see everything's going great," he said, smiling to the men.

"Yes, sir! The caterers are already downstairs, Mr. Vaughan. They want to know when you want the buffet set up."

"Any time now," Turk said, moving away apparently reassured everything was in order.

"Well, what do you think?" He turned to her, a question in his look.

"Impressive—and I must say a little overpowering, Turk." She glanced around her, noticing several small television units about the room. "May I ask how you can see the playing field from this height?"

"Closed circuit TV," he said, a quizzical look forming on his face.

"Oh? Then why bother to—" She stopped short of finishing her sentence, not wanting to give him reason to quarrel with her, but she had been about to say why not stay home and invite your friends in?

"You were about to say why not stay home? Am I right?" Again she was aware of his uncanny way of reading her mind.

"Well?"

"Good point." He laughed heartily. "I knew you'd feel that way, I just knew it! Any girl who gets a kick out of walking in the rain wouldn't be turned on too violently by pomp and pizzazz." His arm slid around her waist in a warm embrace, making her feel closer to him than she had since his arrival.

"Between you and me, it's the easiest way I have to repay obligations to investors and bankers and my contractors. They go for this." His gesture included the preparations going on at the bar and around the buffet table. "Do you like the decor?"

"Love it! It's in good taste. I wouldn't change a thing about it." Her remark seemed to please him as he gave her arm a squeeze before turning to some of the earlier arrivals.

Turk introduced her to the first guests to arrive. She gathered from their conversations among themselves, they were connected solely with construction. When Turk mentioned she was the architect for his new building, many of them seemed interested. One or two of the older men were familiar with the Lassiter name and had known of her father's reputation.

As the morning progressed, she and Turk became

separated more and more but it gave her time to watch him play host to the different sets of people. It was surprising he could be at home equally well with bank presidents and construction superintendents. They seemed to have a warm regard for him too as he moved among the men and women. The women especially were enchanted with their host.

Myrhia drifted toward the bar, thinking she would have a bloody Mary and perhaps a snack, since she had barely eaten since yesterday. She and Turk could eat more later and besides, she enjoyed talking to the groups in little clusters around the room. From her observation she noticed there were more single men than those accompanied by women. Possibly their wives or sweethearts did not like football and took the opportunity to renege on the day's activities.

Bloody Mary in hand she moved toward the buffet table and joined two other couples. They were older with the air of success about them. Myrhia looked up when the portlier of the two men spoke.

"I understand you're Walt Lassiter's daughter." She smiled in acknowledgement. "I knew your father quite well, Miss Lassiter. He was a fine architect. In fact he designed an apartment I was interested in down in Houston. It had great lines and has always been a moneymaker for me." Before she could answer his wife spoke.

"And you are an architect too? My dear, how proud your father would have been to know you are becoming well known in the same field. Turk was just telling us what a beautiful building he was erecting and he owed it all to you. He thinks rather highly of you." Her soft brown eyes hinted of a double meaning in her comment.

"Thank you," Myrhia said, a warm glow enfolding

her. Was it possible that Turk did say complimentary things about her work—at least to others? It gave her satisfaction to think so.

The two couples, after other bits of small talk, left her alone at the sumptuous buffet. She was helping herself to the shrimp when a strong hand closed over hers, knocking the shrimp back into the ice.

Myrhia had sensed Turk's nearness even before he had touched her hand. It was always that way when they were together. It was as if his magnetism pulled her into his special aura and she became part of him. She turned now to look into a pair of sensuous blue-gray eyes that were dangerously close to her own.

"Now, see what you've made me do!" she said, not daring to look too long into his eyes or she would be in his arms voluntarily. "I had a hard time spearing that shrimp in the first place." She laughed, reaching for another.

"Just wait a minute and I'll join you." He smiled, taking the shrimp from her hand and popping it into her partially open mouth. "You've made a hit with these people, darling. I'd better keep a chain on you from now on." His face grew serious. "I do thank you for circulating around. You are a natural hostess."

The compliment pleased her. "Thanks, but I find them all very interesting. Now, hurry up and get something to drink and let's eat. I'm starving and it grows worse the longer I stand here looking at all this food."

"Will do," he said, stepping to the bar for his usual Scotch on the rocks.

Myrhia heaped her plate with something of everything and dropped into one of the chairs to enjoy her lunch. Turk's plate was almost overflowing when he joined her, drink in hand. "I'm not too hungry," he said deadpan.

"So I noticed." She grinned.

By game time the fifty or sixty guests settled into the comfortable chairs, their appetites appeased at last. The buffet had been filled with the lavish assortment of canapés, smoked ham and turkey, imported cheeses, Gulf shrimp. There were hot foods served in large chafing dishes, spiced meatballs, smoked sausages, and Texas chili for the heavy eaters. For dessert there was chocolate mousse, ripe melons, and petits fours.

As the Cowboys trailed behind, Myrhia became conscious of Turk's restlessness. He seemed unable to sit still for long, but rose from her side to make several trips down the terraced steps to the window for a better look at the playing field. For some reason she was feeling his anxiety for the team. Turk seemed to be steeled for the outcome, as if reliving the game through his buddies on the field.

As the whistle blew for the half, Turk took hold of her arm and started up the terraced steps. "Come on, Myrhia. I've got to get out of here. Besides, we'll never be missed."

She would readily agree on the last statement, as everyone was starting for another drink or refill of snacks. She was puzzled, however, by his sudden behavior and allowed herself to be pulled into the elevator and down to the ground floor of the stadium before she spoke.

"Just where are we going?"

"To the locker room—or at least I am." He stopped outside the locker room door. "Wait here, darling. I won't be long." As if he suddenly realized his behavior demanded some explanation, he said, "The Sky Box is for my business associates, but my friends are in there." He gestured toward the locker room.

She watched him disappear into the room, suddenly

feeling very close to him again. Here was a warm, friendly personality—vital, loyal—this was the real Turk Vaughan. He was not a man to seek prestige and wealth just for what it represented to be able to afford a Sky Box and entertain his friends. No, he belonged down here and in that moment she did too.

She could even breathe better out here in the open, she thought, as she took in a deep lungful of air. When Turk found her, she was watching the halftime crowds, beer and hot dog in hand, discussing the game together.

"Do you mind if we wait and follow the team back to the field? One of the players had extra tickets for the first row. I told the guys I had brought a good luck charm." His eyes teased her. "You!"

From their new vantage point, it was impossible not to become a part of the cheering, roaring crowd. She found she stood more than she sat, screaming for one player after another. When, in the last two minutes of the game, the Cowboys kicked a field goal to win the game, she threw her arms around Turk, who lifted her off her feet in his excitement.

"We needn't go back to the box, if you don't want to, Myrhia. They won't miss us. Since we won, they'll be pretty high before the crowd thins."

It was close to seven when they entered her apartment. "Whew!" Turk said, sinking down onto her couch, his long legs sprawled before him. "I hope you weren't too bored."

"On the contrary—I loved it. Especially the second half. I liked being closer to the action," she said, joining him on the couch. He turned to look at her. He was quiet as his eyes traced her face and she could feel a warmth flush over her cheeks at his silent scrutiny.

"I think you mean that." He put his arm behind her

and pulled her head down to his shoulder. "I can't deny I miss the game. It was part of my life for too many years and no matter how far removed I am as the time goes by, I want to go back occasionally."

A companionable silence settled over them for the next few minutes. It was Myrhia who broke the quiet, rising from his side to step to the kitchen. "How would you like a cup of coffee?" she asked over her shoulder.

"I would like it," he said stretching languorously and leaning back on the cushions of the overstuffed divan with a sigh.

By the time Myrhia returned, he was asleep. She set down the cups and saucers, poured herself a cup, and carried the carafe back to the kitchen. He probably needed the sleep more than the coffee as the jet lag back and forth between the islands and Dallas was possibly beginning to bother him.

As she sipped her coffee, a comfortable lethargy settled over her too. It was good to stretch out with nothing pressing on her time for an hour or so and look across the room at Turk. As her thoughts deepened she slept but was not aware of it until she moved somnolently to the surface of a dream, surrounded by soft bubbles, as if she bathed in a pool of warm water. As her eyes opened she was looking into two blue-gray pools focused softly on her face, the owner's lips not inches from her own.

Turk smiled, pulling her slowly to her feet. "Guess we both enjoyed a nap. I woke to find you had deserted me for the armchair." She could feel his soft, warm breath on her cheek. The last rays of the September sun had long before pulled back over the horizon, she noticed from her wide window.

Turk glanced at his watch. "Darling, I have to go. We overslept. I have another meeting tomorrow afternoon on Maui.'' He reached to trace her cheek with his fingers and said, ''Is it possible that you just might come for a few days? Could someone else handle the building for now—perhaps Muldrow or your building superintendent?''

''No!'' she answered too emphatically, feeling him tense. ''No,'' she said more softly. ''You know that's impossible. I'm responsible for the building. I'm also responsible to you and the other investors but mostly to the people who will be spending eight hours of every working day in that building. It has to be safe and I will see that it is.''

He let her go away from him then. ''I might ask you the same question, Turk. Isn't there someone in your office or on your commission who can handle the condos for you?''

''No. There is no one.'' He turned away from her, picked up his cowboy hat, and started toward the door. ''I guess that's the way it will be.''

''I just wanted you to know that I consider my work as important to me as you do yours. That's all, Turk. The sooner we both accept that fact the better it will be for us. Perhaps you need to come to terms with what I am too.''

''I'm beginning to wonder if I'll ever know that.'' There was a definite note of sadness in his remark as he made ready to open the door.

She wanted to run to him to pull him back, to throw her arms around him and tell him it was easy to understand her. She was just a simple architect, who liked what she was doing, but had fallen in love and didn't know how to handle it. Instead she turned away from the finality of his leaving.

While she waited for the inevitable closing of the door, her legs grew jellylike and she was on the verge of sinking onto the sofa, when strong arms encircled her waist from the back and Turk pulled her against his hard body once more.

"I won't be back for so long. I had something I wanted to ask you tonight but now it will have to wait. We need more time and I want to be damned sure you're receptive to what I have to ask. I hope you miss me and long for me and need me as I will you," he added softly and she was aware of the trembling in his thighs.

His lips found hers, sealing once again on an unspoken agreement between them before he pulled away and was gone. She stood a moment longer, feeling desolate and lost before falling onto the couch to mourn him in quiet tears. She wondered how much she would miss him before he came again. The weeks would weigh heavily before the skeletal frame of the building reached its twenty-story height. Not until then could they hold the topping-off party. And then she might see him, but would he want to hold her in his arms again? Would she feel his lips warm on hers? There was no whispered answer from the corners of the lonely room. Once again she tried to steel her emotions against the heavy longing she would have.

Myrhia had come from having lunch with Carl, halfway promising to go along with his invitation to date Belinda's cousin from North Carolina when he came to visit them in Dallas within the next few weeks or so. Now wishing she could withdraw her acceptance, she removed the mail from her mailbox and entered her apartment earlier than usual, since she had taken the afternoon off.

Sinking down on the couch, she riffled through the mail, mostly bills, when a stark white envelope postmarked Maui, Hawaii, and addressed in a masculine hand caught her attention. With shaking fingers she dropped the other letters unsorted onto the coffee table and tore open the envelope.

My darling,

It has been eight weeks—more like eight years—since I held you in my arms. Have you forgotten? Myrhia, I try not to push too hard, but it seems I can't control the feelings I have when I'm with you. I expect to be back in Dallas by the end of January or February at the latest. I have not changed my mind about you, nor do you dare forget me. I want to prove once and for all what you mean to me. You just better be receptive and wanting or else.

Turk

The single sheet of paper slipped from her fingers with a soft rustle and floated down onto the blue carpet, where she and Turk last stood together lost in the wonder of their emotions.

Chapter Ten

Myrhia was in the same position thirty minutes later, sprawled on the couch, when the telephone rang. It was Alicia reminding her of their lunch date the following Saturday, which was day after tomorrow.

"I haven't forgotten, Mother." Inadvertently she again used the term *mother,* reverting back to a childhood need for the moment. "I won't be able to stay for a round of golf, though. I have too much to do on my new project and I'm running ads for an apprentice architect to help out with the extra work."

"I must tell you I'm beginning to read and hear about you. I'm delighted." Alicia gave a little laugh. "I must say, though, I was truly sorry when you and Turk Vaughan didn't hit if off. Is that completely over?"

"Nothing can be over if it never began in the first place. Now, can it?" She tried keeping her voice light.

"It didn't look as if there was nothing started that Sunday at my home, Myrhia."

"Well, Turk's in Hawaii, has been for some time—and I don't know when I'll see him again. But don't worry, someday I just might surprise you." Myrhia was smiling when she put down the receiver. Alicia was trying, but she would always be the romantic.

Myrhia picked up Turk's note from the carpet. As

she reread its brief message, it didn't take much imagination to visualize his taut expression while he wrote it. He was possibly frowning so the dark eyebrows came together to make a frame for his fascinating eyes. She tried to fight off the strange, desolate feeling she was having. He was somewhat highhanded even in this note, threatening her with lovemaking, expecting her to wait all this time. She had never allowed any man to be that domineering with her, but even as the thought crossed her mind, she smiled. Turk was not just *any* man.

She would continually be filled with conflicting emotions about him. She knew he desired her sexually. She could relate to that but there was more to her own need. It was growing harder each time to hold out, and perhaps next time she would find out how wonderful it could be with him.

By the time she entered the office next morning some of her anxiety had left her. Trish looked up. "You have an early visitor. Carl Muldrow is in your office."

Myrhia stepped into her office, smiling. "Carl, this is a welcome surprise. What brings you out so early?"

"Well, Myr, I thought it would be better to tell you this than to call it over the telephone." His amber eyes clouded with worry.

"What is it, Carl?"

"You didn't get the convention center commission, Myr. Almost, but not quite. You were second choice— if that's any consolation." He started toward her but stopped as she sank into her desk chair, feeling dumbfounded. Was it possible she had counted on it too much? She was disappointed and unable to answer him for a second.

"I worked so hard on those plans, Carl. I really put my heart into that proposal." Turk's words came back to haunt her: "It looks like a romantic spot." Was it possible his reaction to the plans had clouded her thinking, made her expect to win in the competition? Carl looked distressed and she couldn't have him feel that way. He had done all he could. "Oh, well, Carl, win some, lose some," she said trying to be flippant, but she knew Carl wasn't fooled. He knew her too well. "Nevertheless, Carl, I thank you for giving me the chance."

"We'll find something else soon, Myr, don't despair," he said kindly, looking around the room at her renderings and her cluttered drawing board. "I think you have plenty to do anyway, don't you?"

"Yes, I'm keeping busy. I guess the convention center would have pushed my hours into late evening anyway. How's your family?" She was glad to change the subject.

"Fine. And that brings me to another matter. Belinda's cousin will be in Dallas in two weeks. I'm confirming our invitation for dinner. Bea is certain that the two of you might have lots in common. By the way, Frank's holding his own showing in Houston this winter."

"Oh?" She couldn't refuse Carl; she owed him too much already. But before she could continue the conversation, he interrupted.

"Besides, Myr, I think it's high time you washed a certain football player out of your hair. Don't mind my meddling, but he's not the man for you."

"You don't need to worry." Myrhia laughed. "He beat me to the shampoo and washed me out of his hair first. He's not interested in M. Lassiter, Architect, in a romantic way."

"Good! Then it's a date for Saturday two weeks from now?"

"Fine, Carl." She hoped she was properly enthusiastic. "By the way, I've set up my office trailer on the lot at the Tarrington site and pulled all the shop drawings from this office and left them on the site with my architect-in-training. I'm lucky to have Doug out there to keep tab. He's a real help." She rose and began picking up two or three fresh pencils and a drawing pad and slipping them into her briefcase. "Everything is quite handy out there in the trailer. Come see for yourself sometime. You'll find me there most of the mornings."

"Sure thing. I'll be over. Maybe this morning. I have to be out that way. I understand the concrete trucks will be arriving at ten fifteen for the first pour. Right?"

"Yes, and I've got to run. I want to be there in plenty of time." She glanced at her watch. "See you later."

Carl no sooner left the office than she experienced a letdown—first, disappointment of not getting the convention center, which she had thought was a cinch; second, anger at herself for denying her real feeling for Turk, although it would have been difficult to explain to Carl the on-and-off courtship they had going with all its pain and trauma; third, dread of her ready acceptance of a date with Belinda's cousin. She did not want to spend an entire evening with a stranger.

She had turned down two very personable men in her office building within the last month. One was a lawyer with an oil company. He had a promising future and after his persistence wore her down, she did agree to meet him for cocktails. It was a failure, as he was too freshly wounded from his wife's walking out on him to be good company. It was easy to say no the second time he asked.

By the time Myrhia maneuvered her car through the

morning traffic, and pulled onto the building site she was feeling better. It always brought a little thrill to see the Tarrington project coming through its various stages. Two large cement trucks were pulled up close to the base of the structure. They reminded her of giant insects, their fat stomachs rolling hungrily as they digested the cement mixture, keeping it rotating constantly.

Stepping from her car, she waved at one or two of the workmen, who had nodded greetings, and hurried into her office trailer to find Doug replacing the telephone receiver into its cradle.

"I was just calling your office to tell you the trucks were here." He wore a wide smile on his slender face.

Grabbing up her blue hard hat, she left the trailer at a run, taking the three steps down from the doorway with one graceful leap. She hurried to where Mac Blount, the superintendent of construction, was motioning the first cement truck into place in order to begin the pour into the steel cages needed to reinforce the piers that would hold the enormous twenty-story structure above it. This was an important moment and one she needed to check thoroughly. As the architect she had the final approval of everything.

"Morning, Mac! How's it going?" she asked, stepping to the super's side and leaning over to look into the first pier hole. It was fortunate, she was thinking, that the Dallas area had very little underground water and they had drilled the twenty-two necessary feet to the limestone without difficulty.

Although the first pier hole looked wide enough to her at first glance, she was having a queer feeling that something was not right about it. She glanced sideways at Mac, who appeared to be his old confident, sardonic self. Myrhia stepped closer and leaned over the hole, peering nervously into its depth. She had to be certain all the holes were the proper width to hold the steel cages. If the holes were too narrow, even by an inch, they would not hold the necessary amount of cement for safety and it might mean disaster.

"Have you rechecked the width of the holes, Mac?" She walked around the gaping opening, glancing at the other holes about the lot. "Are you sure they're thirty-six inches in diameter?" He ignored her, signaling the truck driver to back closer for the pour.

"Hold it, Mac! Hold up the pour! I want to measure the hole.' Her voice was tight and controlled.

"No need for that. Do you think I'd let them pour the cement if the damn things weren't wide enough?" He snorted in disgust. "What d'ya think you're erecting here, *Ms.* Lassiter? The Empire State Building?" Some of the workmen standing near chuckled at his humor.

"I said hold it!" She could feel the hair on the back of her neck rising in anger and her knees were shaking, but she stood her ground. "I said hold it!" She was surprised at her own vehemence. "I'll get the shop drawings and check it out." She ignored the workmen who had stopped to listen.

"That won't be necessary, Miss Lassiter," Doug said, coming up behind her with her drawings. "I've brought the shop drawings."

She gave him a nervous smile and turned to the others. "I'm the one responsible for this building and it's to be erected as I planned. Don't you do another damned thing until I look at my plans, Mac."

Turning her back on his exasperated face, she spread the drawings on a stack of wood pilings in front of her. "See that?" she said pointing to the figure on the sketch. "Thirty-six inches wide!" She turned to find pure hatred sparking from Mac's deep-set eyes.

"It's unnecessary, you know," he said crossly. "I checked these holes myself. They're plenty wide. I've been in this business thirty years and I ought to know what I'm doing."

"I would think you would by now—then, why don't you follow instructions?" she said sarcastically, wishing she were a few feet taller and could look him in the eye.

"Hey, you two, let's get on with it. We don't have all day!" The driver of the first truck leaned out of the cab and glared at her.

Myrhia turned to face him. "Hold it, mister!" she said sharply. "There'll be no pour today in this hole until I have it measured. You may have to wait—not today but two or three days if I find it's not right."

"Hell, lady! You know what that means? We'll have to go dump the stuff out somewhere," he muttered, sending a pleading look toward Mac.

"What's the matter here, Myr?" Carl's voice broke into the moment like a shaft of sunlight. "Trouble?" He was approaching swiftly adjusting the back strap of his hard hat.

"It's a good thing you're here, Mr. Muldrow," Mac said, giving her an angry glare. "This—this—lady," he said, biting down on the sarcasm, "is holding up our construction schedule. These holes are okay. I've sunk many a steel cage in such as this."

Carl ignored him and bent over the shop drawings. "This calls for thirty-six inches. Get a tape measure," he commanded Mac.

"Come here, Julio." Julio Marcias was the pier excavation foreman. "How wide did you make these?" Carl asked tersely. "Never mind, just get out your tape and measure to be sure."

Julio shook his head as he knelt at the hole. "It's not thirty-six, more like thirty-four, I think." He stretched the tape over the opening. "Yep, thirty-four," he said, standing again and looking at Mac.

"Dammit, Mr. Muldrow, you know as well as I do that's wide enough. Just because some darn fool girl got a degree in architecture from some fancy college, she has to throw her weight around. Some of us here have been in this business since she was in diapers, I 'spect. Do we have to follow through on everything?" He glared at Myrhia.

"Yes, you do!" Myrhia said, standing firmly on her rights. "Now, I suggest you call off these trucks and tell the drivers to go dump the cement."

Swearing under his breath, Mac turned to signal the first driver. "You heard the lady. Now get the hell off somewhere and dump the cement. Call you in a day or two."

"No!" Myrhia took one step forward and held up her hand. "*I'll* tell you when to call, Mac. As soon as I see that each hole is the proper diameter and not before."

She walked away not glancing back, feeling Mac's hot anger directed at her back, but she held her head up. As she neared the trailer office she could feel her knees beginning to weaken and prayed they would not buckle under her until she reached the haven of the office.

She made it finally and just in time as she sank into her desk chair and hot tears of anger poured from her eyes. This was her first major confrontation challenging her ability. She couldn't let it upset her this way each time she had a difference with the men under her. She took off the hard hat. She was wiping the perspiration from her forehead and back of her neck and dabbing at the tears on her cheeks as Carl and Doug walked in.

"Nice going, Myr!" Carl said, patting her on the

back and trying not to look at her red-rimmed eyes. "You'll come out okay. They'll get in line soon enough when they find out they can't railroad you."

Doug gave her a shy smile. "I sure like the way you handle things, Miss Lassiter." His eyes were shining with the excitement of the incident.

"Thanks, Doug, but from now on we need to watch for any deviation from our shop drawings. Understand?"

"Yes, ma'am, I sure do," he answered politely, making her feel ancient somehow.

Carl stayed a while longer until she felt some of the anger leave her. She hated to lose her control the way she had and would have to overcome that weakness. There would be further differences she knew, but her reputation as an architect depended on the exactness of her drawings.

After Carl left, Doug sauntered out onto the lot to give her some breathing space. Her mind drifted to Turk. She wondered where he was and what he was doing at this moment. It would be wonderful to be lolling on a white sand beach with him, listening to the waves lapping the shore. She shook off the picture, forcing her mind back to the problems at hand. It might be interesting to get Turk's opinion concerning her battle with Mac. No doubt he would hear about it, as he was in touch daily with the progress report of the building.

She remained at the site the rest of the morning until satisfied her orders were being carried out and the holes were being opened wider. Then, leaving Doug in charge, she returned to her office in Lemon Park.

Trish had a list of calls waiting for her when she entered. Some were from prospective architects in answer to an ad she ran in the Dallas newspaper. She set

those calls aside for later, curious about one call from
Vaughan Associates. She was certain it was not from
Turk, he was planning to be away longer.

As Myrhia dialed his office she steeled herself, drawing a curtain over the memory of his face. Just dialing
his number made her hand tremble. She shook off a
slight apprehension as a familiar voice answered on the
other end of the telephone. "This is Myrhia Lassiter
returning a call from your office."

"Yes, Myrhia, this is Letty Chappel. I'm wondering
if I can take you to lunch tomorrow. We could meet at
the lunchroom around the corner from Lemon Park,
the Pink Pantry—that is, if it's all right with you? Say
twelve o'clock?"

Surprise wrestled with curiosity but the latter won
out. "That will be fine, Letty. At noon," she heard
herself say.

She purposely avoided asking what the lunch get-
together was about, dreading Letty would want to talk
about Turk. There could be no other link between her
and Letty.

Shrugging off the puzzle of the call, she decided to
devote the rest of the afternoon to contacting the appli-
cants who had called about her ad. She was not impressed with the first two, but two hours later she knew
she would hire Jack Carter.

He was young, Trish's age, tall, and thin to the point of
being slightly emaciated. Myrhia couldn't help thinking
that a good meal or two would fill out the lean lines of
his face. She wondered if he had been having a rough
time of it since coming out of the University of Texas.
His portfolio was excellent, showing a great deal of
promise in designing, something she considered important.

"How soon can you report for work?" she asked,

looking up into his eager face. "Business is coming in fast and I can't afford to turn down anything if at all possible."

"I understand and I can report Monday, Ms. Lassiter," he said, shifting from one foot to another.

"Okay, you're hired, Jack. And it's Myrhia from now on. Be prepared to work hard."

"I'll do it. I'm glad for the opportunity, Myrhia." His smile assured her she had made a good choice.

After the salary was set and he had left, she felt pleased with her decision. The three of them would get along well.

Next morning Myrhia was still wondering why Letty wanted to have lunch with her. She assumed it concerned Turk but was it something she wanted to hear? She started to call the Vaughan office to tell Letty she would be too busy to make it. After all, she did need to stay on top of things at the building site since her run-in with Mac over the piers. She would be relieved when there was a better rapport between the superintendent and her.

There was no particular reason for her to dress as carefully as she had for her luncheon date, but for some reason she had taken extra care with her hair and makeup. She chose an ultra-feminine cream-colored blouse with a lace jabot that contrasted well with her new fall suit of soft brown. It was good suit weather, more like a continuance of Indian summer than the approach of winter.

She was the first to arrive at the Pink Pantry. Taking a seat at a table for two near a window, she had too much time to worry over this luncheon. What had made her accept in the first place? Her introspection was short-lived as the door opened and Letty, smiling brightly, came toward her.

As Myrhia watched the redhead's approach between the crowded tables of noontime diners, she knew why she had taken pains to dress well. Letty, she admitted grudgingly, was a head turner, the focus of all male eyes as she walked on well-turned ankles, a timid half-smile on her small rosebud mouth. As she sank into the seat opposite, she caught her lower lip between her teeth, indicating to Myrhia she also felt insecure at their meeting, and in that moment Myrhia thawed toward her.

"It's a good thing you were early. The place is packed," Letty said breathlessly. "Pay day for most of them. We all feel we can dine out with a little solvency, don't we?" Letty gave a light laugh as some of her nervousness disappeared.

"Yes, I know the feeling," Myrhia said.

"I suppose you're curious why I called. I only met you one time before, remember? The Benihana—I was with Turk." She looked away from Myrhia as if wondering what to say next.

Myrhia remembered only too well the last time they met and the catty remarks that Letty had intentionally said out loud. She realized now the other girl was recalling those same remarks and trying to rationalize them in her mind so Myrhia would understand.

"I'll begin with an apology. I mean nothing to Turk—that is, nothing like I led you to believe that night. I don't know what came over me. I think I smelled trouble—trouble that we would lose the attention my family has come to depend on. It was a selfish, mean trick to pull on Turk. He cautioned me about it coming from the Benihana." Her eyes filled with unshed tears. "Turk has been and will always be our best friend, I know that. He and Ted have come a long way together—through hell after Ted came home so battered he wasn't the same man. If it hadn't been for Turk—"

Letty fumbled in her handbag for a handkerchief and made a timid wipe of her eyes with it before continuing. "It was Turk who stood by us and brought Ted home after finding a male nurse for me. He even pays half of the man's salary. I haven't been able to talk about this before, but now I see it's necessary for you to understand. He has been the salvation of my sons and me—not only as a friend but in giving me a job and taking me out to dinner from time to time."

She looked at Myrhia a long time, searching her face with pale blue eyes. "I think you understand what it means to be treated like a woman—invited out for dinner, wine, dancing, and male attention. That is what Turk has done for me. He has kept my female vanity intact—nothing else."

Myrhia started to speak but Letty held up her hand. "A moment more. It's hard to tell you this. I was jealous at first when I realized Turk was in love. He is, you know—even Ted in his lucid moments is aware of the change in him. He kids him about you, such as: 'When will he get to kiss the bride?' and so on. Turk doesn't mention your name often but when he does it is with a softness that's a telltale sign. He's never been sentimental about the other women he's dated."

With an apologetic shrug she said, "I don't mean to imply he has lots of girl friends but he does date frequently but never the same one for long. I know this for a fact—that since meeting you Turk has not been out with another woman."

"You could be wrong, you know. I'm certain he's not in love with me. Our infrequent dates end in disagreements almost always. We never spend an entire evening without tangling over something." Myrhia wondered why she was confiding this way, but it was good to have someone to talk with. Letty was studying her intently.

"That's what I mean, Myrhia. Turk's fighting this new emotion with all he's got. The big lug has fallen and can't accept it yet." A sadness mirrored in her eyes before she looked away. "I wanted to explain my position to you. There has never been any lovemaking between me and Turk—not even on Maui, as you probably suspected. I would have in your place." She laughed suddenly. "Also, I want to explain why I did the calling for your date. Turk had tried several times to get you and was called back to the condo site. He was as mad as an overgrown bear and stalked out telling me to place the call. One of his partners overheard the discussion and said something funny just as I reached you by telephone. Please overlook it. I'm sorry, it's a short-coming of mine. Laughing at the wrong time."

It was Myrhia's time to smile, as she felt a growing affection for this woman who had so little to smile about. It was true the call had angered her. "I'm glad you told me. Naturally I wondered and it did make me angry, I'll admit."

"I'm sure it did. As for suspecting a love affair between me and Turk—there has been none. He's too much a gentleman, a brother, a friend, to even think along those lines. I'll admit there were times I'd given anything if he would have put his arms around me." She paused, looking off into the mall. "Not that I love him in that way, but a woman needs a man some-times." She looked back at Myrhia, a sad smile on her lovely face. "But it won't be Turk. He would never see me that way."

Myrhia had felt a growing pity for Letty's situation. Here she was saddled with a sick husband and two growing boys, though she was still young and very beautiful, and Myrhia understood. Impulsively Myrhia reached for the woman's hand and touched it lightly. Letty turned tired eyes on Myrhia.

"You'll be so good for Turk. I'm happy he has found you," she said easily.

Myrhia withdrew her hand, shrugging her shoulders at the last remark. "You could be wrong, Letty. Turk is not the least interested in my comings or goings anywhere. I have had one terse note from him since he left."

Letty laughed out loud, a small, tinkling laugh. "That's so like him. He covers his innermost feelings. I shouldn't be telling this on him, but Turk is a pussycat under all that muscular bravado. He has always been the top star athlete—in college and on the Dallas team—but it never has gone to his head. He's gentle underneath, and very artistic."

A small gasp escaped Myrhia's lips. "Artistic?"

"You are surprised?" Letty continued. "He is quite a modest but very proficient pianist. Only his closest friends have ever been treated to an evening of entertainment in his apartment."

Myrhia's expression must have mirrored doubt as Letty looked at her for some time before continuing. "I can see you don't believe me. I know it's hard to visualize Turk playing the piano but he's way above average—almost terrific, I'd say. I found out after many years that his mother was musical but there is the crux of Turk's personality flaw. His father was a hard, domineering man who thought the gentler arts were for weaklings—that included his wife. From what Turk told Ted years ago, his mother would have had a breakdown if she had continued to live in the oil fields on leases with the opinionated man she married. They were separated—never divorced—when the mother moved back into her modest musical career. Before she could send for her son, she died at an early age.''

Myrhia was beginning to understand Turk better as Letty talked. These things gave her a flash of insight into what she had suspected about him. But why had he not told her about playing the piano? Was he unsure of her reaction or ashamed to admit a talent? Bits of memory flashed back at his keen perception regarding art. At the time it had surprised her, as he presented a hard, tough attitude on occasion.

"This is all very surprising, Letty. I'm glad to know these things about Turk, but—'' She squared her shoulders preparatory to rising from the table. It was time to go back to the office and she didn't want to hear anymore. Her heart was too full now with longing. She wanted to tell him it was all right to let her know his deepest feelings, to be able to cradle his head on her breast and tell him there was no weakness in accepting beauty. Music and art and dancing were part of the expression of man's deepest strength.

Letty looked at her, waiting for the unfinished sentence that was still dangling on the *but*. "I was going to say, it really doesn't concern me. Turk is not interested in me romantically, I assure you. We have been thrown together because he happened to select my proposal for the Tarrington Building.''

As she rose from the table, so did Letty. "Don't be hard on yourself! Turk needs someone like you, Myrhia. Don't forget I've known him a long time. I think I would be a good judge of whether he was in love or not.''

Fighting to keep the pulsing emotion out of her voice, she said, "I've enjoyed lunch, Letty. The next one will be on me. Is there anything I can do for Ted and the boys?''

"No, but thanks anyway. I do want Turk to bring you over one evening after he returns from the Far East. I'll plan something then."

"Far East?" Myrhia said, incredulous at the news.

. A frown creased Letty's pale forehead. "That man! It's so like him to be secretive about everything. Sometimes I don't know what to make of all men. I thought he would at least have told you."

By way of explanation she continued. "He's been in Shanghai, Hong Kong, and the Phillippines so far. I don't know where else he plans to be. He intends to invest in projects in one of those countries." She gave a light laugh. "Would you believe it? He doesn't always tell the office before he goes, but after he arrives we get a call telling us how to reach him."

Later, as Myrhia entered her office, she was still having mixed emotions concerning Turk. Listening to Letty had given her more to think about. She realized she had felt alienated from him these past weeks. Was it possible her subconscious mind knew he was not in Hawaii? She sighed as she laid a fresh sheet of paper on her drawing board. It would be difficult now to concentrate on the work at hand.

Chapter Eleven

"I see you're busy, Myrhia. I'll come back another time. I happened to be in your neighborhood and thought I'd drop by instead of calling." Carl had come in unannounced just as she was pinning a fresh sheet of drawing paper onto her board.

"No, I'm not that busy, Carl, that I can't chat a minute." She turned, moving back toward her desk and indicating for him to take her other chair.

"No, I won't sit, I don't have much time. Just want to know how you feel about the Tarrington. Any more trouble with Mac and your shop drawings?"

"No, we seem to have come to a truce between us. He's coolly polite but the men are friendly." She walked to the window to stare unseeingly into the sky. She was happy for the interruptions in her thoughts. It had been two weeks since she had lunch with Letty, but some of the things she had said about Turk lingered in Myrhia's mind. She had been thinking of him when Carl came.

"I'm here for two reasons. First in importance: Belinda wanted to remind you about Saturday. Frank is already here and anxious to meet you. He likes to dance I understand, so we're going somewhere to dance. Second, the ground-breaking for the auditorium is set up for the first Monday in December." He joined her at the window. "They plan to start the building right away, hoping for another mild winter in Dallas." He paused. "I understand the Tarrington is going up pretty fast now. I expect you shook them up a little." He chuckled.

"Well, Mac promised the skeletal frame will be up by February sometime. I'll enjoy the topping-off party, I know, since it will be my first big one." She didn't admit that she looked forward to the party for one big reason. Turk would be here. "I spend a lot of time out there now. I should stay with it eight hours a day, but Doug is really helping me."

Carl patted her shoulder. "Well gotta run! See you Saturday!"

No sooner had Carl left than she decided to call Letty and invite herself out for the evening. She might feel closer to Turk that way and she had found Letty to be a very nice person. Letty seemed pleased that she wanted to come and meet Ted and the boys.

"This will be a treat for Ted, Myrhia. He's feeling good this week. Why not come for supper? That way the boys will have a chance to know you. They have so many places to go each evening, basketball and all that."

"Oh, I couldn't have you go to all that trouble unless you let me bring something."

"I promise it will be simple, just family food. Come about six and that way you'll see Ted at his best," Letty said.

"Okay, but I'm bringing the wine."

"Fine, Myrhia, if you'd like."

The Chappel home was a small frame house painted white and tucked away at one end of a one-way street in the older part of town. It was neat and attractive with trailing vines over the doorway. In summer it must look like a storybook house, she thought to herself, as she used the brass knocker. There were spaded flower beds around the front stoop and trellises across the picket fence behind the house, where roses must bloom in profusion.

Letty met her at the door, a bright floral apron over her jeans. "Come in, Myrhia. Ted's anxious to meet you. Thank goodness, he's thinking straight today." She glanced quickly over her shoulder, her voice falling to a whisper. "You do know, don't you, that he is blind?"

"Yes, Letty, Turk told me," she answered quietly.

"Well, well, look who's here, Ted!" Letty turned brightly to the large man sitting in a wheelchair in front of the fireplace. "It's Myrhia. Turk's Myrhia," she added, ushering Myrhia toward him.

He turned vacant, staring eyes toward the sound of his wife's voice, a smile lighting up the corner of his lips. "I know, Letty. I know. Turk is always talking about her. I'm glad we can meet her at last." He held out a large hand toward them.

Myrhia stepped toward him and took his hand in hers. "How are you, Ted? I'm happy to meet you at last."

He turned his head to one side as if listening, while the hand she was holding closed down in a strong grip. He turned her hand over until it was lying in his palm secured by his heavy fingers. He stroked her smaller hand with his for a few minutes before speaking again. "A good hand, a capable hand. You are artistic?" The stare focused on her face.

"She's an architect, Ted. Remember? Did Turk's building?" Letty explained patiently.

"That's it. I knew it. I like you, Myrhia. Turk will be happy with you." He released her hand with a sigh.

Myrhia looked at Letty, feeling a mixed sensation

spread over her. They were so certain Turk and she would find something together and she had nothing tangible to hold to, making it necessary now to deny their relationship. "Turk's a good business partner in my project—nothing more, Ted. I only wish—" She stopped, horrified at what she had been about to say. Her voice had even broken a little on the unfinished statement. How could she lie to this perceptive friend of Turk's whose blindness made him more aware of insight into another's heart?

She glanced at Letty for help, but found her smiling as if she too knew more than Myrhia did about her relationship with Turk.

After a few minutes Ted said, "It's all right to be in love with him, Myrhia. He loves you back. It will be all right," he repeated. "You'll see."

"Well, I'll just put the hamburgers in the skillet and we'll see about supper pretty quick." Letty kissed the top of Ted's head and headed toward the kitchen.

Myrhia followed Letty, surprised at the bright cheerfulness the room seemed to broadcast from the yellow, starched plaid curtains at the window to the scrubbed white cabinets and soft yellow and brown tile floor. "This is a happy place, Letty. How do you do it?"

"I don't know, Myrhia," Letty said in answer to her question. "I don't really know if there is any way to explain happiness. I suppose it's just accepting and going on from day to day. I have the boys and Ted. So many people don't have anyone," she added simply as she stepped to the back door and called in the direction of the garage.

"Boys, I need you. Myrhia's here." She turned back with a smile. "They're busy grinding the lens for an eight-inch telescope. Uncle Turk bought the necessary equipment but they have to grind and polish the parabola first. He promised he would help them silver it when he comes back again.''

Good-natured scuffling and stomping preceded the two teen-agers up the back steps and into the kitchen where they stopped and stared, suddenly embarrassed by a stranger.

"Well, boys, where are your manners?'' Letty teased them.

"Hello!'' It seemed to Myrhia they chorused it. "I'm John'' the shorter of the two spoke up. If Myrhia had wanted to know what Ted had looked like before the accident, she had only to look into the good-looking face of his younger son. He had large limpid brown eyes and a round face with the hint of one dimple as he smiled.

"Hello, John,'' she answered, turning to the taller of the two, who looked like his mother. Red wavy hair framed cheerful blue eyes in a slender face.

"I'm Ted Junior,'' he said, reaching out to shake hands with her. "Everyone calls me Teddy.''

"Okay, boys, go wash for dinner,'' Letty instructed.

"Okay, Mom,'' they said, bounding from the kitchen at the same time and having a good-natured tussle for supremacy at the narrow kitchen door before they disappeared.

"Man! Uncle Turk finally found him a good one.'' Teddy's voice floated back to them.

"And she's an architect!'' John said, voicing a little doubt.

Myrhia laughed. "Are they always like this?''

"Usually. They quarrel, make up, and tease one another, but there is nothing that can ever come between them.''

"I envy you,'' Myrhia said sincerely, wondering why she had never thought of children this way. They were

Turk's buddies, she could tell. Would he want children of his own someday? Her thoughts were interrupted as the boys returned and began to help their mother load the hamburgers with onion, pickle, and all the necessary items.

Supper had been a jolly affair with boy talk, an occasional remark from Ted, and Letty's lilting laugh as she included Myrhia in some family incident that had amused them all.

"You're a real architect?" John asked after they had cleared the table and Myrhia and Letty were enjoying a small glass of wine with Ted before the open fire that Teddy had skillfully built for them.

"I am. Are you interested in architecture, John?"

"I think so—if I can make it in math."

"Math's easy for me," Teddy said proudly. "I intend to become a physicist." He looked at his brother disdainfully.

"I wouldn't worry too much now, John. Math may get better as you go along."

"Well, see you," the boys said, rising and bidding everyone good-night. "Come back again," they called to Myrhia.

They were gone in a flash to their bedroom to watch a basketball game. Myrhia looked at Letty as the door closed behind them, finding her blue eyes were filled with pride.

"They're great!" Myrhia spoke softly. "I see now why Turk likes to come here. You're a real family."

Ted was asleep an hour later when she and Letty came from the kitchen after cleaning up the dishes. It was time for her to leave. As she said good-bye to Letty and walked toward her car, it was as if Turk walked by her side. It was the closest she had come to him since they first met. A wave of guilt spread over her that she had doubted Letty and Turk. Jealousy was a destructive trait. She hoped she was above it now.

When she arrived home, she felt lonely; the apartment seemed emptier now than before her visit to the Chappels. The cut glass hurricane lamp responded brightly as she raised its wick and lit it before setting it down on the marble-topped table. A flare of brightness appeared, falling across the table and spotlighting Turk's last note to her. Impulsively she snatched it up and held it to her breast for a second before unfolding the brief message to reread it once again.

"I have not changed my mind about you." The statement left her confused. What conclusions had he come to concerning her anyway? Was this his way of saying he loved her? She dared not dream that way. He hinted he wanted to continue his sexual pursuit at the point where he left off and try as she might she could not erase the tantalizing memory of his mouth and hands touching her body.

"Damn!" she said aloud to the empty room, striding toward the TV to turn it on—anything to break the silence. At least there might be a newscast to bring another voice into the void. As she sank down on her couch and was in the process of kicking off her shoes, the picture appearing on the screen startled her upright; one shoe was left still dangling off her toe.

Turk was standing a head taller than two smiling Japanese, who were having to look up to him. He was speaking through an interpreter to one of the men. The announcer from NBC broke into the conversation.

"That was Dirckson Vaughan, known as Turk to his teammates and fans, one of the Dallas Cowboys' greats until his retirement from football a few years ago." He poked the microphone at Turk. "Old knee injury, wasn't it, Turk, that forced your early retirement?"

"Something like that," Turk ventured.

"I realize you're here in Yokohama to invest in the proposed hotel that will be one of the largest in Japan. Since you're the biggest foreign investor, you're to pick the designer of the hotel. Who is the architect, a Japanese or an American? Can you tell us?"

"Not yet," Turk said without hesitation. "There's only one architect in the United States I would trust to design a building of this size and class. We investors have in mind a well-structured building at the cost of several million dollars. After commissioning that architect, I'll release a statement."

The news changed abruptly to foreign exports, leaving Myrhia in a state of wonder and mixed emotions. She was longing to see him and at the same time she was experiencing a growing anger at what he had said. Only one architect in the United States, he had said smugly. No doubt that would be his old faithful, T.L. Blight, who had been architect for all the other buildings with the exception of the Tarrington. While she was impressed by Blight's form and style, there was too much sameness in his work.

With an angry twist of the television dial she turned it off and began pacing about the room. She would have to stop this seesawing back and forth over him. She couldn't afford to lose her own identity now when she had begun to be recognized in her profession. These past few months her thoughts about her image had become cluttered and confused for the first time since she had become M. Lassiter, Architect. Yet, his remembered touch, his smile, his unusual eyes that could change like the sea with his many moods, returned each time she tried to erase his picture from her mind's eye. And yet, why did she have a mystifying feeling at this moment that her life was just beginning?

Chapter Twelve

Myrhia was still having an argument with herself on Saturday when she was dressing for the dinner with Belinda's cousin, Frank. There was only one sustaining thought about the evening before her, and that was it might dim the memory of Turk somewhat. However, she doubted it would.

She decided to dress carefully and pay attention to her hair, letting it fall as a cascade of black silk to her shoulders where it curled inward just enough to give it bounce. Her pale gold ultrasuede jumper was offset by a deeper gold blouse. She uncapped her perfume and started to apply it to all the sensitive areas on her neck that Turk found so appealing. Bottle poised in the air, she stopped, put it back on the dresser, and reached for another fragrance instead. The L'Air du Temps would be a painful reminder of Turk throughout the evening and she wanted to forget.

The door buzzer sounded as she turned for a final glance in the full-length mirror before opening the door to meet her date. Frank Sawyer was good-looking in a tall, angular way with naturally fair skin. He had light tousled blond hair that gave him an interesting look.

It was easy to see that Frank was not too disappointed with her either from their first introductions. The thought occurred to Myrhia he was probably having second thoughts about the impending evening as she had. But she and Frank fell into a friendly conversation immediately about art and art shows, which seemed to set Carl and Belinda at ease somewhat and the evening got off to an easy start.

Myrhia had not seen Belinda for months and was pleased to see how happy she appeared to be in her husband's presence. Belinda had taken care to highlight her brown hair for tonight and it shone with gold lights and the sheath fit her well-formed body, making it appear more slender.

Myrhia wished that Carl had not chosen Elan's for the first part of their evening. Memories of Turk rose up to cloud her enjoyment. She would find herself only half listening to Frank's explanation of his art as her eyes scanned the crowded room, searching for a pair of blue-gray ones.

"I understand you also paint, Myrhia," Frank was saying. "I should like very much to see some of your work."

Myrhia forced her mind back to the present. "I'll be happy to show you what little I've done, Frank." Why did Turk's unseen spirit hover about the two of them? "Carl tells me you'll be having a gallery showing soon. Tell me about it." She hoped he wasn't aware of her preoccupation; he was a very nice man and deserved her full attention.

"I'm aiming for January. At least I've given myself a deadline. You probably understand how difficult it is to regulate time when you paint," he said, his pale blue eyes warming toward her.

"I think I do, but you see, my designing is in structural art and I have to conform to a time element, more or less. My delay is when I'm deadlocked on a new idea for a building—stymied so to speak. After that it goes easily." This was pleasant, Myrhia was thinking, having a normal, unheated conversation with a man. There was no controversy to mar their evening. Marriage with a man like Frank Sawyer would be pleasant and restful—though uninspiring. Would she ever be happy with the placidity and dullness of that type of marriage? Why was it she felt lost without the fire and lust of an encounter with someone like Turk? Was it possible now that a little of his aura had remained behind at Elan's to haunt her, keep her from enjoying the unruffled evening with Belinda's cousin?

Myrhia was still pondering about this as Frank deposited her at her apartment. She knew he was disappointed she had not invited him in for a nightcap, but there was no use in prolonging the evening.

The old home on Lakeside had not looked so Christmasy in years. Myrhia had admired the extravagantly decorated porch arch as she walked across the Exall Lake bridge Christmas Eve on her way toward her home for Alicia's holiday celebration. The interior was festooned in similar fashion with greens and poinsettias everywhere.

This year she had related closely to Alicia, feeling some of her mother's loneliness for her husband. Not that her loneliness for Turk could ever be the same, as they did not have what her parents had all those years together. Would they ever know that kind of happiness? Even so, she missed Turk more than she liked to admit to herself.

With all the catering done Myrhia was left free to help Mattie and Brady see that the tables were kept replenished. Some of Myrhia's friends came, making the party more gala for her. With Cleo around, things were always lively. One of her regrets was that Ted had not felt up to the party. For Letty's sake she hoped they would be able to come for just a short time anyway. She felt that having Turk's dearest friends near her would help ease some of the loneliness.

The party was a success socially, she supposed, as she looked over the sparkling crowd. From the candles to the tables loaded with delicacies to the fountain of champagne punch, tended by an ever watchful Brady, it was going well. Alicia moved from room to room like a pretty tree ornament herself, laughing, teasing, and enjoying the party. To see her mother sparkling this way lifted her own spirits.

As had been her custom the past two years since her father's death, Myrhia spent Christmas Eve in her old home. It was less lonely for both of them this way as she and her mother would have each other Christmas morning to share in a traditional exchange near the tree. Myrhia's gift of a mauve sweater set from Neiman's had pleased Alicia. "It's just the exact color of my wool plaid skirt, dear. I must say you've always had good color sense."

Tears sprang to Myrhia's eyes when she accepted a familiar velvet box from her mother, knowing what lay inside. "Grandmother's pearls! Alicia, I'm so thrilled." She had hugged her mother's neck fiercely.

"Your father said I was to give them to you on your wedding day, dear, but—" She hesitated before continuing. "I really feel you should be wearing them now, while you're young and lovely."

Myrhia wished with all her heart she could tell her mother she just might be wearing the pearls as her father wanted her to, but there was really nothing she could say about Turk, nothing concrete to hold to, and there was no use stirring up these hopes in her mother.

Alicia had plans for Christmas afternoon, leaving Myrhia free to go home. At her mother's insistence she left with a tray of hors d'oeuvres wrapped in foil and an entire chocolate cake that were left from the party the night before.

"Myrhia, dear, please take them and anything else you see in the kitchen. Mattie and Brady and I will not be able to eat it all. Besides, you can take it to your office or have a friend or two in yourself." Her unlined face drew a frown between the penciled brows. "I still wish there was some nice young man in your life."

She was juggling the loaded tray and the chocolate cake as she turned the lock in her apartment door and entered. Standing just inside the door, she had looked about the empty room, once again recalling Cleo's words. "It's restful and calm like a quiet pond. Like you, Myrhia."

"Damn!" she said out loud to the quiet pond. "I'm sick of calmness and peace. I want more than this."

Turning on her heel, she fled back into the hall, locked the door behind her, and, still carrying the food, took the elevator down to the first floor again.

She had been in her car driving endlessly and aimlessly for miles before she realized that subconsciously she had a definite destination in mind. She was headed for the Chappels'.

Not waiting to reconsider, she pulled into their driveway behind the van that had been equipped especially for Ted's wheelchair. She had pushed the buzzer when it occurred to her she might not be welcome. This, after all, was a family day and they probably were enjoying it together.

She was turning away when the door opened. John

grinned at the sight of her. "It's Miss Lassiter, Mom," he called back to Letty, who came across the room, her arms outstretched toward Myrhia in greeting.

"Merry Christmas!" Letty said, smiling.

"Merry Christmas to all of you." Myrhia said, handing the cake and tray of hors d'oeuvres to John, whose eyes lit up at sight of the cake.

"Chocolate cake! My favorite!" He bounded off to the kitchen carrying the two trays.

Letty laughed. "That boy! Honestly, you'd think he had a bottomless pit for a stomach. I can't fill him up for over thirty minutes at a time." She spoke fondly, looking back at her son's retreating figure. "I'm glad you dropped by," Letty said sincerely, her smile backing up the cordiality of the words, making Myrhia feel comfortable.

"Come over here, Miss Lassiter." John had returned from the kitchen, a big piece of the cake on a plate. "Come see what Uncle Turk bought us." He motioned her toward the television set. "See—Pac-Man! And all these other games can be played through the set too. We just got it set up. Wanta play a game with me and Teddy? Winner plays the third man?"

Myrhia turned to Letty with a laugh. "Okay with you, Letty?"

"Sure, that way I'll be spared for a while. Here, let me take your coat." She took Myrhia's coat from her and looked at her quizzically. "You know, we were just talking about you. Have you heard from Turk?"

"Yes, I have," she answered, wondering why there was no embarrassment now in talking about him to Letty. "I also have the loveliest jade statue you've ever seen."

"Good for Turk! He's improving. Just you wait—I have an idea things are coming to a head." She walked from the room, carrying Myrhia's coat as her teasing laugh trailed behind over her shoulder.

Myrhia noticed Ted was not in the room with them, but she said nothing, hoping that he was not worse. An hour or so later she and the boys were in the middle of an exciting game in which she was trailing when she looked up to see Ted being pushed into the room.

"Myrhia's here," Letty said softly, taking his hand. "You remember—Turk's Myrhia."

"Turk's Myrhia"—even though it might not be so, just the sound of it pleasured Myrhia.

It was suppertime, and they were exhausted from Pac-Man and hungry. Myrhia insisted she go for pizzas, and with the two boys directing her to the nearest Pizza Hut, she bought two enormous ones along with Cokes.

Later, as she was leaving, they followed her to the car. Letty gave her a hug. "Hurry back," she said sincerely.

"You'd better practice somewhere, Myrhia, if you don't want to get skunked again," John teased.

"We challenge you and Turk sometime, if he ever comes home," Teddy said.

When she returned home her apartment didn't seem as bleak and lonely this time.

The passing of the holidays no longer concerned her now, three weeks later, as she let the batiste drape fall against the window and blot out the bleak day of sleet and ice. This was Dallas's first heavy weather of the winter. It would slow the traffic along the arteries of travel in the city, and definitely slow down construction, delaying the final raising of the framework for the Tarrington, which had been scheduled for completion in three weeks.

Stepping into her living room, Myrhia's full attention fell on a lilac jade statue that stood like a slender thread of hope on her small credenza. Even in the darkened room it offered a measure of reassurance that with this priceless gift had come love. Turk's card had read.

Darling,

I'm desolate that we can't share Christmas together. I wanted to present this in person and I had scheduled a trip home, but something has come up that requires my attention in Bangkok. Christmas is not the same over here, of course, and business as usual. The statue's beauty doesn't compare with yours, my beautiful Myrhia, but it's a small token of my deep affection and ever-growing need for you. I'll expect full payment for this extravagant frivolity when I return. I never knew that months could be so long.

I understand from my office that you handled our super in a fine manner. I wish I had been there to observe M. Lassiter in action defending her shop drawings. Letty informs me the topping-off party will be on schedule. She also tells me you and she have become friends and that you visited her family. She and Ted appreciated it and have fallen under your spell, as have I.

Turk

P.S. You are to remind me I have something very important to discuss with you that will influence our futures.

A thrill of expectation ran through her mind as she reread the brief note from Turk. Did she dare hope that what was important was a declaration of love or a commitment of some kind. She dared not opt for marriage, as Turk did not impress her as the kind of man who would want to assume responsibility for a wife and perhaps a family. What he wanted to tell her probably related to the building—a change in the outer facade or something of the sort. Since it was no doubt business, she could not allow her heart to take hope.

As she turned the statue over and over in her graceful hands, she felt the cool smoothness of its lines with sensitive fingers. Whose ancient talent had created this beautiful work of art and had that person dreamed of the pleasure his carving would bring to others as he chipped and polished each tiny curve of the twelve-inch figure of a Chinese woman? The lilac jade statue was one of the rarest pieces Myrhia had ever seen.

Turk had known what would delight her, his perception surprised her—one of the qualities she had adored in her father. No doubt her father would have approved of Turk as a son-in-law. From her architecture studies of early Oriental cultures, she had learned about the jade carvings. This piece, due to its lilac color, was jadeite and one of the rarest kinds, more valuable than nephrite jade.

With a final caress of its cool exterior Myrhia set the priceless statue back on her credenza, wishing the giver was close enough for her to run her fingers over his finely chiseled face and sensuous lips. It had been so long. Would she feel the same racing of blood along the telegraphic responses of her body at sight of him?

Three weeks could be an eternity and with the bad weather settling in, would Turk decide to postpone his return until he was assured the party for the building was scheduled on time. She had so little to cling to during these four months. But then, why did a spark of hope, weakly nurtured in his absence, suddenly take on new life, gaining strength with each short, terse note from him?

With a sigh Myrhia turned and walked to her kitchen to make her single cup of coffee and drink a small glass of orange juice. She had lost what little appetite she had these past months. She had been working too hard, she reasoned, but each time she tried on a favorite skirt or pair of pants and found them sagging a little, she wondered if Turk would notice she was too thin.

Determined to change her habits this morning she toasted two pieces of cinnamon bread and found it tasted delicious to her. This was a good sign that everything, in spite of the inclement weather, would be coming out all right. The growing hope, so long dormant, rose again. Was it possible that Letty was right? Was Turk unable to express love in words? Surely he had led her to believe he loved her many times and on occasions it hadn't been all sex and body chemistry. There had been times of tenderness when they were not touching physically yet sharing the same room, and the closeness between them was warm.

These thoughts were quickly forgotten when she reached her car and headed onto the Central Expressway. She concentrated on keeping her car going at a moderate rate of speed along the highway and staying in the proper lane. Fortunately the sleet was not sticking to the pavements, but by nightfall driving would be hazardous if the temperature continued to drop as it often did in these January spells. She would have to close her office early to allow Trish and Jack to get home before that happened and do likewise herself.

Trish and Jack were both apologetic when they arrived an hour later than she had. Laughing off their concern, she thanked them for coming at all, feeling grateful for their loyalty. They made a big pot of coffee and Myrhia produced some fresh honey buns she had picked up at the small bakery near the office. A spirit of camaraderie prevailed among the three, as was so often true when the first bad days of winter drew people together in companionship.

Carl surprised her with a call midmorning to tell her that the work on the Tarrington Building would not be hampered much by the surprise storm and all was still on schedule for the topping-off party on the fifteenth.

"This will be a big occasion, Myrhia," Carl said. "By the time you have attended a dozen topping-off parties, it will be old hat."

Myrhia laughed at that. "I wonder if there will be others. So far just the idea of attending this one is enough excitement for a lifetime. Tell you the truth, I never thought I'd get the opportunity."

"By the way, Myrhia, Frank will be in town by the middle of February. His showing has been moved to New York. He wanted you to know. I'm sure he'd like to see you again. Have you heard from him?"

"No, I haven't—that is not recently." She had been negligent in continuing a correspondence with him. Should she tell Carl that she had discouraged Frank from further communication? Not that she didn't find him attractive and likable, but there was nothing between them—no spark or fire. It would be a waste of time for either of them to try for something more.

"I doubt he figures me into his love life, Carl."

"Don't be too sure about that, Myr. I saw how he looked at you last time. Besides, you and Frank would have a lot in common to start on."

"I know," she sighed, weary of the conversation. "If Frank does come, tell him to call. He knows where to find me. Who knows? It might be better this time around."

As she set the receiver back in its cradle, Myrhia wondered why she had said that. Frank's coming would certainly interfere with Turk's return to Dallas. She could become involved in strange mix-ups. One man was interested in her for certain reasons only and the other would probably ask her to marry him for their common interests.

She started into the outer office, when the buzzer sounded once more. "I think it's Mr. Muldrow again."

"Yes, Carl?" she said, smiling into the receiver. "Did you forget part of your lecture?"

"Now, that's being unfair." He sounded grim. "I hope you don't fly off the handle. Just had a call from Mac at the construction site. He'd tried to get you, but I had your telephone tied up. It's like this—a trailer transport just pulled onto the lot and the guys are trying to unload the first pile of curtain glass out of the piggy-back. Mac said he's trying to hold them off until he hears from you. I hope I stopped it by telling Mac the commission voted for precast concrete slabs as your shop drawings specified. Not curtain glass!

"Doug raced out there to show Mac and the driver of the transport your drawings. They're waiting now. Shall I call Mac for you?" he asked worriedly.

"No!" She bit down on her words as anger engulfed her. "Only one man could have given the order for curtain glass. Turk Vaughan! He's trying to discredit me! I'll call Mac myself." She hung up on Carl, cutting off conversation abruptly to dial her trailer office.

Mac, apparently waiting for her call, answered the telephone. "Miss Lassiter, the order came from the office of Vaughan Associates. It was requisitioned two months ago by someone there, the driver said."

Her thoughts were whirling. That could mean only one man—Turk. He had tried to override his own commission in his usual highhanded manner. She was strangling on disappointment. Turk had seemed more compatible with her on their plans lately, but now she was quite certain he was merely softening her up after all.

"Thanks, Mac, for holding off out there. Do I need to come?"

"Not necessary. Your assistant showed the drawings to the driver. He's turning around now—not happy, I assure you, but he's going back for now," he said, his voice less raspy than usual, almost as if he was amused over the incident.

At least this incident had passed without altercations so far. She had no idea how Turk would react when he found out the truck had been turned around with its first load of curtain glass. It was a blow to find out how far Turk would go to get his way. Now she knew this was the important matter he wanted to discuss with her and she suspected the lilac statue was just a peace offering to smooth over the trick he had tried to play on her.

She walked to her wide office window and stared unseeing into the sombre atmosphere. The sleet had almost disappeared but a heavy mist hung over the city. She shuddered, trying to rid herself of her thoughts, which were as bleak as the day had been, then turned and made ready to go home.

The cold spell lasted a short two days. As was often normal for the southwest, a gradual warming crossed over Texas, leaving clear days with the temperature in the fifties. Myrhia had counted on the erratic weather change to help in the erection of the frame of the Tarrington.

For the past few weeks she caught up on her work load, thanks to Jack's recent addition to her office. He had freed her to spend more time in the trailer office where Doug tried loyally to hold off Mac and his assistants over small matters that meant right or wrong with her plans.

Before she realized it, February 14 had arrived. The topping-off party had been confirmed, but there had still been no word from Turk. Even Letty had not heard from him, as she called the office from time to time to see if there was any change in plans for tomorrow. Myrhia had succeeded in packing her emotions concerning him in angry ice, talking herself into believing she no longer cared if he was here for the big event or not. She dared not think along those lines for long, as she felt momentary lapses of memory that caused her pain.

She was about to leave her office Friday when Frank appeared. He looked well, a bright flush on his normally pale cheeks. Myrhia sensed the glow about him had something to do with his New York showing.

"I can see you're pleased with your show, Frank," Myrhia said, walking toward him with her hands outstretched. "How many attended?"

"About two hundred," he said, taking her hands in his. "I sold several hundred dollars worth of originals—twelve pictures in all—and have been commissioned to do a mural for one of the newer federal buildings in New York State. It will be built sometime next year." His face was radiant with his enthusiasm. "I tell you, I was almost overcome by it all."

She could relate to the feeling; it was akin to her own feelings when a design proposal was accepted. "I think this calls for a celebration," she said, turning him around and pointing him out the office door. "I've a bottle of wine cooling in the refrigerator for just such an occasion. We'll toast your future success."

"I came to invite you out for dinner tonight. That is, if you don't have other plans."

"Some other time, Frank. I'm really beat tonight, but come on to the apartment anyway. I'll fix us something to go with the wine."

"If you feel up to it, Myrhia, it will be fine."

They parted outside the building entrance to go to their separate cars. As Myrhia started to the parking lot, her heart did a flip at sight of a blue Mercedes pulling away from in front of the building. She was certain the driver was Turk or why would her nerves be jangling this way? Why hadn't he called to tell her he was in town? Had he seen her come out of the building with Frank and jumped to conclusions? All these questions raced through her mind.

Still feeling the electric awareness he brought to the surface in her, she drove thoughtfully homeward. If she didn't hurry, Frank would be there first. The situation could be awkward if Turk decided to stop by too. She hoped not. After weeks of silence she had plenty to say to him if he did, but not in front of Frank.

Frank was waiting for her when she entered her apartment foyer. They rode the elevator and stepped out onto her floor. Frank turned suddenly, one arm circling her waist, his eyes bright and full of warmth. His free hand cupped her face and his lips were gentle on hers.

"I don't make bells ring for you, do I?" he said sadly.

"It's not your fault, Frank. The fault is all mine. I just can't handle it now." She lay a hand on his arm.

He held her close a second more before releasing her but not before his lips brushed her cheek once more. "Myrhia, I—"

His sentence hung suspended between them as the second elevator door opened and Turk stepped out into the hallway. He took a long look and stopped moving, surprise exploding over his handsome face. Slowly the surprise faded to be replaced by anger, and his eyelids closed to narrow slits over the steel-gray behind them.

"I see you don't waste time between men, do you, Myrhia?"

Frank's arm tensed around her waist, pulling her back against him as if to protect her from Turk's fury. "You have no reason to speak to her that way." Frank's terse words must have struck a blow to Turk as he winced before turning away.

In that moment Myrhia found strength to vent all the pent-up frustration, disappointment, and love she felt for Turk and it burst like a dam over him.

"You—you—" she spluttered. "How do you have the nerve to face me at all? Of all the sneaky tricks! Overriding your own committee's vote and sending in curtain glass to be used on the outside of the building after all. What did you do that for?" Taking a deep breath, she plunged in again. "Besides, I've only heard from you twice in all these months and then you try to soften me with a bribe, sending the statue. Well, you can just take it back. If you'll wait right here, I'll get it for you. Now!"

Frank was standing uncomfortably, rocking from one foot to another, shocked by her tirade and staring first at Myrhia and then at Turk. He was not the only one who was stunned by her attack, she noticed, as a perplexed look replaced the anger in Turk's face.

"Curtain glass! Did you say curtain glass?" he repeated angrily. "So you think that I—I don't know what the hell you're babbling about, but now is not the time to air our differences. I'll just bow out and wish you and your new conquest a good evening." Turning to Frank, he said coldly, "I hope she's more receptive to you."

Spinning on his heel, he caught the next elevator at

the right time and stepped inside. While the door closed she continued to stare at him, imprisoned on blue-gray spikes that no longer reflected anger but a sorrowful pain. In that moment she knew he had not ordered the curtain glass siding for the building. The mistake was someone else's.

She stood seconds longer staring at the closed elevator door, conscious of Frank's stare at the back of her head. He spoke first.

"Myrhia, I'll take a raincheck on that glass of wine. You're too upset for now."

He took her gently by the shoulders and turned her to face him. "I don't know who that was or what it was all about, but I do know what I witnessed is more than just a business quarrel between two people. I can understand why I'm not making tracks with you myself. You love him, don't you?"

"Yes," she answered sadly, leaning her forehead on his chest. "And I don't know what to do about it."

Frank held her close a moment or two more, stroking her hair as he might a child's. "I think you'll both find a way." She felt his muscles tense as he set her away from him. "I envy the man." Frank took one more long look at Myrhia and with a sad smile punched the elevator button. "Good luck, Myrhia." She felt a sense of loss as she watched the elevator door close.

Her apartment felt cold. Myrhia checked the thermostat and found it above normal heating, walked to her bedroom to slip out of her suit into her warmest robe, feeling the chill creeping into her bones. Why was she trembling? Was it possible she was coming down with something? She was never sick, so it couldn't be that. A cup of hot tea would warm her. As she came back from the kitchen, she passed the credenza. The lovely nude statue seemed to glow in the semi-darkness. She stopped, taking the figurine lovingly in her hands to feel again the cool jade under her fingertips.

Carrying it with her, she walked back to her bedroom and set it on the bedside table, feeling that somehow the little china lady would bring her comfort throughout the night. Would she and Turk ever be able to communicate normally with one another, even as two friends might do? They had passed the friendship stage long ago. Now what they had was heartbreakingly tender at times and if they could learn to understand each other, they would have it all.

The hot tea failed to warm her so she set the cup down on her bedside table. A good night's sleep before tomorrow was what she needed. She had almost forgotten the topping-off party because of all that happened. Now she worried that Turk would not make his appearance. It was a traditional affair, a milestone in the erection of any new skyscraper. The dedication party, at the building's completion, would be the formal affair with catered food, champagne, and all the dignitaries with their wives. That would not be for over a year until the building was finished. Perhaps the novelty had worn off for Turk, who had been erecting tall buildings since football days.

She dropped off to sleep quickly in spite of the uneasy turmoil of her mind. Her last thought was guilt that she had not called Turk to apologize for her outburst and had not waited for him to defend himself. Now it was too late. He probably hated her.

Her bedside telephone waked her from a troubled sleep and a glance at the clock showed it was past midnight. Who could be calling now?

She answered sleepily. Turk's voice sounded hoarse and husky. "I'm sorry, Myrhia, but I thought you might still be up. Did I wake you?"

"Yes, but—" Her voice trembled and her heart began a frightening beat.

"I wanted to confirm our date for tomorrow's party. I presume you'll be there? How about four o'clock?"

"Fine—that will be fine, Turk." She felt a nauseous excitement at hearing his voice now so calm and cold as if he barely knew her. "Turk, I'm sorry. I jumped to conclusions about the panels. It's a bad habit of mine."

"That's all right. I owe you several too." He paused. "If we take it carefully, we might be able to settle this between us." Another pause followed by a clearing of his throat. "Did your friend leave early?"

"Quite early. In fact, he didn't stay at all."

"Oh, a paragon of virtue! Am I supposed to swallow that?"

He was baiting her again but she refused to grow angry. "You can believe what you want to, Turk. Besides, I don't need to justify my dating to you. You have no claim on me, you know." She felt suddenly proud of the way she was holding back.

"Are you certain about that? My not having claim? We'll see about that tomorrow." There was a long pause, so long she thought he must have hung up. "It will be a long night without you, darling," he said softly.

Myrhia lay for some time listening to the rapid pounding of her heart while questions surged in and out of her mind. Why hadn't he come instead of telephoning? Was he checking to see if Frank spent the night in her bed? Would tomorrow bring them close again or was his invitation to call for her a gracious gesture on his part and only that? Would he carry out his end of the bargain to see the building through its various stages and then walk away?

Sleep came at last some time in the wee hours. When

she woke, the morning sunlight was sending shafts of gold across her bed and over the lilac statue, giving it an unnatural glow, as if the little lady were alive. Myrhia hoped it was a good omen for the day before her first topping-off party, which she would remember always. But, she realized, with an ardent flutter inside her, that she was looking forward to seeing Turk even more than the party, important as it was to her.

Rising, she picked up the small statue and, cradling it in her hand, carried it back to the dining room to its usual place of honor while she whipped through breakfast. A glance at the kitchen clock told her she had slept most of the morning and she was starved. It would have to be brunch now with a sweet roll, bacon, and scrambled eggs added to her usual juice and coffee.

Feeling better with each bite, she made up her mind not to let anyone or anything spoil this day. With this thought in mind and a tidy kitchen left behind her, she would have time for a shampoo and leisurely bath. Today she would take time to towel dry her hair, curling the ends under at the last minute. She intended to let it fall shoulder length, shining and slightly waved.

As the bath bubbles rose and burst in their foam, the fragrance floated about her. Jasmine always reminded Myrhia of moonlit nights in a summer garden where fireflies played their lantern games as she lingered, naive and innocent, to wonder about love and what it meant. Her mind turned to Turk as always. His angry, beautiful face now reflected in her mind's eye seemed close enough to reach out and touch. Would he want to make love to her again? This time she would not turn away—not even if she knew their love would be short-lived. She had come to a decision to experience the ultimate with the man she loved, the man she would remember all her life.

She stepped from the warm tub, almost reluctantly, to begin toweling her hair. With quick deft rubs she managed to dry most of the moisture from it before wrapping the bath sheet around her body. As Myrhia stepped into her bedroom, the door buzzer sounded. Twisting the towel turban fashion around her damp hair and tightening the twist of knot in the bath sheet above her breasts, she stepped to the door.

"Yes, who is it?" she asked through the closed door.

"Turk, Myrhia. Let me in!" As usual his voice held the ring of authority she had come to accept as part of his personality.

"Just a minute," she said, sliding back the bolt to peer through the narrow opening at him.

Turk was dressed impeccably. It took her breath away to look at him. If anything, he was more attractive than she wished him to be at that moment. They stared at one another through the crack in the door. "Well, darling, are you going to open the door?"

Forgetting she wasn't dressed in her excitement, she released the catch and they flowed together. She was in his arms as his lips came down hard on hers. He lifted her off the floor with his compelling passion. Her lips were responding, giving, touching as her tongue traced the beautiful contours of his mouth until she was gasping for breath.

As they broke apart her turban fell, releasing a cascade of dark silk to her shoulders. Loosened by the embrace, the bath sheet followed suit and she stood before him not unlike the lilac statue observing them from the credenza. With a groan Turk swept her up, fastening his lips to hers as he carried her to her unmade bed and laid her down gently, then eased his big frame down beside her. His smile was sweet as he looked at her, his hands warm and vibrant as they touched and teased her skin, stirring and creating a desire in her she had never known possible.

His movements became catlike, smooth and fluid as a dreamy quality engulfed them. His eyes, shining with passion, moved over each seductive curve of her body as his warm hands played over the silken skin. "You are as I imagined, my darling," he said huskily, "lovely and so beautiful."

"Don't you think you'd better remove your clothes?" she whispered, beginning to untie his silk maroon tie.

He rose slowly, not taking his eyes from her and calmly and methodically removed each piece of clothing. She continued to watch, fascinated by the muscular beauty of his body, until he stood before her like some Grecian statue of old. There was no embarrassment between them. This was the way it was destined to be.

"You're one gorgeous male, Turk Vaughan," she whispered as he lay down beside her and took her in his arms. "Someday I want to sketch you."

It was her turn to touch, to feel, to trace the curve of his body over his shoulders and down his back, feeling the small ripples of pleasure her touch brought him as his flesh responded. Soft moans of enjoyment followed the course of her fingertips and she felt the tremble of desire as his flesh quivered under her hand. "I love your body, Turk," she whispered against his cheek, finding it hard to speak with the new emotion almost choking her.

He pulled her close, his hands doing their own seeking and fondling, until they reached a peak of desire together. It was then he claimed her in a timeless rapture of love that would be forever young.

After the explosion of ecstasy had subsided, they clung together. It was Turk who finally broke the silence between them. "My darling, I've dreamed of this for months." He fingered the damp strands of her hair as they lay in each other's arms, passion momentarily spent.

"You'll never belong to another. You're mine! Understand?" he said, nuzzling below her ear with his lips, giving her a pleasant tingle.

Surely he must *love* her as she did him, Myrhia sighed contentedly. She could read it in his eyes but still she longed for him to say it. Tracing his lips with her fingertip, she felt his body tense once again and marveled at this need between them. Once again his passion claimed her, more binding than before. No matter what happened after today or in the future, she knew there could never be this closeness with anyone but the man now lying spent with his arms around her. They were linked in a new awareness, neither wanting to break the spell, but it was Turk who glanced at his watch.

"Myrhia, my darling, it's high time that M. Lassiter dons her finest casual togs and makes herself beautiful for her party—the first of many like it."

Slipping his arm around her shoulders once more, he kissed her gently as she reached for his face to pull it down to her throat again. "No," he said, "that will have to wait for now. We'll continue this scene in my apartment after the party. Then I have something to ask you. Two very important questions." His eyelids almost closed, hiding their secret, tantalizing her.

"What's wrong with right now?" she asked, sitting up.

"No, it'll bear waiting. You'll see," he said, teasing her.

As Turk rose, pulling her with him, his hands slid lovingly over her body and came to rest in the mass of raven dampness. "You'd better dry your hair." He pointed her toward the bathroom and gave her a gentle shove and a pat.

Grabbing her towel, Myrhia fled to the bathroom, calling over her shoulder, "You'd better dress in the living room. I won't be able to concentrate with those eyes watching every move."

"This time only I'll submit to being henpecked and abide by your request. But from now on I intend to watch every minute detail of your preparations for the day." He blew her a kiss, grabbing up his shorts and trousers to stride from the bedroom.

While the blow dryer hummed, she could only imagine what he was doing in the other part of the apartment. She was tingling all over from the wonder of what had just happened to her body. A glance at her face in the mirror told her all the world would know she loved him. Her green eyes were halfway glazed with lingering passion, and her lips, fuller than usual from the not so gentle kisses, gave her a sexy look.

Not daring to look at herself further in fear of running back into his arms and forgetting the whole afternoon before them, she began to apply a light touch of makeup to camouflage the glow in her face. Her hair now blown to a glossy sheen turned up just right above her naked shoulders. Turk had found her beautiful. That was enough—to be beautiful for the right man.

As Myrhia returned to the bedroom, she noticed that Turk had made the bed but was nowhere to be seen. She felt as if she were walking on air some minutes later as she entered the living room clothed in designer jeans and a silk blouse, which had been another extravagance bought at the time of the center commissioning. She had celebrated in her usual manner, indulging herself in a token frivolity. She wore the small emerald drop her father had given her on her sixteenth birthday. Somehow she felt today he should have a share in her good fortune. With the tiny gold earrings and gold bracelet to complete her jewelry, she walked with a spring in her step.

Turk was standing with his back to her, staring out of the window when she entered the living room. Outlined in the sunlight, his broad frame would be a perfect model for the mature male figure and if she only had the gift of sculpturing she would capture him as he was today.

He turned, a low whistle escaping his lips, to watch her walk toward him. "You're unreal! It's hard to believe that you can be all things to me." He circled her with his arms and buried his face in her hair.

"You smell so good! But most of all you feel so good in my arms."

Myrhia raised her lips for his kiss. "Don't tempt me! You'll release another torrent within me," he said, kissing her cheek instead. "We'll need to be a little early." He gave her another intimate hug before releasing her and turning her to the door. "I could stay here all day, you know, but this is your big moment." Taking her arm, he led her toward the door.

"By the way, darling, Letty said to tell you she takes all the blame for the mix-up about the curtain glass. She gave the wrong set of orders to the company. Should have gone to a building in Fort Worth. She asked me to tell you how sorry she was and wished you the best of luck at the topping-off party. She won't be able to be with us, Ted is not feeling well."

"Oh, Turk, to think how I came down on you about the mix-up. I'm ashamed of my behavior, but you'd been teasing me so about it all along."

"No more about it. I would have jumped to the same conclusions about you if the problem had been reversed. I guess I had been tormenting you pretty hard about the siding."

"Poor Letty and Ted," Myrhia said sadly. "I certainly will forgive her. It's a wonder she can keep her mind on anything as it is."

"That's quite a family," Turk said with feeling.

Chapter Thirteen

As they drove toward Turtle Creek, a shaft of light reflected back on one of the tall girders at the twentieth floor of the building. A thrill passed over Myrhia and she reached for Turk's hand.

"Did you see it?" she asked, her excitement mounting.

"Yes, and it will be beautiful when it's finished—" He cut his eyes away from the traffic briefly to give her a wry grin. "I was going to say with the proper facade—the precast concrete. You're one hell of an architect, darling."

His sincerity touched her. "I didn't think you'd ever say that. You mean it, don't you?"

"You'll find I seldom say things I don't mean," he added, giving her hand a squeeze.

In spite of the reassurance his statement gave her, a small doubt crept into her mind, drawing away some of the afternoon's perfection. He had never said he loved her. Was she to believe he only needed her physically as he had just moments ago? The sweetness of their passion still lingered about them. Was love the one word he could not say in honesty? The pain of this thought caused her to remove her hand from his.

Turk turned to look at her, a puzzled frown marring his clear forehead. She made no explanation for her action and he looked away again, concentrating on driving into the parking area near the building. She could not let the fact he had not committed himself to saying he loved her ruin this afternoon. He had come back in time to be at her side during the ceremony.

Turk maneuvered his Mercedes through the other cars and into her reserved parking space. A crowd was already assembling as she and Turk joined the others. Carl had brought Belinda, who appeared to be excited over the event too. She said, "Myrhia, I am thrilled to be here. Carl invited me and it's the first topping-off party I've ever attended."

"Mine too," Myrhia said, laughing. "I just can't believe I've had a hand in all this."

"This is your moment, Myr," Carl said, giving her arm a squeeze. He looked deep into her face as if searching for something. She hoped her smile was reassuring, although it was difficult to conceal the soaring rapture her body had undergone so recently. It was hard to believe her heightened stimulation didn't show at this very moment, but perhaps others would attribute it to her excitement over the party.

The pressure of Turk's hand in hers was reassuring as they moved onto the cement floor supporting the tall girders. Several kegs of beer were being rolled onto the flooring and lifted onto huge wooden racks. At one end of the slab she could see several portable ovens already in operation and from the fragrant aroma of the barbecue turning on the spits it would taste delicious. Catering trucks were still arriving as uniformed waiters were kept busy carrying baked beans, buns, and relishes of all kinds to go with the barbecue. The food was spread on long makeshift tables, made by laying large sheets of lumber over sawhorses.

She looked up at Turk. "So this is the way it is! This is going to be some party."

"I'm glad I could be here with you. I wouldn't have missed your excitement and enjoyment for anything." He pulled her close and kissed her cheek. "This is an important send-off for any new skyscraper. It's a ritual in a way. A good luck party for the building. You'll find this is different from the dedication party at the end. I think I enjoy the topping-off party best."

"It couldn't be better," she said, feeling almost giddy with the thrill of it.

This afternoon's party was for the workmen who erected the building: the superintendent, his assistants, and all the crew. The hard-hat bunch and their families were all gathering now. As the architect she had a special place at the party. She knew that later they observed an old custom of hoisting an evergreen to the top of the framework. The custom, which had come over from Europe decades ago, was to ward off evil spirits and ensure the dwelling's good fortune. She had learned also that the Europeans often hauled a tree or branch of evergreen to the rooftop of their new homes for good luck.

The party was in full swing by four o'clock. Carl was acting as master of ceremonies and stepped to a make-shift stage to call for silence. As the crowd quieted he announced from a small podium in front of the group, "This is an exciting occasion. You men and your superintendents on the job should be congratulated for raising the framework of the Tarrington in record time. Most of you and your families have attended these get-togethers before, but today I want to share a proud moment with our architect. This is her first topping-off party. Myrhia Lassiter!" He motioned for Myrhia to join him on the platform. She was standing off to one side with Turk and was surprised at Carl's announcement. She had not been expecting to be called forward.

"Come on up, Myrhia. I want you to be standing up here when they raise the tree to the twentieth floor of your building. This is your first tall structure—but it most certainly won't be your last."

There was a round of applause as she started toward the platform, but Turk laid his hand on her arm, detaining her for a moment as he whispered, "I'm proud of you. Go to it! You've earned the praise."

Myrhia watched breathlessly as the rope was untied from a pulley and a small fir tree was fastened securely before making its climb upward toward the twentieth floor. With each tug of the rope she could feel her heart rise in her chest. The excitement was overwhelming in that moment as the spectators watched quietly below, their faces turned upward, following the slow progress of the evergreen. Myrhia knew this moment would be forever etched in memory. Oddly, she felt a sense of complete accord with Turk in that moment as if she could feel his support, but she did not dare turn to face him, afraid she might give herself away.

When the tree reached its height, it swung like a tiny toy. Now the city would see a new building would soon be added to Dallas's skyline. Myrhia looked down at Turk then, her eyes seeking his agate ones, and felt rewarded by the warmth she found there. As he stepped closer to her, reaching up to take her hand, she saw something more shining from their depths, a soft, unreadable look she had seen on other occasions when she had expected him to say he loved her.

Carl reached her other side at the same time. "Well, Myr," he said, wearing his lopsided grin. "You're on your way!" He turned to Turk who was looking at him quizzically. "Vaughan, old fellow, you'll have to go a long way to find another architect as good as Myrhia."

Turk's expression broke into a dazzling smile of his

own. "Don't I know that? I'm aware of my good luck in many ways, Muldrow." He looked into Myrhia's face as if making certain she was reading his meaning. She felt a shiver of delight at her own immediate understanding.

Turk gave Myrhia a light hug and stepped onto the platform between her and Carl. "I'd like to make an announcement. I had thought I'd keep it from Miss Lassiter until later, but now seems to be a good time while enthusiasm is high." He waited until the crowd became attentive and moved closer to the platform. Myrhia felt her nerves begin to tingle. What was he about to announce? It was difficult to tell as he gave her a disarming smile and held up his hands to quiet the group of guests who were looking from her to Turk, questions on their faces.

"For those of you who have been working close to our architect these past months and those of you who are her good friends, I'd like you to know I hope to commission M. Lassiter as architect for a multimillion-dollar hotel in Yokohama, Japan. Plans are for the building to be erected within the next four years." Turk turned toward her, his gray gaze burning into hers. "That is, if she'll accept the commission. There is no one more qualified in our country, as far as I am concerned."

Myrhia gasped. He wanted her to design the hotel. The short news flash returned to mind.

"There's only one architect in the United States I'd trust to design a building of this size and class," he had said. Now she went hot and cold. Would she be able to please him? As friends crowded around to congratulate her, she suddenly knew that with Turk's confidence in her she could design the most beautiful hotel Japan had ever seen. This was his surprise he had promised, a chance to show what she could do in a foreign country.

While her mind soared with the excitement of his announcement, she tried to reassure her heart she really couldn't expect more from him, but her contrary heart wouldn't listen.

It was fortunate that everyone believed her answer would be in the affirmative, she was thinking, as at this moment she wouldn't have been able to answer Turk at all. She was having difficulty breathing and to speak would be out of the question. This excitement would never come again. A hotel in Japan! How many architects had that opportunity to be chosen without having to enter competition and be judged and wait all those agonizing months for a committee to decide the fate of their design. Her eyes blurred with unshed tears as she looked into Turk's intent gaze. The eyes were warmly gentle.

She nodded and acknowledged the congratulations and comments from many of the workmen and their wives. Most of them she recognized on sight, having seen them on a daily basis.

"I see you've won over most of the men who work with you." Turk had been standing to one side, watching her move among them. "I expect some of the young ones are madly in love with the lady architect. It's easy to see that your assistant is smitten." He nodded toward Doug, who was wearing a grin as big as a slice of melon.

"Oh, not Doug! He's just proud of the way the others have come around. It wasn't that easy at first."

"I just wondered how much competition I was having from all these guys. I think there's one exception." Turk gestured toward Mac Blount, who was standing off to one side talking to one of the subcontractors. "He's probably capitulated, but doesn't want to admit it." His eyes held a hint of humor. "Some of us are like that. I learned from Carl he tried to override you a time or two. Carl told me you handled him like a pro." Myrhia looked up at Turk, surprised to find his eyes warm and passionate. He looked at her caressingly. Thank God! There was no more jealousy of Carl.

"I hope I can please you and your Japanese partners, Turk. I'm going to do my best. By the way, I saw you on television, towering over the two Japanese. You can't imagine how I felt seeing you like that." She smiled up at him. "I wish you knew how excited I feel now."

"I do know how lovely you look just now and as far as pleasing my partners and me, you needn't worry on that score. They'll be enchanted with you, but, darling, you've already pleased me in more ways than you know." He pulled her close.

Suddenly a crooked grin sparked a devilish look in his face. "Did you know at the time you saw the TV broadcast that I meant you?" He stared down at her. "No, I can see you didn't. I hoped you would be watching and could just see you stomping over to your television set and furiously turning the off button. I could almost hear it snap." He chuckled.

It was odd he had imagined her striding to the TV to turn it off. She had done just that, erupting like a volcano at his announcement. Now she could confess her reaction to him and laugh about it.

"Let's just say I was upset with you when you said that only one architect in the U.S. could handle the hotel design. Naturally I had no idea you thought of me at all—now, how could I? You and I have fought over the Tarrington Building since we first met."

His smile was sardonic. "Don't you know why?"

"Perhaps now a little, but not at the time." She laughed in answer.

"As soon as we can comfortably break away from

here, I'm going to kidnap you. I have plans for you." The remark tempered her former disappointment that he had not told her he loved her. Perhaps this was his way—to throw the biggest prize in her direction, giving her the honor of creating something beautiful in a country already known for its artistry. She would learn not to expect the usual from Turk. Perhaps he would never be able to give her love. He might never be able to say that to anyone. She would have to be satisfied he had accepted her professionally.

It seemed to Myrhia gallons of beer were consumed and pounds of barbecue eaten before the workmen began to drift away from the party. She felt warmed by the sometimes grudging remarks of a few of the men, who had been hardened by years of construction jobs and were accustomed to taking their orders from a man. She hoped now it would be easier between her and the super until the final dedication party—with luck, possibly next year. These men risked their lives at times and she could understand their need to believe in the person responsible for the way the building was constructed.

"I think we can slip away now." Turk had her arm in his firm grasp as he made a hasty move toward his car with her.

As they drove out into the traffic again, Turk reached over for her free hand. "I'm taking you home with me for a change," he said, bringing her hand to his lips. "I've already spilled one of the things I had to tell you. I still have the most important one."

Myrhia's heart raced in anticipation. This had turned out to be quite a day, full of surprises, and it wasn't over yet. Anything could happen from now on.

Chapter Fourteen

Turk's apartment was large and masculine, like the man who occupied it. Myrhia noticed his excellent taste in choosing soft, warm colors of browns and rosy beiges, complimented by rare art objects from different countries he had visited. He had laid two logs in the gray stone fireplace that reached to the ceiling. Two overstuffed sectional sofas, covered with matching cushions, faced the fireplace. It was definitely a bachelor's playground and she couldn't help wondering how many women had been seduced by his charm on the soft carpet before that fireplace.

A strong impulse to run flew a warning flag in her mind—to run before she became another conquest. But even as the thought surfaced she knew she could not leave him. Her pulse raced at the sight of his broad shoulders bent toward the fireplace as he worked the logs.

As she turned away her gaze fell on a lovely Steinway piano at one end of the long room. She had forgotten that Letty had told her of his ability to play the piano. She had called his touch professional. Would he play for her? She would wait a while to see if he felt at ease enough to share his talent with her.

"Myrhia." Turk looked at her strangely when she turned back to him. "Do you like my apartment?"

"I do. It's quite beautiful. In fact it feels warm and friendly." She was discovering a different Turk underneath the big, strong football image he presented to the public. She was fortunate to find the quiet, thoughtful, and often tender side of him. She glanced around the room, surprised there was no sign of a trophy or plaque to indicate what a star he had been in his Dallas Cowboy days.

He kissed her gently on the forehead. "You can freshen up in my bedroom, darling. I'll fix us a drink."

His bedroom was almost as large as the living room. Here was the celebrity. One end of the room was covered with pictures, mementos, silver cups, and trophies accumulated over the years. Here was the football image, the man who could turn women's hearts. Now she had come full circle around the two sides of the man she loved.

Myrhia lingered longer than necessary, browsing over the many pictures of Turk. In high school—a tall, long-armed, gangling boy with a haunting expression in his eyes. Later, in college, the pictures showed him more filled out, handsome, and sure of himself as if he knew where he was headed. Then the army pictures surrounded by his comrades, a look of compassion and determination etched in their young faces. Then there were a few pictures of his Dallas Cowboy years where he looked big, confident, cocky, and proud. All the chapters of his life to date lay before her. She wondered if she would be a part of the final ones.

Myrhia reached out to touch a portrait of Turk made toward the end of his outstanding football career. While her fingers traced the outline of his face, she heard piano music coming softly from the living room.

Excitement crowded previous thoughts out of her mind as she stood immobile, too fascinated to move for the moment.

As if compelled by the chords of music, she walked softly from the bedroom. Turk had his back to her as she moved toward him, watching his long fingers move skillfully over the keyboard. He was playing a medley of love songs that drifted into "Lara's Theme."

She walked up behind him, placing her hands on his shoulders, feeling his flesh tremble through his clothing at her touch. She marveled she had that effect on him. Turk looked over his shoulder and smiled at her as he changed from the familiar love songs she knew to one she didn't know. His long fingers began a melody that was hauntingly beautiful. Myrhia stood transfixed listening to its seductive quality. When he finished, she found her voice.

"That lovely melody! What is it?"

"My own composition. It is called 'Love Song to Myrhia.'" He turned and pulled her into his lap as his arms crushed her to him and his warm lips found hers. "That was the only way I could tell you, Myrhia. I love you. Will you marry me?"

Words strangled in her throat but there was no need for words. "Yes, Turk, I will marry you." Her eyes misted with unshed tears. "I love you too."

She could feel the rapid beating of his heart as he held her close, conscious only of a similar beating of her own. "How long have you known, Turk?" Myrhia asked, her head still cradled on his shoulder.

"That I loved you?" he whispered softly, his warm breath teasing a spot below her ear. "I have loved you all my life, but never found you. That's how it's been with me—ever since I found out M. Lassiter, Architect, was the woman I wanted to spend my life with. I confess, darling, I fought it. I had to come to terms with my weakness and acknowledge it. Then I—'' He stopped talking to brush the hair back from her forehead and kiss her gently.

He continued, his voice low and husky. "I discovered what I had considered weakness was my strength. I had been misled into believing anything artistic or beautiful was produced by weaklings. It took me some time to learn from a very beautifully designed package of feminine wiles that artistic talent and strength of purpose go hand in hand." His mouth claimed hers preventing an answer at the moment.

They walked silently arm in arm, to the sofa before the fireplace. Two wineglasses were waiting with a bottle of Château Lafite cooling in a silver bucket on the glass-topped fireside table.

Before releasing his hands from around her, he leaned closer; a flicker of amusement passed across his eyes. "Besides, I decided it would be good business to keep Texas's most promising architect in Vaughan Associates."

As the logs sputtered and crackled into life, they sipped their wine with Turk sitting at her feet, the long fingers of one hand laced through Myrhia's. She was awash with contentment as the hearth flames grew stronger and burst in a shower of sparks, making the only sound in the room.

She released her hand from his to pull his head close to her knee while she ran her fingers through his hair, tousling it in a captivating disarray that made him look even more sensuous and desirable to her.

Turk finally stirred beside her, turning to look into her face. "Do you know how much you mean to me?"

"Can you tell me?"

"I can show you better." He eased her effortlessly onto the soft carpet in front of the fire.

"You were made to be loved, and I intend to spend my remaining years doing just that."

"I can't think of any objections to that at the moment," she teased, beginning to unbutton his shirt. As each button was released she pulled him over to kiss the exposed portions of his chest. When the last came undone, she let her fingers roam over his muscled shoulders while he sighed with pleasure.

Turk pulled back slightly and drew her face up to his, his gray eyes gleaming in the firelight. One hand came up to gently caress her cheek before he allowed his fingers to descend, featherlight, to her neck and breast. His eyes continued to devour her as his hands began to undo the buttons of her blouse. His lips and fingers made love to her by the merest touch as he continued to undress her. When she lay before him in silk panties and bra, he moved to be free of his own hampering clothing, never taking his eyes from her lips.

When at last he was unencumbered, he slipped the small scraps of silk from her body and stared. "You're all woman, my darling." His lips crushed hers, weaving a sensuous web of love around them as the firelight shadows danced over their bodies.

Caressing her breasts and raining kisses over the sensitive areas of her body brought her to a frenzy of desire that matched his as they came together in intoxicating ecstasy. The touch of his bare flesh on hers stirred emotions in her she never dreamed existed.

Myrhia lay with her head on his wide chest, reveling in the pleasure she felt. She thought there was a tigress hidden somewhere in her, as she had felt primitive when Turk masterfully carried her to heights she had never known existed and her body had arched wildly to meet his desire.

Turk rose to sitting position to look down at her, his hands roaming over her shoulder and down over her breast, causing another wave of pleasurable impulses to dart over her, "We have plans to make and much to do. First, I have a little dinner surprise for us to eat before the fire. We'll toast our marriage, our bright future, and above all our love."

As they slowly rose together, Myrhia was almost reluctant to end the perfect harmony that existed between them during the past hour. Picking up her scattered clothing, she started for his bedroom but stopped suddenly to glance back. The sight of Turk caused a wave of pleasure to wash over her.

He was standing with his back to her, still nude and leaning against the mantel staring into the fire. The firelight wavering in the background framed his beautiful body like an aura. She would remember this moment the rest of her life. Soon she would be married to this dynamic man but in reality she had been married to him mentally for a long time. From that first moment at Élan's when his daring look crossed the room to hold her captive she had felt destined to be a part of his life.

It was difficult for Myrhia to believe they had been married now two weeks and half of their precious honeymoon was over. She had not visited Maui on her Hawaiian trip two years before and now she found it the Pacific paradise it was touted to be. She had risen early, leaving Turk's warm side, to sit on the balcony and enjoy the early morning. Small fishing craft left their overnight moorings to put out to sea. Off in the distance a navy cruiser bound for some other port was silhouetted against the dawning light.

Turk had been right, she reflected, in saying they had much to do before the wedding was set in motion and still find the time to manage their offices and meet previously scheduled commitments. The stepped-up wedding date had been Turk's idea for two reasons. He wanted her now without further barriers between them and he wanted a prolonged honeymoon on Maui where he could oversee the completion of his condominiums and arrange a meeting with the two Japanese, who were partners in the hotel building, in order to introduce them to their new architect.

Turk had leased a condo for them on a six-month basis so they would have a place to come to on their frequent trips back and forth to the mainland. It would be impossible for Myrhia to stay away from her office and particularly the Tarrington Building for great lengths of time until she could give the final approval of its completion. Turk was understanding the first time she had to leave him but the second time he insisted on going back too. She knew these problems would work themselves out in time but the main thing was their complete happiness.

She smiled thinking of the whirlwind week of activities prior to their wedding. Alicia was the only one really flustered by the suddenness of it all but she became reconciled when she was allowed to have a lavish reception for them at the Dallas Country Club, where she and Walt Lassiter had held membership since first coming to Dallas. Here she could display her new son-in-law to her old friends, most of them from the area around Turtle Creek. She was ecstatic over Turk, saying smugly she had spotted his interest in Myrhia first.

The occasion seemed complete with Letty and Ted and the boys at both the wedding and the reception. Noticing Turk's happiness at having them there, she understood him more. This was his family, and the compassion and love toward the man in the wheelchair was wonderful to see. No longer would she have doubts of his gentle side.

She rose from her deck chair now, thinking to slip quietly into the kitchen for some bread crumbs for the doves and pigeons who frequented their balcony for handouts, apparently spoiled by former tenants.

As she rose, Turk's arms closed around her waist. He had come up behind her quietly without her knowing it. "What's wrong, darling? Couldn't you sleep?"

She laid her head back against his broad shoulder. He still felt warm from sleep.

"How is it possible to be so happy?" she asked, reaching over her shoulder to stroke his face with her fingertips.

"I just hope you feel the same way ten years from now—twenty-five years from now and—" He tightened the grip on her waist.

"Hold it, Turk! I may want to change partners after the first fifty." She whirled around in his arms to lift her lips for his kiss. "He'll have to be the sexiest old man with the most devilish gray eyes and the most provocative kisses or I won't even take a second glance."

As his mouth joined hers, desire flamed between them once again. It was a marvel to Myrhia that such gentle kisses could develop with such speed into an all-consuming passion each time when she was held over and over again.

"I hope you always feel something—just half of what I'm feeling this very minute for you, and it's growing stronger by the second."

She could see that any plans for breakfast or a turn at sight-seeing would have to wait awhile as their bodies seemed to flow back to the tumbled bed.

Toward the end of the idyllic month she was allowed to see the finished condominiums. Turk had wanted the outer facade finished before she passed judgment. As he drove the curving shoreline road toward Hana, she caught sight of a sweeping structure that followed the line of sandy shore.

"That's it, isn't it?" she asked him, excitement rising at the sight of the beautiful buildings.

"How could you know?" He smiled at her, pulling the car to a stop on top of a rise behind the condos.

"It's beautiful, just lovely!" The concrete was tinted a rosy cast that was not unlike the shore sand stretching out for yards before it. "It's marvelous! How did you ever find someone who could capture the beauty of the surroundings and follow through in the design this way?"

"I'd like for you to meet him sometime. He's an Austrian and very capable. To tell the truth, we changed the plans somewhat." He was looking at her skeptically now. "It was soon after meeting you. You made some reference on how they were spoiling the natural beauty of Honolulu, in your opinion, with all the towering skyscrapers of cement. Remember? Well, I came back and told the architect we needed to make our condos conform even more than he had in his prospectus. This is the result, stolen in part from your creative mind."

His remark touched her heart, bringing him even closer. "It's just perfect. I hope we can spend some time here someday." She leaned against his shoulder.

"We will. We have first choice of the apartments for our second home. I've already chosen one. It faces the ocean and it's on the curving end—right there." He pointed to the last apartment as it curved outward. "Do you like my choice?"

"I'm sure I will." They sat together in silence as she nestled closer to his shoulder, neither anxious to destroy the moment.

"Tomorrow you'll meet the two Japanese who'll be partners in our hotel. They'll be on Maui for an evening only."

She gave a little start and pulled away to look at Turk. "Oh, I'm apprehensive about that meeting. Will they like me?"

"Of course they will. They'll be enchanted with you."

"I want them to have confidence in me, and above all, I hope they like my prospectus." She felt the palms of her hands grow clammy at the thought of meeting the two men.

Later, as she looked back over the dinner with Mr. Tokunaga and Mr. Mikosu, Myrhia felt the meeting had gone rather well. After their initial shock of finding she was a woman and the wife of their American partner, they warmed toward her and agreed to let her have free reign in her design. They would submit a rundown on what they wanted the hotel to look like and she could submit her design proposal sometime within the next four or five months. She had to admit that Turk's confidence in her carried her through the dinner quite well.

Afterward, when they returned to their leased condo alone, it was like heaven again. They had wandered along the beach in the moonlight, made love in the sand, lay wrapped in each other's arms, breathing the fragrance of the plumeria and pikake blossoms and listening to the cooing of the small brown doves at nesting time.

Standing before the wide mirror in Turk's massive bedroom now shared by her, Myrhia let the blue-gray silk slip softly over her head like a caress. She had chosen the revealing nightgown for her wedding night over a year ago because the color reminded her of him.

It clung to her soft pointed breasts and rounded hips, and never failed to stir sensuous lights in Turk's fascinating eyes. Tonight she felt like another celebration on the eve of the dedication party for her building as she ran a comb through her hair and went to find her husband.

She started from the bedroom when she heard the soft piano music. Drawn as by a magnet, she followed the sound as she had done the night he had asked her to marry him.

When Turk became aware of her approach, he stopped abruptly and began playing her song, "Love Song to Myrhia," weaving a tighter net around her heart, ensnaring her forever. The melody was full of joy and wonder and passion. Almost reverently, in awe of a strength that could be so gentle, she ran her hands over his bare shoulders aware once again of his masterful build and marveling each time she was capable of making his flesh tremble at her touch.

As her song ended he turned slowly to lift her once again in his arms and carry her effortlessly to the bedroom, where his kisses blotted out all thought but a need for oneness of body and mind that only the two of them could experience together.

As his lips and hands moved over her body, it seemed to her he awakened new delights and feelings each time as he explored every inch of her. She had grown somewhat wanton in her desire for him, finding her own fingers could bring heights of excitement to him as he moaned softly, his lips crushing hers in never ending heat.

His strong fingers played over her body until nerve,

flesh, and cell were in tune before his deft fingers found the intimate places that would be forever his. When she knew she could no longer stand the pent-up longing for him, he murmured, "I do so love you, darling."

After they had consummated their love for each other they rose and walked to the balcony that overlooked the myriad lights of Dallas. Hypnotized by emotion and the lingering intimacy of their lovemaking, Myrhia nestled closer to his shoulder, letting her hand move over the dark hairs of his chest.

"There! See what you have created, my darling?" he whispered.

Off in the distance the first lights of her creation winked back at them as the Tarrington Building rose above the skyline.

Great old favorites...
Harlequin Classic Library

The HARLEQUIN CLASSIC LIBRARY
is offering some of the best in romance fiction—
great old classics from our early publishing lists.

Complete and mail this coupon today!

FREE BONUS BOOK

Harlequin Reader Service

In U.S.A. 1440 South Priest Drive
Tempe, AZ 85281

In Canada 649 Ontario Street
Stratford, Ontario N5A 6W2

Please send me the following novels from the Harlequin Classic Library. I am enclosing my check or money order for $1.50 for each novel ordered, plus 75¢ to cover postage and handling. If I order all nine titles at one time, I will receive a FREE book, *District Nurse*, by Lucy Agnes Hancock.

- ☐ 118 **Then Come Kiss Me**
  Mary Burchell
- ☐ 119 **Towards the Dawn**
  Jane Arbor
- ☐ 120 **Homeward the Heart**
  Elizabeth Hoy
- ☐ 121 **Mayenga Farm**
  Kathryn Blair
- ☐ 122 **Charity Child**
  Sara Seale
- ☐ 123 **Moon at the Full**
  Susan Barrie
- ☐ 124 **Hope for Tomorrow**
  Anne Weale
- ☐ 125 **Desert Doorway**
  Pamela Kent
- ☐ 126 **Whisper of Doubt**
  Andrea Blake

Number of novels checked @ $1.50 each =	$ _____
N.Y. and Ariz. residents add appropriate sales tax	$ _____
Postage and handling	$ _____.75
TOTAL	$ _____

I enclose _____
(Please send check or money order. We cannot be responsible for cash sent through the mail.)

Prices subject to change without notice.

Name _____
(Please Print)

Address _____
(Apt. no.)

City _____

State/Prov. _____ Zip/Postal Code _____

Offer Expires April 30, 1984   31056000000